DREAMS
OF
BRONZE

Camilla Lackberg is a worldwide bestseller renowned for her brilliant contemporary psychological thrillers. Her books have sold over 40 million copies in over 60 countries and have been translated into 43 languages.

www.camillalackberg.com

Also by Camilla Lackberg

PATRICK HEDSTRÖM AND ERICA FALCK SERIES
The Ice Princess
The Preacher
The Stonecutter
The Stranger (previously titled *The Gallows Bird*)
The Hidden Child
The Drowning
The Lost Boy
Buried Angels
The Ice Child
The Girl in the Woods
The Cuckoo

FAYE'S REVENGE
The Gilded Cage
Silver Tears

SHORT STORIES
The Scent of Almonds & Other Stories

Written with Henrik Fexeus

MINA DABIRI AND VINCENT WALDER TRILOGY
Trapped
Cult
Mirage

DREAMS OF BRONZE

CAMILLA LACKBERG

Translated from the Swedish by Ian Giles

Hemlock Press,
An imprint of HarperCollins*Publishers*
1 London Bridge Street,
London SE1 9GF

www.harpercollins.co.uk

HarperCollins*Publishers*
Macken House, 39/40 Mayor Street Upper,
Dublin 1, D01 C9W8, Ireland

Published by HarperCollins*Publishers* Ltd 2026

1

Copyright © Camilla Lackberg 2024
Published by agreement with Nordin Agency, Sweden
Translation copyright © Ian Giles 2025

Originally published in 2024 by Bokförlaget Forum, Sweden as *Drömmar av Brons*

Camilla Lackberg asserts the moral right to be identified as the author of this work.
Ian Giles asserts the moral right to be identified as the translator of this work.

A catalogue copy of this book is available from the British Library.

ISBN: 9780008713676 (HB)
ISBN: 9780008713683 (TPB)

This novel is entirely a work of fiction.
The names, characters and incidents portrayed in it are
the work of the author's imagination. Any resemblance to
actual persons, living or dead, events or localities is
entirely coincidental.

Typeset in Sabon LT Std by Palimpsest Book Production Limited,
Falkirk, Stirlingshire

Printed and bound in the UK using 100%
Renewable Electricity by CPI Group (UK) Ltd

All rights reserved. No part of this publication may be
reproduced, stored in a retrieval system, or transmitted,
in any form or by any means, electronic, mechanical,
photocopying, recording or otherwise, without the prior
permission of the publishers.

Without limiting the exclusive rights of any author, contributor
or the publisher of this publication, any unauthorised use of this publication
to train generative artificial intelligence (AI) technologies is expressly prohibited.
HarperCollins also exercise their rights under Article 4(3) of the Digital Single
Market Directive 2019/790 and expressly reserve this publication
from the text and data mining exception.

*To my sisters Rita, Lena, Aurora,
Eleonora and Isadora
– sisters of blood, sisters of choice*

February

Faye contemplated the snowy yard. She leaned her forehead against the latticed window, her gaze fixed on the high fence that separated the inmates of Stenakull prison from the rest of society. A huge bird circled above the forest before disappearing from her field of vision.

Everything had gone wrong. Soon both her mother Ingrid and her daughter Julienne would be dead, despite all her efforts to protect them. She had to get out, but she had no idea how. Nothing in her life – not her childhood in Fjällbacka, her life as an upper-class wife in Östermalm nor her career as a successful entrepreneur – had prepared her for this. How would she connect to the others and make them trust her – make them *follow* her?

Did she have it in her to start over again? Did she have it in her to break free one more time?

Faye had never felt so alone. She was further away from Julienne than ever before. She already missed her liberty, although she had only arrived at the prison a few hours before.

Voices in the corridor made her straighten up.
She swallowed.
Closed her eyes.
It couldn't end like this. She wouldn't let it.

PART I

Eight Months Earlier

From her suite in Stockholm's Grand Hôtel Faye had a view across the waters of Strömmen. There were clusters of lightly dressed people moving about on the quayside on the far side, below the walls of the Royal Palace. She put a hand to her chest and felt her pounding heart. Had it ever beat that fast before?

A knock at the door made her start.

'Who is it?' she called out. Her voice sounded much too weak; she barely recognised it.

The fact that she had to ask the question at all only increased her anxiety.

'Alice,' said a familiar voice, and Faye exhaled. She was so relieved she almost let out a sob.

Her hand was trembling as she opened the door.

Her friend, who was a key partner in Faye's company Revenge, entered and immediately began to wander around the suite.

'So this is how the other half live.'

'You're not exactly stuck in the slums yourself, Alice.'

Faye managed to muster a laugh even though her heart was still racing.

'Is this the suite they usually put Madonna and Beyoncé in?' Alice said, sitting down on one of the big sofas. 'Or do they have another one that's even more gorgeous?'

'It's this one.'

Faye reached out for the silver coffee pot on the tray filled with delicious breakfast items.

'So right now I'm inhaling their residual DNA...' Alice said reverently.

Faye managed another laugh.

'I dare say they aired it out of here a while ago. Hopefully they erased all trace of bodily fluids too. You'll have to make do with my spores.'

She held out a porcelain cup of coffee to Alice and pointed towards the milk jug with an implied question mark.

Alice shook her head.

'No thanks. I'll take it black – like my lover.'

Faye grinned and poured a cup for herself. Then she sat down in the armchair opposite Alice.

'I don't think that's very politically correct...' she said.

Alice shrugged. Since her ugly divorce from Henrik, she'd exhibited a liberating lack of fucks about what anyone thought of how she lived her life.

'Why did you want to meet here rather than at the office? And how come you're here rather than at home?'

As usual, Alice had cut to the chase.

Faye looked down at her hands. She didn't want to get the people she loved mixed up in her troubles, but she also knew from past experience that being alone was not a position of strength.

'I saw my dad last night when we were at Riche. He stopped outside the window and stared straight through it at me. Then he disappeared.'

She shivered as she recalled her father's ferocious gaze. It was the one that had made her feel small and weak throughout her childhood because she knew that when he gave her or her mother that look, it wouldn't be long before they were punished.

Alice set down the coffee cup with a hard clatter on the saucer.

'Are you sure?'

Faye nodded.

'Yes. I'm sure.'

'I knew there was something up. You went all quiet and left early. Ylva noticed too.'

'Yes, I've got to talk to her as well.'

Faye fixed her gaze on Alice's.

'When I got home, I found marks on the front door of the apartment – as if someone had tried to break in. So I came straight here and checked in.'

'Oh my God.' Alice reached out and squeezed Faye's hand. 'So what are you going to do about Italy then?'

Faye's throat constricted at the mere thought of the beautiful home in Ravi where her daughter and mother were waiting for her.

'I'm going to cancel the trip. I can't risk leading him there. He knows they're alive, because yesterday he held up a photo of them that I gave to Jack before he … died. They must have stayed in touch after they escaped from the prisoner transport, and Jack must have given the picture to Dad and now… I don't know. But I've got to find a new place in town to live. A house. Apart from when I was Kerstin's lodger, I haven't lived in a house since I came to Stockholm. Hopefully that's not something Dad will be expecting.'

'Isn't it safer in the city centre – in a flat?'

Faye shook her head.

'Too many people coming and going. I can be in control of a house. I can monitor it.'

'Let me know if there's anything I can do,' Alice said, getting to her feet. She refilled her coffee cup.

'I'm sure I'll need your help, but first there's stuff I have to sort out myself.'

'Would he really risk attacking you? Evidently he managed to escape. Maybe he just wants to keep his head down? And leave you all alone?'

Faye shook her head.

'No. I know him. He's coming for me. Why else would he have shown the photo? I've got to be ready for him.'

Her arms were covered in goosebumps, as if there were a draught in the elegant hotel room.

'So what do you want to do about the launch? Should we postpone?'

'No. I'll sort this out. We've worked way too hard to risk it all by postponing. You and I both know that if we make it in the American market then we'll be taking Revenge into the beauty brand elite. I'm not going to let Dad stand in the way of that.'

Faye hugged herself; it was even draughtier now. Was it the air conditioning?

'But can you enhance our security at the office right away? I'll have to come in – maybe later today,' she added.

'I'll see to it immediately.'

Alice stood up and hugged her tightly.

Faye inhaled the familiar scent of Chanel no. 5. Alice had always been one for classics.

Once the door had slammed shut behind her friend, Faye went into the bedroom and picked up her phone with some hesitation. This wasn't a call she was looking forward to. She hated lying to her daughter. She'd have to tell her mother the truth. Her mother was perfectly aware of the danger her ex-husband posed and it wouldn't be right to leave her in the dark.

Faye sighed and called them on FaceTime. Her heart ached when she saw her daughter's beautiful face on the display.

'Mum! When are you coming home? I've done a drawing to give you when you get here!'

'That's so sweet of you, darling. I miss you so much, but it's going to be a while before Mum is back. I've got some work things that I have to stay here and deal with first.'

Julienne's disappointed look was all too familiar. Once

again, Faye had broken a promise. It stung even more when she saw her daughter struggling to look nonchalant.

Julienne shrugged.

'K.'

'So how are you?'

'Fine, but I guess you want to talk to Grandma like usual?'

'Oh, Julienne. Right now it's really important that I talk to Grandma, but next time we can...'

'Sure.'

Julienne's face disappeared, to be replaced by glimpses of bright walls and dark furnishings as she walked through the house.

'Grandma!' she shouted.

Faye's mother's face appeared.

'Can you make sure you're on your own?' Faye said in a low voice.

Her mother nodded and Faye watched as she went upstairs.

'What is it?' she said, a little breathlessly after rapidly climbing the stairs. 'You're scaring me.'

Faye took a deep breath.

'I saw Dad yesterday. And I think he tried to break into my apartment.'

Her mother gasped sharply.

'Gösta? Are you sure?'

It was the same question Alice had asked, and Faye had to give the same reply.

'Yes. I'm absolutely sure. And he knows you're alive. So I've cancelled my trip to see you – there's no way he can know about the house in Ravi, but I don't want to lead him there if he's watching me.'

She felt the tears pricking the backs of her eyelids, but forced them away.

'Be extra careful from now on. I'll arrange more security right away. I'm not going to take any risks.'

'Where are you now?'

Her mother's voice was trembling slightly and the phone was shaking in her hand.

That was her father's doing; he could awaken a deep, primitive fear within them. They both knew what he was capable of and the evil that resided within him.

'I've checked into the Grand. But I'm going to sort out a new, safer place to live.'

'Take care of yourself,' her mother said quietly. Faye merely nodded.

She couldn't let the fear take over. She didn't want to give her father that power. And she needed to keep a cool head to plan her next step. He was on the run and a wanted man, which meant she had a certain advantage.

'Take care of Julienne. Love you,' she said, hanging up.

Faye sat on the bed. After everything that had happened in the last few years, she was sick of fighting. But that was just what she would have to do now. She'd have to fight for her life and her family's too. She thought about the photo she'd shown to Jack and that he'd taken with him. It was the one picture there was of her mother and Julienne, and she missed being able to look at it. She'd taken their photo on a Sicilian beach and she could still picture Julienne curled up in her grandmother's arms with her long blonde hair tangled after swimming in the sea, gazing into the camera. Now her father had that photo.

She would fight for them to the bitter end.

She pulled out her phone again and searched for 'estate agent in Stockholm'. The first hit made it clear in their advertising that they were primarily focused on exclusive homes. She tapped on the number on the website to call it and, before long, a man's voice answered.

'Hello, I'd like to buy a house,' Faye said succinctly.

'Okay! Putting you through to one of our realtors now.'

As she waited, she reached out for the bottle of mineral

water standing on the nightstand and took a sip to wash away the bitter aftertaste of the coffee.

'Peter Bladh speaking. How can I help you?' Judging by the sound of the man's surroundings, he was in a car.

'My name is Faye Adelheim and I'd like to buy a house. Fast. It needs to be on a waterfront plot and it can't be more than half an hour from Stockholm city centre. Price is no object.'

There ensued a brief and confused silence.

'Hmm... I do have one house that might fit the bill,' he said. 'It's out on Lidingö Island, by the water. The starting price is—'

'Like I said,' Faye interrupted, 'price is no object. When can I see it?'

'Where are you?' the man asked.

She had to act normal; she couldn't show fear. The attack would come soon enough, and when it did she would have to be ready.

'I'm staying at the Grand Hôtel.'

'I can pick you up from there in twenty minutes. I just have to swing by the office to get the codes and keys for the house first.'

'Perfect.'

After she'd rung off, Faye got up and headed for the shower. She had a lot to do now. She was going to protect her family. At all costs.

The house had been built some five years ago by a Swedish billionaire. Now he'd started a family, sold his stake in a certain well-known finance company and relocated to New York. He had good taste in interior design for a finance bro, Faye reflected as she looked around. Assuming he'd had anything to do with it... The interior alone was worth millions of kronor but it wasn't ostentatiously vulgar. She had no great difficulty picturing herself living there.

A high wall surrounded the plot and a massive electric gate had silently glided aside when they pulled up to it in the realtor's convertible. The house was three storeys high and at the far tip of Lidingö Island. It was positioned to afford views of the water through the huge panoramic window in the rear wall. Below them was a well-kept lawn, a big pool and a sandy beach.

Peter, the realtor, was standing by one of the huge windows. He had stayed in the background while Faye had hastily inspected the house. Outside, there was an archipelago steamer puffing past, sending small waves towards the shore.

'There's no transparency. The windows have been designed to let you see out but no one can see in.'

'Like an interrogation room?'

Peter laughed. He had an attractive, symmetrical smile spread across his face. His teeth were white and even.

'Just like an interrogation room, yes.'

As she stood next to him she could detect the scent of his cologne. He was in his thirties and tall with wavy brown hair combed in a side parting. It was apparent that the man worked out a lot. He was treating her politely without swaggering, and had self-confidence without being pushy. Faye had immediately been attracted to him and the drive out here in the car had been good-humoured and pleasant.

She had the definite impression he was single. At any rate, there wasn't a ring on his finger and he was well dressed in an authentic and deliberate man's way, rather than based on a woman's taste.

'The place has a top-notch security system. CCTV, electronic alarms with a direct connection through to Wadling Security. The seller is very security conscious. Stockholm isn't what it once was. I'm sure you're aware there are gangs who specialise in robbing houses like this one. They're completely ruthless. So it's important to protect yourself.'

Faye nodded, glancing at the chest muscles visible beneath the close-fitting shirt. She had to make an effort not to lick her lips.

It wasn't robbers she was worried about; it was her father. If he made up his mind to try to get at her, there wasn't an alarm system in the world that would stop him. On one of the few occasions when her mother had tried to leave him and had gone to a youth hostel together with Faye and Sebastian, their father had come knocking on the door the very next morning. He was like a bloodhound; he always found them. But a good security system could buy her time.

'What do you think?' Peter said, when there had been thirty seconds of silence.

Faye nodded curtly.

'Are there any other interested parties?'

'I showed Martin Lorentzon around yesterday.'

She knew the Spotify co-founder had deep pockets given his huge success, so she'd have to pull her finger out.

The house was perfect. She'd be as safe as could be here, not far from the city centre but maintaining the sphere of privacy around her that she needed. No nosy neighbours to interfere – that had only got worse and worse in her years in Östermalm. Previously, she'd thought that she'd never be able to live on the impersonal, discreet island of Lidingö. Now that was just what she wanted. And she'd be able to arrange rigorous security around the property in a way that would be impossible while she remained in town.

'I'll pay a premium of five million kronor on top of the starting price on condition that I can move in right away.'

'That shouldn't be a problem. I'll call the vendor.'

He went downstairs, leaving her alone. A few moments later he appeared on the lawn running down to the shoreline, phone to his cheek. Faye stayed where she was, safe in the knowledge that he couldn't see her through the window.

Once again, she shuddered. Her father's reappearance had forced her to change her plans. She was not the mistress of her own existence and that was something she would have to change; she needed to take back control. To do that, she needed to relax.

She placed a palm against the glass and slid her other hand into her panties. She was already wet. She caressed herself, keeping her gaze fixed on Peter with his toned body and confident posture. She imagined his sculpted pectoral muscles. They were probably clean-shaven. With small, hard nipples. It didn't take her long to come. She bit her lip, stifled the moan trying to escape from her throat and closed her eyes as her whole body trembled.

After a while, she adjusted her clothes and sat down on one of the cream sofas. Her pulse slowed. She pulled her Revenge powder compact from her Hermès Birkin and touched up her make-up using the small mirror. Then she undid the zip on the inside pocket in her handbag and pulled out the necklace with the silver locket that she had taken to keeping there now she no longer had the photo. She opened the locket and looked at the tiny, beautiful picture of her and Julienne from when her daughter was very little. It had been taken by the photographer Kate Gabor and it had always been her favourite picture.

After a while, she heard Peter's footsteps coming back up the stairs, so she quickly snapped the locket shut and returned the necklace to her bag.

He stopped in front of her.

'Sorry to keep you waiting.'

Faye smiled.

'No worries. I was enjoying the view.'

She allowed her gaze to wander across Peter's body.

He cleared his throat, his tanned cheeks visibly flushed.

'I spoke to the vendor and your offer has been accepted. When his wife heard you were the buyer, she was over the moon. She asked me to tell you that she's a big fan of you and your products. She always uses Revenge.'

'A woman with taste.'

Faye stood up and Peter indicated with an outstretched arm that she should lead the way out. While he keyed in the code to lock the house and arm the security system, she made her way to the car, got in and pulled the sunglasses down off her head. He got in behind the wheel and used a remote control key fob to noiselessly open the gate.

As they drove away, Faye looked at the house she had just bought in the wing mirror. In another reality, Julienne would one day be able to move in there with her, but in truth it was impossible. As far as the world at large was concerned, Julienne was dead. Sometimes it seemed so real to Faye too; she played the role so well that the thought made her sad.

She'd had no choice. The pictures she'd seen on Jack's computer had been so terrible. He'd subjected Julienne to the most awful things. She'd been forced to get Julienne away from her father and make sure that he never saw her again.

The lifelong deception was a prerequisite for her daughter's entire existence. Faye hoped she would be able to continue it, but sometimes the weight of it felt overwhelming.

After a final flirtatious glance at Peter, Faye exited the realtor's office on Humlegårdsgatan on foot. The papers relating to the purchase of the house in Lidingö had been signed. In Humlegårdsgaten Park Stockholmers enjoying their lunch breaks had spread out picnic blankets or were lying on their backs in the grass. The sun was shining, warming the dark asphalt while small streaks of white cloud were visible in the sky.

Ever since she'd first come to this city to study at the Stockholm School of Economics, she'd loved it. Back then it had seemed enormous to her. Now it suddenly felt suffocatingly small. It was as if every person she encountered was an emissary of her father.

Faye's mood changed so quickly she felt dizzy. One minute everything felt pretty much as normal, and the next she remembered that he was out to get her and worry would claw at her.

She took a left heading for Stureplan and Revenge's offices. Alice had called to reassure her that they had implemented maximum security, but going there still felt like a risk. Her father doubtless knew where it was. But she couldn't hide all of the time.

The receptionist smiled cheerfully and waved as Faye swept past her. Out of the corner of her eye, she saw two guards standing at either side of the lobby looking forbidding and dangerous. The visitors sitting there waiting to be let in raised their eyebrows curiously as she walked by. She was used to the glances. By now, she was a well-known personality both in Sweden and abroad.

Sometimes she loved her celebrity status, but sometimes it was oppressive. Right now, it was not to her advantage to be recognised everywhere she went. At the same time, it was the basis of her success. Faye the legend. The woman who had been cheated on but fought back. That truth was part of her, but the image was one she had carefully created herself.

Faye swiped her access card and passed through the security barriers, then moved quickly towards the lifts, relieved to escape the attention of those around her. This was her fortress; her sanctuary. She had created all this – out of nothing.

She pressed the button to take her to the top floor and let the lift carry her lightly and gently upwards. When the doors glided open, she turned right. Ylva's office was in the corner and had staggering views of the city through its huge floor-to-ceiling windows.

'Oh my God, Faye,' Ylva said when she entered.

She stood up and gave Faye a hug that was as warm and long as the one Alice had given her a few hours earlier in the hotel suite. This time it was the scent of Chloé that wafted up her nostrils. Chanel no. 5 was for old ladies, as Ylva was wont to affectionately tell Alice.

'We've amped up security to the max,' Ylva said as they sat down on the hard, uncomfortable sofa in the corner of the large office.

'I've no idea why you keep this thing,' Faye said, grimacing. 'Sitting on it is such a pain in the backside. And it's prickly.'

She ran a hand across the upholstery and it felt as if she was being stung.

'It's a family heirloom. It reminds me of where I come from,' Ylva said. 'It's dangerous to get too comfortable.'

'My backside begs to differ.'

She smiled at Ylva. Sisterhood. These women she had got to know along the way, who had stood side by side with her through it all: they weren't just friends – they were family.

The road to friendship for her and Ylva had been odd to say the least. It had all started when she'd found her husband, Jack, in bed with Ylva. And they'd then had a daughter together. But there was no anger left between Ylva and Faye. Jack had strung both of them along, and they'd had their revenge.

Ylva leaned in towards Faye.

'What are you going to do?'

'Well, for starters I've just bought a house. I don't feel safe in the apartment. I haven't spoken to Kerstin yet, so I don't know whether she'll want to stay in her apartment or move into the house with me.'

'How much do you need?'

Ylva was tasked with overseeing both Faye's personal finances and those of Revenge. She was a numbers whizz with a brilliance that Faye had never managed to acquire despite her successful studies at the Stockholm School of Economics. Admittedly, she hadn't actually graduated. That was something she'd learned over the years as she'd built her company: to surround herself with people who complemented her.

'Eighty million.'

'Oh, so it's just a small cottage then?'

'More or less.'

Faye smiled. Revenge's success had endowed her with a fortune beyond anything she could ever have dreamed of when she was growing up in Fjällbacka. But money couldn't buy everything. Right now, she would happily have given away every penny to obtain security for her nearest and dearest.

'I'll make the arrangements. Have you got the paperwork with you?'

Faye handed over the glossy-looking realtor's folder and

Ylva stood up and deposited it on her desk. She sat back down next to Faye and took her hands in hers.

'How are you feeling?'

Her gaze was insistent, refusing to waver.

A sob began to form in Faye's throat, and she had to swallow several times. She couldn't give in now. There was no time and she couldn't afford to.

'Shit, if I'm being totally honest. Shit. I've cancelled my trip to Ravi and I had to lie to Julienne and tell her that I had to work. Her face when I said it...' Faye cleared her throat, the words not wanting to come. She took a few deep breaths. 'But I told Mum what's going on. I don't think Dad knows about the house in Italy, but I can't take any risks. I need to find the best security company in Sweden right away and sort out protection for them.'

'We use Secur – they're the best out there. I did my research before hiring them. Do you want me to sort it out?'

'No, I'd like to speak to them myself. Give me their details and I'll get in touch.'

'Sure thing. I'll send them right over.'

Ylva pulled out her mobile and tapped away on the screen. Then she took Faye's hand and squeezed it tightly.

'You're not alone. Never forget that.'

'I know.'

Another sob was burning away in her throat, but once again Faye swallowed it.

As she was leaving Ylva's office, she stopped in the doorway and gazed at the panoramic view out of the windows. Stockholm. So beautiful and yet now so treacherous. Somewhere out there was her father and he wasn't going to give up until she was dead.

He'd come close to killing her mother several times because of all the rage bottled up inside him. It was a rage that could only be expressed through his clenched fists. Through damage and destruction. The only way that Faye had been able to ensure her mother was freed from her father had been to fake her death and make sure he took the blame.

He'd wanted revenge on Faye ever since.

'Good afternoon,' said the woman behind the dark oak reception desk. She was doing her utmost not to show that she knew who was standing in front of her. 'Would you like anything to drink?'

'I'm fine, thanks.'

'Carl won't be a moment.'

Just then, a man in his fifties appeared. He was tall with a stiff, upright posture. It was obvious that he was ex-military, which Faye found reassuring. He extended a powerful hand towards her.

'Carl Novak.'

The handshake was firm without being dominant.

'Faye.'

He showed her into an unexpectedly large office with views over the crowds of people coming and going on Kungsgatan. Secur was doing well.

'How may I be of assistance?'

Faye crossed her legs and removed her sunglasses.

'First I'd like to make sure that anything I say in here won't leave this room.'

She reached into her bag and pulled out a non-disclosure agreement that she'd had drawn up. She slid it across the desk to him.

'You've already signed an agreement with Revenge, but this is a private matter.'

If Carl was surprised then he didn't show it. He skimmed the document before retrieving a pen from his top desk drawer and signing it with a practised movement.

Faye folded the document in half and put it back in her bag.

Despite the fact that he had signed it, revealing her mother and daughter's hiding place went against every fibre of her being. Apart from Faye, only Kerstin, Alice and Ylva – her closest confidantes – knew they were alive. Her father might have that photo, but he didn't have any real proof. Her ex-husband, Jack, had gone down for Julienne's murder and her father had gone down for her mother's. Were the truth revealed, it would not only mark her downfall; she would also be going to prison.

'I own a property in Ravi in Italy. There are two people in that house for whom I wish to arrange bodyguard protection. And I gather you have a division that undertakes international security assignments.'

Carl nodded.

'When do you want it to start?'

'Now.'

He leaned back in his chair and contemplated her.

'Is there any immediate threat towards them?'

'Yes. There is an acute and lethal threat that I want to protect them from using all possible resources. I want you to put your best men and women on this.'

'Of course. In order to protect them, we need…'

'I'll pay whatever it costs. Anyone you assign to this job will have to sign a non-disclosure agreement. And like I said, they have to be the very best you've got.'

He stroked his clean-shaven chin without allowing his gaze to waver.

'The confidentiality issue isn't a problem. All our operatives come from sound military backgrounds. Do you have a picture of the property that the principals are living in?'

Faye pulled out her phone and searched her inbox for the drone images that she'd been provided with when she'd bought the house.

She handed over her device. He reached for a pair of computer glasses, perched them on his nose and examined the pictures.

Finally, he put down the phone.

'It's a large property but from what I can see the perimeter security appears ample, although we'll have to review that on site. What about alarm systems?'

'All of that is already in place. According to the security company I work with in Italy, the kit I've got is the best money can buy. But that won't be enough. Not anymore. And I want to hire a company I can really trust.'

Carl handed her phone back to her and removed the glasses, carefully folding the earpieces and laying them down on the desk.

'I'll send two of my people tonight. Depending on the situation on the ground and in consultation with them, I'll decide how many operatives are needed. Is that all right with you?'

'Yes.'

A small smile tugged at the corners of his mouth, but his eyes radiated calm.

'They'll be safe. My personnel are soldiers – some of the best-trained ones in the world.'

Faye nodded. Her shoulders relaxed slightly.

'I also bought a property in Sweden earlier today and I need to make sure that it's secure too,' she said.

Despite the fact that Peter Bladh had attested to the security company engaged by the house's former owner being top notch, Faye couldn't rely on that. She couldn't take any chances.

'We'll sort that out as soon as our meeting is over,' Carl said after she'd given him the address. 'You'll have security in place no later than tonight.'

Faye leaned back in her chair.

'Good. But there's also something else I need your help with and it needs to be arranged now and start today.'

She explained to Carl what she had in mind and he displayed no signs of surprise whatsoever. He merely nodded briefly as Faye told him what she wanted him to do.

The Skogskyrkogården cemetery was beautiful even in a grey haze. Faye shivered slightly as she moved briskly towards the grave. She was constantly looking over her shoulder. She still had the feeling that she was being watched, but the only people she met were sprightly pensioners out with their walking poles and mums with pushchairs strolling side by side while chatting.

As was her custom, she took a right to avoid the section with the children's graves – all the teddy bears and all the intervals between dates of birth and death that were far too short were more than she could handle. She slowed down as she got closer to Chris's grave. It was always painful yet comforting to visit her. Today was her birthday. Faye didn't want the best friend she'd ever had to be alone on a day like that. The world might be on fire, but she would still come and spend a while with Chris, and for a spell feel her closeness.

They'd met at the Stockholm School of Economics and for a long time they'd been inseparable. There was no one she'd had as much fun with, laughed so much with and loved as much as Chris. Her friend had been joie de vivre wrapped up in an effervescent personality, and Faye still struggled to comprehend that she was dead.

Chris had found love before she passed away, which was

always a source of comfort for Faye in her darker moments, when she missed Chris so much that it felt like she would shatter into pieces. Before she had been taken from them by cancer, she had wed her beloved Johan. He was a good man, and a man who had loved Chris in sickness and in health until the very end.

At times, Faye wondered whether she would ever experience a love like that. She'd thought so when she had met Jack. But he had betrayed her in every way that it was possible to betray someone. Now he was dead, and before that he'd been sent to prison for killing their daughter Julienne. All according to Faye's carefully devised and executed plan.

For a short time, she had thought that she might have found love again, but she had been betrayed once more. Now she confined herself to brief, nocturnal encounters with young, fit men who gave her what she wanted in bed but weren't let in anywhere except between her legs.

Faye crouched beside the grave. A beautiful bouquet was lying next to the headstone.

It's your day today. But really every day is yours. Will always love you! Johan.

Faye gently touched the handwritten card. She pictured Johan and Chris at their wedding, just a day before Chris had died.

'I miss her too,' said a voice behind her, making Faye start.

'How did you find me?'

Faye stood up, brushing the needles and leaves from her knees, and embraced Kerstin. Wonderful, amazing Kerstin, who had always saved her when she was at rock bottom. Broken, despondent and destitute, she'd rented the upstairs of Kerstin's detached house in Enskede and they'd been very close ever since.

'You weren't at the office. And I know it's Chris's birthday today. So I took a chance.'

Faye brushed away a stubborn tear.

'I wish she was here. She would tear my dad apart with her bare hands.'

'Only after she'd cut his balls off,' Kerstin said dryly, before laughing. Then the older woman turned serious. 'Your mother called and told me what you had said. And there's a removals company at your flat packing it up.'

'Sorry, I should have called. I just had a few things to sort out first. And yes, I'm moving. It's not safe for me to stay there any longer, so I've bought a house. On Lidingö. I've already got the keys. It's up to you whether you want to stay in your apartment or move in with me. But right now I think it's probably safer for you to stay on Karlavägen, if I'm honest.'

'I'll do as you wish,' Kerstin said softly, caressing her cheek.

In many ways, Faye considered herself to have two mothers. There was the mother she had grown up with, and there was Kerstin. And she knew that Kerstin regarded her as a daughter.

'Why don't we pop into Delselius for a piece of cake to celebrate Chris? If you've got time? And if it's safe?'

Faye linked arms with Kerstin.

'I don't really have time. And it might not be safe. But there's nowhere I can be completely safe right now. And Chris would want us to eat a couple of thousand calories at her place.'

As they walked through the picturesque cemetery arm in arm, the pressure in Faye's chest eased for a moment. She was going to figure this out. Together, they were going to figure this out.

'You've made quick work of it!'

Peter Bladh looked around the house in surprise. The removals company had packed up the whole apartment and then unpacked it in the house. Some things hadn't ended up in the right place, but at least it was now habitable even if there wasn't enough furniture to fill the place. Not that it mattered – interior design was the last thing on Faye's mind right now.

Carl Novak had kept his word. The new security setup had already been installed. He had suggested bodyguards, but even though she realised it would be for the best she'd turned them down. In order to do what she had to, she needed freedom. It was a risk she would have to take. But she knew that even the slightest movement outside her house at night would trigger the alarm and that the security company's people would quickly be on site. There was also a panic room in which she would be safe until help arrived. It was a calculated risk, rather than a foolhardy one.

Faye regarded Peter.

'I'm a competent orderer of services – and I'm willing to pay my way.'

They were in the large kitchen with the custom cabinets, shiny marble and premium Gaggenau appliances.

'Fancy a glass of wine?'

She pointed to a bottle of Châteauneuf-du-Pape that was already open to breathe.

The realtor hesitated before shrugging.

'I guess I can take a taxi home and pick up my car tomorrow?'

There was a subtext to his question and Faye responded to it by pouring two big glasses of wine.

'Here's to your house,' he said, raising his.

'Here's to your commission,' Faye said, taking a big swallow of the expensive wine.

They looked at each other in silence. Faye set down her own glass and then his on the grey marble worktop and took a step towards him. His lips tasted of the wine they had just drunk and she tentatively inserted her tongue into his mouth. When his tongue met hers, she felt the warmth begin to spread between her legs. It was liberating to stop thinking and let desire take over. Everything else disappeared and the only thing she was focused on was his tongue against hers and the intensifying throbbing in her sex.

Peter's hands began to caress her body. She paused in the middle of a kiss and hopped up onto the edge of the kitchen table to allow herself to wrap her legs around him. He pressed himself against her as they began to kiss intensely again, and when she felt his hands on her breasts she gasped.

Faye pulled off her top and bra and began to unbutton his shirt. Just as she had imagined, Peter's toned pectorals were waxed with not even a strand of hair, leaving every muscle clearly defined. He let out a low moan as she ran her fingers across his nipples, before gently biting her lip. Faye's hands slid further down between his legs and she relished feeling his hard cock through the thin fabric of his trousers.

'Slowly, slowly,' he said thickly, but she ignored him and carried on stroking his member with increasing pressure.

Peter stepped away and got down onto his knees in front of her. With his gaze fixed on hers, he slowly removed her tights and panties from underneath her skirt. Once he'd discarded the garments, he pushed her skirt up and splayed her legs. Now she was completely laid bare for him. She loved the feeling of knowing that what was about to happen was as yet unwritten. This was a man she didn't know – she had no idea what he was like in bed – but now he was going to work her over with his tongue.

A second later, she felt the gentle application of pressure on her clitoris. Slowly and purposefully he used his tongue in a way that revealed he knew what he was doing. She parted her legs even more to give him full access. He switched up the pressure and circled around and around with his tongue while she felt herself getting wetter by the second. When he started caressing her with his fingers while still licking her, she could no longer take it. She wanted him inside her, now.

Faye grabbed his head and pulled him up towards her. He tugged off his trousers and underwear and then his socks while kissing her harder and harder. She could taste herself and that only made her want him more. She tore off her skirt. Now they were both naked. His cock was bigger than she had thought. She grasped it in her right hand and was rewarded with a deep groan as she moved her hand up and down.

'I want to fuck you,' he said in a low voice, pushing her hand away. He gently pushed her down so that she was lying with her back on the table.

In one quick movement, he pulled her towards him so that her behind was right on the edge, and parted her legs again. He took time to gaze down at her and stroke her breasts before slowly pressing his cock against the opening. Faye bit her lip hard as Peter penetrated her. Then she relaxed and let him slowly enter her fully. They moved together, in unison, as if they had done it many times before.

'Touch yourself – I want us to come at the same time,' he panted, watching as she obediently lowered her hand and began to rub herself.

When he picked up the pace, so did she. The orgasm came almost too soon.

'Now,' she gasped and he sped up even more as he thrust into her.

She tilted her head back and moaned loudly, and he pumped hard a few more times before grabbing her hips with a roar and holding himself deep inside her. Then he collapsed on top of her and lay there on her stomach, both of them perspiring.

A few seconds later, Peter propped himself up on his elbows and grinned.

'Time I was on my way or are we going again?'

Faye smiled.

'Let's have some wine. Then I thought you might fuck me from behind.'

As he pulled out of her, she gazed through the window at the dense darkness broken only by the odd dot of light. She wanted to put off being left alone with her fears for as long as possible.

Faye was sitting in an armchair in front of the panoramic windows with an espresso on the armrest and her laptop perched on her knee. She really ought to focus on Revenge. On her father. But instead, she was scrolling through articles on the criminal gangs that Peter had told her about; the ones that assaulted wealthy people in their homes. Apparently they meticulously scouted out their victims before striking. How long would it take for them to catch wind of this house?

Faye raised her gaze and looked down towards the water below her. She'd spent her first night in the over five-thousand-square-foot house – alone, after Peter had finally gone home.

It had taken a while for her to work out how to operate the coffee machine, a silver contraption the size of a steam locomotive.

It was raining. The sky was grey, merging shade by shade into the water outside.

Right now, she missed Julienne almost more than she could bear.

She'd accomplished her most important and pressing task: to ensure the security of her mother and daughter. Now she had to deal with the other. Her life's work. She wasn't going to let her father stand in the way of her plans for Revenge. They were working flat out to launch the beauty empire in the USA, with the plan being that she would go to New York to lead the expansion. That would be impossible as long as her father was at large.

She didn't know what he was planning, but he was definitely looking to take his revenge on her somehow. This realisation not only made her uneasy, it also pissed her off. She'd spent half her life running away from him, and the other half trying to erase all trace of him from herself, be it mentally or physically. She'd thought she'd made it. That she was free. But now everything had been turned on its head.

A movement out of the corner of her eye made Faye jump before she realised it was just a boat passing by below the house. Her thoughts returned to criminal gangs. She was one of Sweden's wealthiest women; she'd practically lost count of how many billions of kronor she was good for. She was the subject of ample coverage in the press, and gossip magazines were always working hard to concoct headlines with her name in them. She lived alone, which she assumed made her a worthwhile target. Of course, there was another possibility: that the people she was certain were following her had been sent by her father. But until she had a clear understanding of the situation, she had to consider both options.

She went to the Aftonbladet website to dispel the thoughts about herself and the situation she was in. The tabloid proclaimed that a notorious criminal had been shot dead in his home in Tullinge. According to reports, he was a leading figure in one of Sweden's most influential criminal networks, headed up by the infamous Zoran Rakitic. Rakitic himself was apparently cleaning up his ranks.

While Rakitic is currently doing time in Hall, his influence extends far beyond the prison walls, said a police source.

Hall? Faye squirmed. That was the prison her father had escaped from. But Hall was a big prison that housed some of the country's most hardened criminals. It was probably just a coincidence.

The police press spokesperson quoted in the article said

there had been no trace of the perpetrator or perpetrators who had gained access to the house.

This is a new approach that we are seeing and we are very troubled by this development.

Faye scrolled down to see what related articles were recommended on the site.

The life of gangster kingpin's wife Milenka Rakitic while her husband is inside: the parties, the kids, the clothes!

The photo showed a strikingly beautiful woman and Faye was about to click on it to read the piece when a chiming tone resounded through the house. She jumped. Was that the doorbell? She hadn't yet learned to recognise the sound.

Faye put down the computer and looked around before getting to her feet. She went to the kitchen island, pulled out a big knife and held it in front of her.

She went downstairs while looking around; the whole time she was gripping the knife in her hand.

Her heart was pounding.

At the front door, she discovered that someone had in fact pressed the doorbell button at the main gate. On the monitor, she saw a red sports car and standing next to it a young man in a cap. She realised that her new car had arrived. She couldn't bring herself to contemplate how much it had cost to have it delivered so quickly.

The guy pressed the bell again as Faye searched for the button to unlock the gate. She finally found the right one and then watched on screen as it opened. She laid the knife on the floor out of sight but still close to hand and then opened the front door.

It was at that moment she realised she was wearing nothing but a black negligee with nothing underneath or on top. She found herself smiling.

The car, a Porsche Carrera, pulled up outside the house.

The guy opened the door and got out. He was cute with his peach fuzz moustache and his baseball cap worn backwards.

'Morning, I'm here to deliver this beauty,' he said, running a hand over the bodywork.

Then he stopped mid-movement, leaned forward and rubbed the paintwork frantically with his t-shirt. He barely seemed to have noticed how scantily clad she was; he only had eyes for the car.

'I didn't realise,' he said in embarrassment. 'Sorry.'

Faye laughed.

'I think the beauty can handle it,' she said. 'It wouldn't be much of a car otherwise.'

He walked over to her and handed over two sets of keys.

She closed her left hand over them while proffering her right hand and introducing herself.

'Markus,' said the young man, his gaze wavering as he began to blush. 'Would you like me to show you how it works?'

She looked up at the sky; the rain had passed.

'Okay.'

She walked barefoot across the wet gravel towards the car while he hurried to open the driver's door. She got in behind the wheel and Markus adjusted the seat. As he leaned forward and explained with tremendous enthusiasm what all the different buttons on the dashboard did, she couldn't help but feel rather hot and bothered. There was something about young men that turned her on. She'd noticed this increasingly of late and wondered when the shift had occurred. In her teens she'd always fantasised about older men, but now it was younger men who occupied her fantasies.

She let the negligee slide up her thighs and enjoyed the way he began to stumble over his words as he remained hunched forward.

'The windscreen wipers are… Er, it's this button. It's an interesting…'

She pretended not to notice his plight, preferring instead to interject with the occasional dutiful follow-up question in a serious tone.

She wished she had learned earlier in life how easy men were to control – at least the majority of them. At the same time, she was fascinated that she was still able to think about sex despite the serious situation she found herself in. She interpreted it as a show of strength, perhaps even a defence mechanism. Perhaps her contempt for men was beginning to turn her into a man herself, or at the very least she'd taken on some of their views of sexuality. For a second, she toyed with the idea of telling him to be quiet, grabbing him by the scruff of the neck and guiding his face down towards her pussy.

She wondered how many young women had experienced that kind of encroachment by men in positions of power while they were just trying to do their jobs. How many secretaries, cleaners and maids in global history had been subjected to this kind of strong-arm stuff?

What was stopping her? She didn't know. Perhaps it was because she understood that she couldn't pursue young lovers and similar pleasures in the near future if she wanted to stay alive and save her business.

A couple of minutes later, the introduction was complete. Faye got out of the car.

'What are you going to do now?' she asked.

'Erm, I'll just walk to the tram stop,' Markus said, blushing again.

'If you can wait half an hour then I'll drive you into town.'

'For real?'

'Oh yes,' she said. 'It would be a pleasure.'

Anything to make her forget reality for a while.

Zagreb, 1982

I was standing on a chair since I couldn't otherwise reach the sink. I was using a sponge scourer to clean a glass. The dirty dishes smelled of alcohol, smoke and washing-up liquid. I put the glass down on the drainer and set to work on a plate. I didn't have anything against doing the washing-up; it gave me a feeling of control. What was more, I liked the transformation. Something ugly and dirty could become clean and beautiful. I was like a mini conductor and the crockery was my orchestra.

The dishes were always the first thing I got started on once I'd picked up my five-year-old brother Zivko from the ground floor where Aunt Majda looked after the neighbourhood's little kids. Zivko was often afraid and black and blue all over. I would take him by the hand and lead him up the five flights of stairs to our flat. His clothes would stink of cigarette smoke.

I always dressed him in fresh clothes, even if they smelled bad too. Then I would wash what he had been wearing in the basin in the small bathroom and hang it up to dry. In summer, it only took an hour or so to dry in the heat, but in early December, as it was now, the top and trousers from the day before were still hanging there, sodden. The whole flat was cold and damp.

It was Friday. Both Zivko and I hated Fridays. Mum and Dad worked at the steel plant, which meant they would be at home for two whole days. During the week, Zivko and I took care of ourselves. While I did the washing up, he would flip through a picturebook we'd borrowed from the library a couple of blocks away. The books were always well-thumbed and worn-out, but he loved them.

Once I was done with the dishes, I would read aloud to him from one of my books. I always read from the adventure books that Mum and my teacher at school claimed were written for boys, because they were what I liked reading best. After I'd read to Zivko for a while, we'd usually be hungry and if we were lucky there would be some unappetising leftovers from the day before for us to fill our bellies with. Otherwise we had to wait for Mum to come home, since she would do the shopping on her way back from work.

She was usually tired by then and had a headache or a sore back, so she had taught me how to cook from a young age, and ever since, that had been my task while she sat on a chair watching me. Sometimes she would offer succinct comments or instructions.

On this particular Friday, Dad came home first. He was a silent, self-contained man who never said much at all. Not at home and not when we were out and about. Mum had once told me that he hadn't always been this way, but with the passing of the years he'd become increasingly taciturn. And the quieter he got, the more the blows rained down.

My earliest memory was of when I spilled juice by the dining table. I can't have been more than three years old. I remember the sound of the plastic cup bouncing on the floor and the yellow liquid splashing everywhere. Then there was silence. The next sound was the rustle as Dad put down the newspaper. Then the scraping of the chair legs as he got to his feet, took a step forward and slapped me. The impact was like an explosion and I screamed loudly. Mum picked me up and carried me away. On that occasion, the shock stung more than the pain.

On this particular Friday, he came home just as I'd finished doing the washing-up and had started reading *Gulliver's Travels* to Zivko on the living room sofa. Suddenly there he was, standing in the doorway, watching us.

'Hi, Dad,' I said.

He didn't answer, but went into the bedroom.

I picked the book up again and continued reading. More quietly, almost whispering, because Dad wasn't to be disturbed. If we were lucky, he'd fall asleep. If we were unlucky, he'd start drinking.

Zivko had shifted closer to me. He was sitting so close that it was as if he wanted to blend into my body to be protected from Dad. But my skinny nine-year-old body didn't offer much in the way of protection, even if I did my best.

I stopped reading when I saw that Zivko's fingers were black. I reached out for his hand and brought it closer for a better look. It was black ink.

'Have you been painting?' I whispered.

He nodded.

'At Aunt Majda's?'

His eyes widened and he nodded.

I closed my eyes, hoping it was true. I shut the book and was about to take him into the bathroom when Dad came out of the bedroom. He came up to us. Zivko hid his hands under his thighs.

'Who's been drawing on the wall?' Dad said quietly. It sounded almost as if he were pleading.

'Me,' I replied.

'Show me your hands.'

Slowly and reluctantly, we both held them out. Dad scrutinised them and swallowed. For a second or two, I thought he was going to let it go. Maybe he would just order me to wipe it off, and make do with a slap each. But then Dad yanked Zivko off the sofa by the wrist and dragged him into the bedroom.

I don't remember what I yelled, but I did yell. Zivko was crying loudly. I grabbed his other arm and tried to pull him free. 'It was my fault,' I said. 'I gave him the pen. I didn't think he'd draw on the wall. I'm sorry.'

Dad didn't reply. Instead he kicked at me to make me let go. He hit my stomach hard, winding me. I wheezed and panic took hold of my entire body as I was unable to fill my lungs with air. Still, I managed to take a few stumbling steps after them. I reached out towards the doorway just as Dad slammed the door shut. My forearm was stuck between the door and the frame, and Dad pushed harder. It felt as if the bone in my arm had broken and I screamed in agony as I fell backwards.

The door closed before me. My forearm was protruding at an odd angle, as if the bone inside wanted to penetrate through the skin. Stunned, I stared at the fingers on my right hand. I tried to move them and realised I couldn't. My hand wouldn't obey.

From the other side of the door, Zivko screamed as Dad began to give him the belt.

I must have fainted. When I came to, Mum was stooping over me, bags of shopping in her hands. She put them down and gazed at my arm in horror. The pain throbbing from my wrist up to my shoulder made me scream.

'We have to get you to hospital, sweetie,' she whispered.

She gently helped me up. Then she leaned against the door. Zivko had stopped crying, but the sound of the belt striking his body was still audible. That was good. Dad was triggered by our crying; it made him hit us harder. Zivko had finally started to learn that. Soon it would be over. For this time.

'We're off to the doctor's,' Mum said, a little louder this time so that Dad would hear.

I shook my head.

'Not yet.'

'We have to. Your arm's broken.'

'We can't leave Zivko alone with him.'

Mum looked from me to the closed door and then nodded.

'You're right,' she said.

She led me to the sofa. I closed my eyes, trying to push away the pain in my arm and the sound of leather striking a child's fragile skin.

Mum went into the kitchen to put away the shopping. Finally, the door opened. Dad shoved Zivko into the living room and then closed it again. Mum came back and took him by the hand.

I got up and followed. I couldn't put my coat on – it hurt too much – so Mum took a towel from the bathroom and draped it over my shoulders.

'You can't say what happened – what your father did,' she said to me as we emerged onto the street.

Of course. I already knew that.

'I'll say I fell.'

'Fell how?'

'Off the sofa. Me and Zivko were jumping on it and I stumbled and fell with my arm under me.'

Mum thought about this for a while, as if she were visualising the contrived story in her mind's eye.

Then she nodded.

'Good,' she said, smiling at me. 'You're a sensible girl, Milenka.'

I tried to answer, but my arm hurt too much.

Once she'd dropped off the car guy, who had stuttered his thanks for the lift, Faye was once again overcome by the seriousness of the situation. With nothing to distract her, her father came to mind again.

She stopped the new Porsche outside Revenge's offices on Birger Jarlsgatan to pick up Alice. Her friend got into the passenger seat without saying a word and shut the door. She must have sensed Faye's mood.

They drove in silence along the rainy, glistening streets onto Strandvägen and onwards towards Djurgården.

Despite the grey sky lowering over Stockholm, there were a few housewives and young upper-class ladies out and about exercising on the verdant island. At least that was how they looked. Maybe they were happy in their lives? Faye hoped so, but she suspected that they too felt cooped up, afraid and controlled. Their lives were completely in the hands of men.

They passed the Nordic Museum, the Gröna Lund amusement park and the Skansen outdoor museum before she turned into a car park close to the Manilla School. Faye switched off the engine and a heavy silence settled upon the passenger compartment.

Alice's fingers with their red-painted nails began to play with her blonde hair just as they always did when she was nervous or worried.

'How are you?' she said cautiously.

'Better now that I've moved, but that's only the first step. There's a lot left for me to do to protect myself from my father.'

Alice shook her head.

'What does he want? Money?'

'In that case it would be easy.' Faye sighed and looked seriously at Alice. 'He's a very violent man who has always terrorised his family.'

'And now he's on the run from prison.'

Alice's voice was suddenly small.

'And now he's on the run from prison,' Faye repeated, nodding slowly. 'He's filled with so much anger, Alice. So much aggression. I'm not just scared of what he might do to me, but also what he might do to Mum and...'

Her voice faltered.

An index finger with a red-painted nail caressed the back of Faye's hand.

'And Julienne,' Alice said in a low voice.

Faye could only nod.

'How safe do you think they are?'

'I've cut contact with them for the time being, but he'll find them – sooner or later. He'll never give up. Revenge is all he has left to live for.'

Alice shivered and Faye could also feel the goosebumps spreading up her forearms.

'What are we going to do?' her friend said.

Faye held up her hand.

'I'm afraid that's not all.'

Two women power-walking passed by on the pavement, while some way behind them two Filipina nannies were pushing prams that doubtless contained their charges.

That could have been Alice and me, Faye thought with a shudder. In another life, when we were still confined to our gilded cages.

'I've got a feeling that I'm being followed. By my father or by someone else; I'm not sure. Maybe he's got someone else doing the job for him. Maybe someone is going to attack me, or maybe someone is just staking me out. But I'm absolutely certain that someone has eyes on me.'

'You're sure it's not just paranoia?'

Faye smiled. She couldn't escape the feeling that time was running out. At the same time, she knew she couldn't allow herself to panic. She had to be ready – had to have thought of everything. Otherwise, she would be done for.

'Yes, unfortunately I'm sure. Someone is following me and I need to know who. For as long as I remain in company and stay in my house, I'm safe from my father, at least for the time being. I think. I hope. But I have to find out who is following me.'

'How are you going to do that?'

'You and I are going to do it right now. And I'm afraid we'll have to carry on with it for the rest of the day.'

'So we're acting as bait right now?' Alice said with a smile that Faye interpreted as sincere. She saw no signs of fear on her friend's face.

'Something like that. Why do you think I'm driving around in a brand-new Porsche?'

'Say what you like, Faye, it's never boring being your friend.'

She parked the Porsche on Brahegatan – one of the smaller side streets not far from Östermalmstorg – and they strolled along Nybrogatan, down towards Brasserie Astoria. Despite the fact that the restaurant was packed, the maître d' arranged a table for them upstairs within moments. He showed them to it and Faye couldn't help but notice heads turning towards her as she strode across the room.

'Do you remember that interview request that you turned down from TV4?' Alice said once they'd sat down and champagne flutes had been delivered to them.

Faye tasted the champagne while they waited for their Caesar salads.

'Yes?'

It had been a request for a longer, more in-depth interview, and they had discussed whether or not Faye should do it. In the end, they had agreed that it wasn't critical enough to merit postponing her trip to Italy. But the situation had now changed.

'You said no because you were going to Italy. The fact that you're still in Stockholm will be noticed. The journalists will sense that something is up. Maybe you should accept the request and explain why you've stayed? The market can be sensitive to signals, as you know.'

Faye gazed at the other lunch patrons. Most were businessmen in expensive suits. She and Alice were splashes of colour in a sea of dark jackets. She couldn't detect anyone who seemed interested in her presence beyond the curious glances that she had always attracted in more recent years. As usual, part of her enjoyed the attention, while another part of her detested it. But she also realised that for as long as she lived, she would be the subject of such looks. And there wasn't much she could do about it. Her success was based on her creating reactions and emotions. Her life story was the reason behind Revenge's improbable success and billions in sales.

She thought about what Alice had said and realised she was probably right. Her name was charged; her presence would be noticed and it might be questioned. Better to anticipate the speculation and control the story.

'You're spot on. Let's do it.'

'I'll ask one of the PR girls to get in touch with TV4 right away to set it up.'

Alice pulled out her phone and stood up.

Faye watched Alice walk away with quick, confident footsteps. She took another sip of champagne. As always when she was left to her own devices for a few minutes, her anxiety and thoughts of her mother and Julienne grew. Now she feared that others who were close to her also risked being threatened.

Faye longed for Julienne with every fibre of her body. When would they next see each other? Was all this worth it? Perhaps she should just go to Italy, retrieve Julienne and her mother and then fly far, far away. At least that way they could be together. At the same time, she knew that sooner or later her father would find them. He would never give up. He wouldn't rest until he'd exacted the revenge that he'd wanted for so many years.

A couple of minutes later, Alice returned and nodded to indicate that everything had been arranged.

Their food arrived and they ate the delicious salads in silence. Faye glanced towards Alice's smooth face. She seemed to be utterly unmoved by what Faye had told her, and exhibited no signs of being nervous or repelled. On the other hand, Alice's Botox-smooth face was always so hard to read.

Suddenly, panic made her feel a little nauseous. What if Alice was hoodwinking her? What if her best friend was in league with her father? For the money? To outmanoeuvre Faye and seize control of Revenge?

She looked at Alice and took a big swallow of champagne. She had to get a grip. These suspicions were absurd – she realised that – but the fact that she'd even contemplated them proved just how much her father could mess with the contents of her head.

It was probably exactly the kind of uncertainty he wanted her to feel. He'd taught her through his words and actions that there were few people who could be trusted. Yet later experiences had taught Faye that there were some people in whose hands you could lay your life. Friends who did everything for each other. Who came through, who offered support, who defended. Sometimes, when life felt at its most hopeless and burdensome, she would return to that thought. To Kerstin, Alice and Ylva.

Once they had eaten, Faye went to pull out her purse to pay. But where was her handbag? It wasn't on her chair and it hadn't fallen to the floor.

'That's weird...'

Alice looked at her quizzically.

'I can't find my bag. I must have left it in the car. Unless someone's stolen it...'

Without a word, Alice pulled out her purse and placed her black American Express card on the silver platter the waiter had put in front of Faye.

'Thanks. I don't care about the purse. I'll block the cards and get them replaced. But I've got a necklace in my bag...'

'Don't worry. It's probably just in the car.' Alice got to her feet.

Once the payment had been taken, they made a quick exit from Astoria.

They returned to Brahegatan and were approaching the car when Alice's phone rang.

'It's TV4,' she said, answering.

After a few moments, she turned to Faye. 'They're really pleased the interview is going ahead. They'd like to broadcast it as soon as possible. Does recording at eight o'clock tomorrow work for you?'

Faye nodded. It would have to.

Then she came to an abrupt halt. The uneasiness in the pit of her stomach was back. A hole had been smashed through the window of the Porsche.

Alice turned and looked askance at her.

'What is it?' she whispered.

Faye pointed.

'Someone's broken into my car. But look: my handbag's still there.'

Alice pointed to the phone.

'Thanks. I'll let Faye know,' she said, quickly ending the call.

She stood next to Faye and peered through the shattered driver's side window.

Faye started when her phone began to ring. She pulled it out of her jacket pocket and answered without looking at the display.

'Yes?'

'It's Novak.'

It took Faye a moment to realise that it was Carl Novak, the CEO of the security company she had contracted.

'It's best you come here,' he said.

'Now?'

'Yes, right away.'

Faye gasped. For a moment, she was convinced that her mother and Julienne were dead.

Novak must have realised that he'd chosen the wrong words. He cleared his throat.

'Everyone in Ravi is fine. This is about you and the other assignment you tasked us with.'

After noting that the Birkin bag was still in the car, Faye looked inside and found that her purse and all her credit cards were still there, as were her keys and everything else. The only thing missing was the necklace with the silver locket on it. She suddenly felt sick.

They walked to Secur's offices on Kungsgatan. For some reason, neither of them found it an appealing prospect to get into a car that had just been broken into.

It was three o'clock in the afternoon by the time they reached Secur. They were shown straight into a meeting room. Carl Novak was waiting next to a conference table together with a man in his thirties who had a laptop tucked under his arm. He was tall and muscular with close-cropped hair. He neither introduced himself nor greeted them. Faye thought that Carl and he might have been father and son.

As soon as the secretary had closed the door behind them, the room was filled with the humming sound of the electric blinds lowering over the glass walls.

After exchanging curious glances, Faye and Alice sat down next to each other on one side of the table while Novak and the other man sat opposite them.

Upon a gesture from Carl, the younger man tapped on his keyboard and his screen appeared in enlarged form on the projector screen at the far end of the table. On it, there were three black and white faces. Two men and one woman. Faye had never seen them before.

'You asked us to look into whether you were being followed and the short answer is yes, you are,' Carl said. He stood up and approached the projector screen. He nodded to the muscular man. 'Fredrik has headed up the work. These three individuals have been following you since yesterday evening on rotation.'

Images began to scroll across the screen. They had been taken in locations across central Stockholm that Faye had visited over the last twenty-four hours. She recognised Brasserie Astoria and Birger Jarlsgatan. Some had been taken from a car.

'Do you know who they are?' Alice whispered.

Faye shook her head.

'No, I've never seen any of them. That much I'm sure of.'

A thought occurred to her.

'Was it one of them who broke into my car?'

Silence. Carl looked at the man he had referred to as Fredrik and Faye couldn't help thinking that it was probably a made-up name.

Fredrik cleared his throat.

'My team followed these three individuals and none of them accessed the car. What's happened?'

'While we were having lunch earlier, someone smashed the window and took a piece of jewellery from my handbag. They left my purse. And the bag, which is worth a fair bit.'

The man called Fredrik and Carl Novak quickly exchanged glances again.

'As I said, it wasn't any of them and you'll understand in a moment why it wasn't them who broke into your car.'

Faye turned to Carl.

'You're saying you know who they are?'

He nodded. Then he reached for a glass of water and took a couple of sips.

'Yes, they're undercover cops.' He gave Faye a long look. 'You're under police surveillance.'

Zagreb, 2 May 1995

I was working as a waitress in a small greasy spoon called the Rose not far from the Flower Square. My plans for the future, which had included books or at least some form of education, had been ruined by four years of war. Communism was gone; Yugoslavia was dissolved. Since 1991, we had been Croatia – a young, wounded nation. Our troops had been on the offensive in Slavonia as part of Operation Lightning, and the old men I was serving coffee to in the Rose were talking of nothing else over their newspapers and cups. Personally, I was sick to death of the war. I was completely exhausted. All I wanted was peace. I wiped my hands on my apron and glanced at the clock, which showed it was a quarter past nine in the morning.

The door chimed as it opened and when I looked up I saw, to my surprise, that it was my own mother. She was in the company of a pale woman of about the same age. They sat down at a table and beckoned me over. I hurried over to them, embraced Mum and asked them what they wanted.

'You were right,' the other woman said with a smile after scrutinising me. 'She really is very beautiful, is your Milenka.'

I raised my eyebrows.

'My name is Jadranka,' she added, spotting my surprise.

Mum leaned forward.

'Jadranka has a son who lives in Sweden,' she said. 'His name's Zoran.'

Jadranka eagerly reached into her bag and pulled out a purse. From it she produced a photo which she handed to me.

I examined it. It was of a tanned man with a jaunty smile. He looked to be a year or two older than me, and I couldn't help thinking he was handsome.

Jadranka and Mum looked at me expectantly. I handed the picture back without saying anything.

'Well? He's a good boy. A diligent, hard worker.'

'I'm sure he is,' I said. 'Too bad he lives in Sweden.'

Jadranka tucked the picture back into her purse.

'He wants to get married – but not to a Swede. He wants a Croatian wife who knows how to take care of a man. The women in Sweden are all beautiful but cold.'

Mum had lit a cigarette and was glancing at me with a furtive smile.

Three men came in and I excused myself. While I was absent-mindedly taking their order, I thought about the conversation I'd had with Zivko the evening before. He was in the army now but was home for a few days' leave, resting up in the flat. We'd talked about leaving Croatia together. Seeking out happiness elsewhere.

We were both tired of the war slowly squeezing the youth from our bodies, making us older without giving us time to live because of the bloody violence and killing.

Zivko was now a man in uniform who had perhaps killed other soldiers – I didn't dare ask since he made it so clear he never wanted to discuss the war – but it was still me protecting him. At the same time, I wanted to live – I didn't want to grow old and look back and think that I'd thrown away my life.

I knew many of my compatriots had fled to Sweden and

from what I had heard, it was paradise. Cold, sure, but there was no war, no killing.

But there was nothing to suggest this Zoran guy would want me. Perhaps he had his hands full with the Swedish girls and had only said he wanted to marry a Croatian to make his mother happy.

I was often told I was beautiful. Men would give me long, covetous looks and whenever I was out with my friends we were rarely left in peace because of the constant stream of young men approaching me. And I suppose I'd gone with one or two of them to their rooms. But I didn't want to be someone's wife just because I knew how to take care of a man, as Jadranka put it. Besides, it would feel like I was betraying Zivko. We were going to get out of here together. But he couldn't go anywhere because of the war. Actually, it was only for his sake and for Mum's that I was still here.

Just as I was heading back to the table where Mum and Jadranka were sitting, there was a loud bang that made the whole building shake. Everyone stopped what they were doing. Then came the next one. The patrons started to cry out and suddenly I realised I was doing so too. Later on, we found out that it was a Serbian rocket attack on Zagreb.

I rushed to the cellar door, yanked it open and shouted at everyone to get downstairs to safety. A couple more people came in off the street and I led them down to the cellar.

We all sat there on the floor, backs to the wall, close to one another. To begin with, everyone was tight-lipped and terrified, but after an hour or so we fell to talking again. The bombardment was unrelenting and occasionally a hit close by would make the cellar shake.

I closed up the Rose at four o'clock in the afternoon when there was a break in the shelling and everyone emerged from the cellar to head for home. Mum and I said goodbye to Jadranka and hurried the almost two miles on foot to our flat. Several buildings had been destroyed, there was a power cut and no vehicles were out on the roads apart from the emergency services. There were people lying on the pavements, injured and maimed.

As we approached our ten-storey block of flats, we found to our relief that it was undamaged and still rising into the blue sky. Outside the main door, we bumped into Zivko who was also on his way back inside. He was in uniform and seemed agitated. He embraced us tightly. As we separated, I saw that not everything was as it should be.

'What is it?'

'Dad ... he's been injured. They've taken him to the Dubrava.'

I glanced at my right forearm. There was still a white scar on it where he'd once broken my arm. Conflicting emotions coursed through me. Dad was older now; it was years since he'd beaten any of us. Not that he didn't want to – it was just that Zivko and I were too big. He still worked at the plant, where he was now a foreman. In spite of everything, I didn't want him to die. I was still hoping for an explanation and an apology for everything he'd put us through.

The hospital was in a complete state of chaos. Zivko and I saw dusty and bloodied civilian Zagrebers sitting and lying on the floor of the hospital corridor. Grim-faced doctors and nurses rushed past; they were bloody too. We didn't know where our dad was or whether he was alive and it would be hours before we got any clear information. Mum spoke to a neighbour whose daughter had suffered minor injuries and was waiting to see a doctor.

Zivko and I left her and found a staircase leading to the hospital roof. We stood there by the railing gazing out across the city. There was black smoke billowing into the sky in several places.

'What a hellscape,' Zivko said gloomily. 'I'm probably going to be called back to the front tonight.'

I was disappointed, but it had crossed my mind that this

might happen. I turned away, not wanting him to see my tears. I was terrified that he was going to die. Or that I would and we would never see each other again.

'Why did Mum go to see you at the Rose today?'

I wiped away my tears and laughed shakily. I'd forgotten about Mum and Jadranka's visit that morning; it all seemed so distant now.

'She's met a woman who has a son in Sweden.'

'Oh?'

'He wants to marry a Croatian, or so his mother claims. I saw a picture.'

Zivko shook his head and laughed. He had such a beautiful smile.

'So was he handsome then?'

I shrugged.

'Milenka,' he said, fishing a pack of cigarettes from his pocket and proffering it to me. I put one between my lips, as did he, and then he produced a lighter and lit both of them. 'Get out of here if you can. Your life is slipping past you.'

'He might not even want me. And maybe I won't want him.'

Zivko exhaled a cloud of smoke and looked at me.

'Every guy wants you. You know that.'

I smiled. Zivko was unusual like that. He never seemed bothered by the fact that his mates or other men were always courting me. I thought it was nice of him. He saw me first as a human being and second as a sister.

'I might not want him.'

'Whether or not either of you wants the other, get out of here. Go to Sweden. Live. Get away from...' He made a sweeping gesture towards the city with the hand holding the cigarette. 'This.'

'But what about you? We were supposed to do it together.'

'I'll come later – when the war's over.'

'And what if you die?' I whispered.

He shrugged.

'If I die then I die regardless of where you are. Not even you can protect me at the front, although I expect the enemy would be terrified if we sent you in.'

I punched him gently with my left hand and took a long drag on my cigarette.

'We'll see,' I said, and at that moment the shelling resumed.

Faye and Alice crossed Stureplan and entered Sturehof, where they asked the maître d' if they could be accommodated in the private dining room. They didn't want to go to Revenge's offices, but they needed to talk undisturbed.

After ordering a drink each, they sat down side by side. At first, they were silent, each one of them devoted to their own thoughts, and before long the waitress brought their orders.

The fact that Faye was being followed by the police was the worst possible news. It could only mean one thing: they suspected her of being involved in the murder of her ex-husband, whose charred body had been found in a burnt-out summer house outside the town of Köping.

'I would have preferred it if they were thieves,' Faye said at last, taking a sip of her gin and tonic.

Alice glanced at her.

'Are you sure about that?'

'Yes, because you can fight back against them. With security, money, bodyguards. But the cops... I don't know. They must still suspect me of being involved in Jack's death.'

'What are we going to do?'

Faye had spent the short walk from Secur's office to the restaurant pondering a response to that question. It was perfectly clear that if she was arrested and then found guilty of murder, Revenge would be in danger. There was only one thing to do: build walls and moats between herself and Revenge. She had to legally distance herself from the company, otherwise it risked being smashed to pieces and then she would be destitute. She'd been born poor and married rich. When she'd divorced she'd become poor again and then slowly built up Revenge with the money she'd managed to save from her dog walking business. She was *not* going back to poverty. Only someone who had been poor knew what that entailed. She'd only ever met people who claimed that money didn't matter among the upper classes. People who were born with money. They had no idea what they were talking about.

Faye took another sip and tried to calm herself down. She didn't want to show Alice how shaken she was. She felt as if she were being hunted from all sides. She knew very well who was behind the theft of the silver locket with the photo of her and her daughter inside it. While she had to try to save Revenge, she also had to try to protect herself and those she loved most from her father. She was going to have to fight a war on two fronts.

She pushed aside the half-empty glass.

'I have to distance myself from Revenge,' she said grimly.

Alice shook her head.

'No – that's impossible. You're the very soul of the company, we—'

Faye held up a hand and Alice fell silent.

'Obviously I'll be back, but I need to do it temporarily. If I'm convicted of ... what happened to Jack, then we might lose everything. It'll damage the company too. But if I'm out of the game then you and all the other women who helped me are safe. Otherwise, you're just as exposed as I am. You have kids, Alice. Think of them.'

'But...'

Faye took another sip of her drink. The ice cubes clinked together as she tilted her head back to finish it.

'I have to go. I'll come back once I'm out the other side. But I have to win the war first. I need to buy time.'

Alice leaned forward.

'Who are you going to sign your stake over to?' she said.

'I don't know yet.'

They sat in silence for a while. Faye stared down into the empty glass, trying to gather strength for what was to come. The tasks and challenges that lay ahead of her seemed insurmountable.

'Oh God, why is this happening now?' Alice wailed, raising her glass and downing the last of her own drink.

Faye smiled sadly at her.

'Are you sure you want to do the interview?' Alice said.

'I can't say I'm thrilled by the prospect,' Faye said. 'But we've got to carry on as normal. We can't show the outside world what's about to happen.'

Alice raised her empty glass towards Faye's.

'We'll have to get through this with a smile. Fuck it, it feels like I'm married to Henrik all over again.'

Faye laughed. There was no one she would rather be going through this moment with than Alice. She knew that when push came to shove, neither of them would leave the other's side. They would fight for each other until the end.

Alice stared down at the ice in her glass and then glanced at Faye.

'How long do you think we have?'

'I've no idea. We've got to plan and prepare for the worst, but we don't know for sure that anything is going to happen. I can't really see how they could turn up any evidence. There's nothing to lead them to me. In a couple of months we might be back here laughing at the whole thing.'

'I hope you're right.'

'So do I. But we've still got to be ready to fight for our lives.'

Alice sighed, leaned forward and rested her forehead on the white tablecloth.

'Do you remember what it was like?' Faye said.

Alice lifted her head.

'When?'

'What you said before. When I was married to Jack and you were with Henrik. Do you remember how unhappy we were? The way they treated us? Humiliated us? Patted us on the head? The way we were constantly wandering through life with the feeling that we weren't good enough?'

Alice swallowed.

'Yes.'

'We might lose everything, but we'll do so as free women. Well, maybe not me. I suppose I'll be rotting in some prison.'

They laughed. Then Faye turned serious.

'Whatever happens, we broke out of our gilded cage. We did it together. I'll never forget that.'

They raised their glasses, whose contents now consisted of melted ice.

'Here's to us,' they said in unison.

After a sleepless night alone in the big house, Faye got dressed and climbed into the car. Once she had buckled her seatbelt and was ready to leave, she winced. What if there was a bomb underneath the car? Would the car – and she – be blown to smithereens when she started it?

She closed her eyes. Clenched her fists. She could not let paranoia be the master of her. She took a deep breath and turned the ignition switch on the left-hand side of the steering wheel. The Porsche started.

Faye exhaled.

How long could she live like this? Constantly on edge, alert to danger, enduring the constant rush of adrenaline. And no sleep.

This could not be allowed to affect her. She couldn't afford to lose focus, not even for a second. And she had at least made an important decision during the night. It was a decision that required her to see Ylva in order to realise it.

She nodded to the guards as she entered the lobby at Revenge. Maybe she should just set up a camp bed in one of the conference rooms? The office was one of the few places she felt fairly safe; it was a place where she could lower her guard for a while.

Revenge was her home, her baby. She'd created it from scratch, building an empire out of nothing but a vision and her keen business acumen, as well as a tremendous understanding of and love for women. The fixed points in her life – the only ones she had been able to trust – were women. Men betrayed. Men struck. Men deceived. There was only one man she could trust – that was what she had eventually realised during the course of her sleepless night.

Ylva gazed up at her in surprise as she stepped into her office. She looked as tired as Faye felt.

'Rough night?'

Ylva's eyes widened and she sighed deeply.

'Have kids, they said. It'll be fun, they said. My God, Nora messed me about all night. *Mummy, I need a wee. Mummy, I want water. Mummy, there's a monster under my bed.* It was never-ending.'

'Julienne went through a similar period at that age. It's just a developmental phase. You can borrow my best motto, which got me through the early years: this too shall pass. I've even got it tattooed on my shin.'

'We'll have to bloody hope it does,' Ylva muttered. 'Otherwise she'll be going cheap on Facebook Marketplace before you know it.'

Nora was Julienne's half-sibling. Her little sister. She had been conceived through Jack's infidelity with Ylva, but that didn't prevent Faye from loving Nora almost as if she were her own. The girl had got the best of Jack. His intellect, his looks. But she'd got Ylva's warmth and empathy.

'How are you holding up?' Ylva peered intently at Faye, who had just sat down on the sofa with a grimace.

'Damn it, this sofa... I'm this close to buying a new one. Maybe something from Svenskt Tenn...'

Ylva smiled and for a moment the fatigue was gone from her eyes.

'Forget the sofa. Do you want some coffee?'

'A litre of the stuff, please.'

Once Ylva had returned with a cup for each of them, she

sat down next to Faye and put a hand on her leg. She didn't say anything but merely looked at her. The warmth of her hand and the love in Ylva's gaze made something in Faye's chest begin to melt. But she couldn't let herself cry. If she got started, she wouldn't be able to stop.

'What with everything that's going on, I've decided I have to step aside from Revenge for a while. A temporary change at the helm.'

'You're not going to ask me to be the CEO, are you?' said Ylva in horror. 'I'm perfectly happy as I am with my income statements and balance sheets.'

Faye held up her hands.

'No, no, I know how you feel, and it wouldn't be possible in time terms either, given you've got Nora.'

Ylva swallowed audibly.

'Alice? Good God, I hope it's not Alice? You know I love Alice, but three-hour lunches at Riche followed by an hour's shopping in Nathalie Schuterman doesn't quite align with the role of CEO.'

'I'm under pressure, not insane,' Faye said, laughing.

'Kerstin?'

'Calm down a bit and I'll tell you what I have in mind. But no, not Kerstin. She's enjoying her retirement far too much. She's got Bengt and the orphanage in Mumbai to keep her busy and just the other week she was talking about doing a pottery course when she's back in Stockholm...'

'If I ever start banging on about a pottery course, please shoot me,' Ylva muttered.

She downed her cup of coffee and reached for the pot to refill it.

'Caffeine. It's crack for the mothers of young children.'

'I thought Johan could step in as CEO.'

Ylva stopped mid-movement and stared at her doubtfully.

'Johan? You mean Chris's Johan? The one who's a teacher? And who has zero business background? That Johan?'

'Yes, that Johan.' Faye held up a hand to stave her off. 'Hear me out. We've got a stable team in place. You've got an iron grip on the finances. The PR and marketing department is doing a fantastic job; we've got good people there. And Alice can always launch a charm offensive on the bank and take those meetings. Our contact at Nordea has wanted to get into her pants for years. I just need someone I can trust. Someone who can hold the fort for a while.'

'Great, an amateur CEO for a major international corporation. Perhaps not one to issue a press release about?'

'No, no. Let's keep this one under the radar.'

Ylva downed another cup of coffee. The crockery clinked as she returned the cup to the table a little too hard.

'Have you spoken to him yet?' she said. 'Does he actually want to do this?'

Faye got to her feet.

'You draft a contract, I'll speak to Johan. This is how it has to be.'

'It's a bitter pill.' Ylva sighed. 'But I suppose I should borrow your motto: this too shall pass.'

'Exactly. Right, I've got to head off to TV4 for that bloody interview.'

Faye blew Ylva a kiss before picking up her coat and hurrying out of the office. She was not looking forward to being interviewed – especially not when she had so much else on her mind. But as they always said: the show must go on.

The atmosphere in the TV studio was relaxed but professional. After spending a little less than an hour in Make-up, Faye had been shown to a green leather armchair positioned on the glossy studio floor. Sitting on a sofa behind the cameras were Alice and a girl from the Revenge PR department who had introduced herself as Teodora. They had so many staff these days that Faye could no longer keep track of everyone who worked there.

Four cameras were trained on Faye and the presenter Rita Dofstrand. She was a popular TV veteran who had been at TV4 since the start of the Nineties. Her loyalty had seen her rewarded with her own talk show, which was broadcast on a Saturday evening. The production team had emailed the questions in advance, but Alice had warned Faye that Rita had a tendency to go off script and improvise.

Faye wasn't feeling at all nervous; she considered herself to be an actress in interview settings. Her task was to sell a dream and a story about herself. Sometimes she would exaggerate, but most of the time she resorted to outright lies. Over the years and with all the training she'd had, she'd become a skilled media operator. So much so that she sometimes even appreciated being interviewed. She regarded it as almost being a form of therapy.

'What does someone who has achieved as much as you have dream of?'

Rita tilted her head to one side.

Faye paused for a moment, as if she were genuinely thinking before she answered.

'I've already lost the most important thing to me: my child.'

Her voice was frail, as if she might fall apart at any moment. Faye paused and glanced into the middle distance as she collected her thoughts. She'd been so convincing that she had to remind herself that Julienne was alive and well in Ravi. At least for now.

'To answer your question, I dream of her being proud of me. Everything I do, I do with Julienne in mind. I try to see myself through her eyes because I know she's watching me from somewhere. And, as I said, I want her to be proud of her mum.'

She could tell that her words had made an impression on Rita, whose eyes had moistened. The presenter cleared her throat and assumed a grave expression.

'Can you forgive your ex-husband for what he did?'

Faye's gaze wavered while in her mind's eye she replayed Jack's final moments.

'No. I can't. And I probably never will. I believe in forgiveness, but not when it comes to someone who murdered your child.'

'He's dead too. Jack was found burnt to death. How did it feel to hear that news?'

That question hadn't been included in the running order, and Faye was annoyed at Rita even though Alice had warned her.

She took a deep breath while pondering how to fend off the question.

'I felt nothing. Nothing at all, if I'm perfectly honest. I think every mother out there will understand. The person who hurt your child is never worthy of your tears or regrets. He'd tormented Julienne and me for so long. This may sound harsh, but I couldn't care less about my ex-husband's death.'

'Do you have any theories on who might have killed him?'

'Jack had a lot of enemies. Being ruthless often has that effect.'

After she'd fallen silent, she discreetly sought out Alice's gaze and got a nod and a tiny, almost imperceptible smile in response.

'Let's move on,' said Rita. 'Revenge, the beauty empire you built up following the divorce from Jack—'

'After he left me for his much-younger co-worker,' Faye interjected.

Rita nodded.

'Yes, quite. A woman who is now part of your team at Revenge, as it happens. Where did you find the strength to do all this?'

'In all the women who have been betrayed by the men who say they love us. You can find us throughout world history. Women who have been deceived, tricked and humiliated. I wasn't going to let him win. I knew that all he cared about was money, so I wanted to show him that I could get richer than him. It was the only way to win his respect. It was my revenge. Hence the name of the company.'

'What's next for Revenge?'

'The USA,' said Faye.

'You're entering the American market?'

Faye shook her head while simultaneously holding up her index finger to reinforce her answer.

'No, we're going to *dominate* the American market.'

Rita grinned at her.

'You've talked about an American launch before – for instance, on an episode of *Skavlan* you appeared on. Is it really going to happen this time?'

Faye straightened up and met the host's eyes:

'It's going to happen.'

'Your confidence is rock solid.'

'Yes. It has to be.'

'Some might call you cocky.'

Faye smiled.

'Who would that be?'

Rita suddenly looked unsure. She laughed and shrugged.

'Rita, let me be honest with you,' Faye continued. 'I believe in myself and I believe in my company. We're owned by women and run by women. This makes us better suited than anyone else to understand what it is that a modern woman wants. Whether that's in the USA or another country. I think women all over the world are fed up with having their lives dictated to them by men.'

Rita nodded.

'Good luck. And thanks for taking the time to join us this evening.'

They sat there until the assistant floor manager came up and said they could move.

After some dutiful small talk, Faye exited the studio together with Alice and Teodora.

She'd parked the Porsche with its smashed window outside the TV4 building.

'What are you going to do now?' Alice asked once they reached the car.

'Now I'm going to secure Revenge's future,' Faye said.

After waving goodbye to Alice and Teodora, who had departed in separate taxis, she got behind the wheel. She quickly headed for the south of Stockholm.

Once she was out of the city centre, she picked up the pace to make sure no one was following her. Phil Collins' 'Another Day in Paradise' was playing on the radio and she hummed along to it. She enjoyed feeling the power of the engine as the cold night air gusted in through the window. The small joys in life had suddenly become much more meaningful. If her time was up then she was going to enjoy the moments of beauty she had left.

Stockholm, New Year's Eve 1995

There were only a few hours left until 1995 would turn into 1996 when I arrived in Sweden. Zoran and I had exchanged letters during the summer and autumn, and in the end I'd made up my mind to travel to Sweden.

He met me on the platform at Stockholm's Central Station when I got off the train from Malmö. I spotted him right away through the window as I was taking my suitcase down from the overhead rack, and I thought at once that he was even more handsome in real life. He wore a white turtleneck and a dark coat. On his feet were heavy boots.

I stepped down onto the platform and was struck by how cold it was. He smiled broadly when he caught sight of me. I'd wondered how we would greet each other, but he simply opened his arms, stepped forward, embraced me and picked me up.

'Milenka,' he said into my hair.

I laughed self-consciously. He smelled of a cologne I wasn't familiar with. Once he'd put me down, he examined me from head to foot.

'You're even more beautiful than in that photograph. But we've got to buy you a winter coat.'

'It's colder than I was expecting.'

He took off his coat and draped it around my shoulders, then picked up my bag.

'It's been snowing all day; the city is completely white. It's beautiful.'

'Won't you be cold?'

He tugged at the neck of his woolly sweater.

'This'll keep me warm. Besides, we're not going far. We're staying in a hotel.'

In the letters, he'd told me that he lived in Växjö, which was a fairly small town, but I had no idea how far away it was from Stockholm. When he said we were staying in a hotel, I became a little worried. I hoped he'd booked two rooms, because while we'd written to each other we didn't really know one another.

He was so tall that the coat he'd given me dragged along the ground as we walked towards the station building.

'Wait a minute,' he said, putting down the bag. 'Hold out your arms.'

I did as he told me and he rolled up the sleeves so that my hands were visible.

Inside the station building it was teeming with people and there was a big Christmas tree covered in lights soaring towards the lofty ceiling. We walked through the building and emerged onto the street. It was half past four in the afternoon but it was already completely dark – except for the snow, which shone. He was right: it really was beautiful. I'd never seen so much snow. The pavements, the roofs, everything was white. We turned left and trudged through the snow. My trainers were quickly sodden.

'I'll have to buy new shoes too,' I said, pointing at them.

He laughed.

'Are you cold?'

'A bit.'

He stopped and bent forward.

'Hop up.'

I laughed but shook my head.

'No.'

He smiled, then he made a loud sound that was difficult to interpret.

'What was that?' I asked.

'I was neighing,' he said, a broad grin still on his face. 'Now hop up.'

I realised he meant it. He bent his knees and I hesitantly clambered up onto his back. He straightened up, picked up my bag and then continued to trudge through the snow. People stared at us but I didn't care. I held onto him and inhaled the scent of his aftershave.

Like Zoran had said, it wasn't far to the hotel. When we stepped into the foyer, he put me down and went over to reception where he spoke to the young woman behind the counter in Swedish. I couldn't understand a word of it and thought I would never be able to learn that language.

He was issued with a key and I realised that we would be staying in separate rooms, since he'd told me on the way to the hotel that he'd arrived in Stockholm the day before. For some reason, this was both a relief and disappointment to me, even though I'd done my best not to show it. He was my only safety net and I feared he would leave me alone and abandoned in my room.

We went up to the third floor and he led the way. He stopped outside room 317, inserted the key into the lock and opened it. He held the door open for me and I went in.

'What do you think?'

I was speechless. I'd never seen anything like it, although I had admittedly never stayed in a hotel before. Everything was shiny and looked new. I couldn't fathom how he could afford this. According to his letters, he was a waiter in a restaurant. Sweden really was a peculiar country if restaurant employees could afford to live like royalty. I could not figure it out.

'It's incredible,' I said.

I went over to the window and gazed down at the white street below, where the traffic was crawling past. He stood next to me. I took off the coat and handed it to him. Then I took off the coat I'd brought with me from Zagreb and put it on the bed. It looked cheap on the luxurious sheets.

I saw him looking at my body but pretended not to notice.

'Where are you staying?' I said.

He pointed to the wall.

'Next door.'

'What are we doing tonight?'

'I don't know about you, but I've got a date,' he said, twisting his wrist towards me so that I could see his watch.

I stared at him and then noticed the corners of his mouth were twitching before he burst into laughter.

'I've got us a table booked for seven.'

'What time is it now?'

'A quarter past five. Meet you down in the foyer at half past six and we'll have a drink before dinner.'

He put the key down on the desk and then left me alone.

I heard the door to the neighbouring room open and close. Then I bent down and opened my bag. Judging by the little I'd seen of what Swedish women wore, I realised I was going to look hopeless.

Suddenly, the telephone on the desk rang. I winced and stared at it. What was I supposed to say? I didn't know a word of Swedish and I only had a few English phrases. I reached out and gingerly picked up the receiver.

'Hello?' I said in English.

It was Zoran.

'Did you wonder who it was?'

I smiled at my own reflection.

'Yes.'

'I forgot to say that Father Christmas was late this year. He couldn't find Croatia.'

I didn't understand what he was getting at.

'So he left a present for you in your wardrobe.'

I glanced in that direction.

'Wait a second,' I said, carefully putting the receiver down on the desk. I opened the wardrobe doors to find a glittering black dress on a hanger. I stared at it. I'd never seen a garment so beautiful, and I didn't dare contemplate how much it must have cost. On the floor there was a pair of matching black shoes.

I took the dress out on its hanger and held it up in front of me while looking in the mirror. It looked like a perfect fit. I grabbed the receiver again.

'What do you think?' Zoran said.

'I love it. I don't know how to thank you. But how did you know my size?'

'I asked your mother. She helped me. The heels are a size 36 so they should also fit, although it'll be chilly. But the restaurant we're going to is right nearby.'

'You'll just have to carry me on your back again,' I said, smiling. 'See you at half past six.'

Faye pressed the doorbell of the small terraced house. A sudden gust of wind made her shiver. This encounter with Johan Sjölander was going to determine her future. If it didn't go well, she'd have to rethink and come up with another plan. But she hoped that Johan was as reliable as she remembered him being. They hadn't seen each other for a long time.

The door opened and Johan stared at her in surprise. His blond hair was, if it were possible, even more tousled than she recalled. The first time she had met him, she'd thought there was something open and good about him, and the same thing still applied.

It warmed the cockles of Faye's heart to see his lanky figure.

'Hello! Can I come in?'

'Sure thing. Sorry. I was just so...'

Faye stepped inside and embraced him.

'I'm sorry to show up like this out of the blue, but we need to talk.'

'You're always welcome here – you know that. Can I get you something to drink?'

'Tea, if you've got it?'

Johan showed her into a small kitchen.

Hanging on the wall behind a traditional box bench there was a framed photographic portrait. Faye's eyes filled with tears when she saw her best friend's face. The final days were so clear in her memory: Chris wasting away and her strong body getting weaker while the doctors were unable to do anything. Faye usually consoled herself that at least Chris had been happy with Johan.

Johan looked at Faye.

'She loved it when I cooked, especially at the end. It was special to her, given that she couldn't eat anything herself. That's why I wanted her in here to keep me company when I'm making my packed lunches.'

There was a lump in Faye's throat. She had no defence mechanisms against her grief over the death of Chris. At the same time, she felt a pang of guilty conscience vis à vis Johan. She should have visited more often; he must be very lonely. But perhaps that was why she couldn't handle it – he reminded her too much of Chris.

He busied himself boiling water for the tea.

'Packed lunches. So I take it you're still teaching?' Faye said, sitting down on the creaky bench.

Johan got out two cups and saucers, added teabags and then set them down on the side while waiting for the water to boil.

'I sure am. Same school. I don't think I'll ever change profession or workplace.'

Faye gave him a long look. This was the man who had inherited Chris's fortune – except the company itself – but who continued to live a seemingly modest life.

He poured the water into the cups and carried them over to the table. He sat down on the chair opposite Faye.

'Are you sure about that?'

'About what?' he said absent-mindedly.

'That you'll always want to be a teacher?'

He laughed.

'Are you offering me a job or something?'

Faye realised that not even in his wildest dreams could he conceive of what she was about to offer him.

She smiled.

'Well, as it happens, I am.'

Johan scrutinised her as if waiting for her to burst into laughter, but Faye's gaze didn't waver.

'Are you serious? What use am I to you?'

'I trust you. That's good enough for me. Actually, that's pretty much the job description.'

Johan blew on his tea but said nothing.

'Shouldn't you be asking what the job is?' said Faye.

He removed the teabag with the teaspoon, squeezed a couple of drops out of it and then deposited it on the saucer.

'What's the job?'

'Mine. I want you to be the CEO of Revenge.'

Johan began to roar with laughter, but Faye remained completely expressionless as she waited for him to finish.

'Are you completely out of your mind?' he said at last. 'I don't know a thing about running a multinational. And I definitely don't know anything about beauty products. Why would you want me to do that job? Besides, aren't I the wrong gender? Isn't the whole thing with Revenge that it's by women for women?'

'Like I said: I trust you. Despite your obvious handicap of having a penis.'

Johan shook his head and rubbed his eyes.

'I'm glad you asked, Faye, although I still think you're joking. Thanks, but no thanks. I think you'd be much better off without me. Things seem to be going pretty well. Anyway, what are you going to do if you no longer want to be CEO?'

'For various reasons, I need to distance myself from the company for a while.'

'What reasons would those be?' There was a flash of worry in his eyes. 'You're not sick, are you?'

He glanced quickly up at the portrait on the wall behind Faye.

'No, I'm not sick. For reasons that I can't go into right

now, I need to create a barrier between me and Revenge but I need to maintain control of the company. To do that, I need someone I can trust on the inside. And since Chris passed away there's only you. She trusted you. Which is why I do too.'

He opened his mouth as if to say something but then closed it again. Faye sensed that he was weakening.

'The salary is nineteen million kronor a year.'

His eyes widened.

'Plus bonus.'

He shook his head.

'I don't know.'

'I need your help.' Faye could hear how imploring her voice sounded. Naked. Vulnerable.

Johan hesitated.

'In that case I wouldn't do it for the money. I've got more than enough to get by on. I'd be doing it for you. Because it's what she would have wanted,' he said, nodding towards the picture of Chris.

'I know that.'

'Isn't there loads of paperwork and stuff? Or some sort of vote?'

Faye shook her head.

'As you know, you're already on the board, even if you haven't been all that active. Those were Chris's wishes when she bequeathed Queen Group to me, to be incorporated into Revenge. So you're already part of Revenge, even if you've never really ... got involved.'

Johan shook his head slowly.

'It would mean a lot if you did this for me,' Faye said. 'I really am in a tight corner. I might lose everything. And if I'm honest, you'll only be a figurehead. An invisible one at that. I'll provide you with clear instructions and you'll have a team around you who'll take care of most things.'

They sipped their tea.

Then Johan nodded.

'Okay, I'll do it,' he said. 'For your sake, and for Chris.'

Faye smiled warmly at him.

'Thank you. Ylva's drafting a contract. We'll send it over to you by messenger by tomorrow for your signature. There's some other stuff to be signed, but then you'll be in charge of a company that has forecast revenues this year of fifteen billion kronor. You'll be able to put Russian caviar in your packed lunch if you want.'

Johan gazed at her forlornly.

'Chris was always the one who loved Russian caviar. Personally, I've always been more partial to squeezing mine out of a tube of Kalles.'

Faye placed her hand on his.

'And that's exactly why I'm able to entrust my life's work to you.'

The very next morning, Johan arrived to settle in at Revenge's offices. The school he worked at was desperate to make cutbacks, so they'd had no problem with letting him go immediately.

'I don't think I've ever felt so out of place in my whole life…'

Johan gently ran a hand across Faye's polished desk.

'If you like, I can scratch some expletives onto the desk so that you feel more at home,' she said.

'That would definitely make it easier.'

Johan laughed nervously.

Ylva swept in with a stack of folders in her arms.

'Here are the accounts for the last few years. It would be good if you could get to grips with the figures as soon as possible.'

'Faye? Help?'

Johan paled and looked like he wanted to get up and bolt.

Faye sat down next to him and stroked his arm reassuringly.

'You're not alone – okay? You'll have Ylva here every day, I'll pitch in where I can, and the rest of the team are at your disposal. Most of it's just common sense. It's not astrophysics. Money comes in, money goes out. Ylva sees to most of the details. You only need to be knowledgeable enough to help make sensible decisions.'

'Sensible decisions about a corporation making billions,'

Johan muttered. 'You do realise that I struggle to decide what to eat for lunch?'

He stared at the folders as if they were snakes preparing to attack him any moment.

'Look at this. You don't need to know all the figures. There's an executive summary at the front of each folder. Here's last year's.'

Faye opened the folder on the top of the pile and laid it in front of Johan. She calmly and methodically explained the various entries. He nodded and she could tell that his fear was gradually beginning to dissipate.

'Here are some more folders.'

Ylva came back in with another pile the same size and the panic-stricken expression was immediately back on Johan's face.

Faye stood up and laid a hand on his shoulder.

'You know what? We can do this later. We've got something much more important to see to now. Something that's vital to your new role as CEO.'

'What?' Johan said in horror. 'Something even worse than this?'

'That depends on how attached you are to your corduroy jacket.'

She pulled out her phone and dialled the number of her stylist, Niklas Berglind.

'Niklas, we've got an emergency assignment. Can you meet me at Nordiska Kompaniet in an hour? In Menswear.'

Johan held up his hands defensively.

'Faye... I... No. I actually happen to like my jacket. I'd rather stay here with the folders. I...'

'The jacket's history. Come on.'

Johan muttered loudly as Faye dragged him out of the office. Somewhere in her own heaven, Faye knew that Chris would be choking with laughter.

It was half past one by the time Faye and Alice met for lunch at the Grand Hôtel. It was a Friday and the dining rooms were full of the rich and beautiful. Faye was hungry and ordered beef Rydberg while Alice went for a fish stew.

Alice was constantly vigilant, and Faye couldn't help but smile at her concern.

'No one's following us.'

'Are you sure?'

Faye nodded.

'We'll have to trust Secur.'

Their wine arrived. Alice sipped hers, looking worried.

'Can't we just forget about the outside world for a little while? Let's pretend we're just two regular friends out to celebrate the end of a successful working week,' Faye said, taking a mouthful of wine.

A week after she'd started preparing Johan for his new job, Faye had started to wonder whether she had been getting things out of proportion or whether Secur had been mistaken in their conclusion that she was under police surveillance. The operation against her appeared to have been paused, that was, if there had been one at all. This was confirmed by Carl Novak and his personnel, who were still monitoring Faye and reporting on any suspicious activities in her vicinity. Things had been calm of late.

Johan had stepped into the role of CEO with great seriousness and had proved to be perfectly cut out for the task. He was calm, interested and friendly, and had quickly become immensely popular at the office. What was more, he was very well dressed in the new suits she and the stylist had picked out for him at the department store.

Faye couldn't help but be impressed by him, although at the same time she suspected that she might have been a little too hasty in drawing her conclusions and taking action. The police must have eventually decided that she was innocent of the murder of Jack after all. But she couldn't help wondering what had caused them to re-open the investigation.

Her father, however, was still out there somewhere – full of hatred towards her. He was probably just waiting for an opportunity to strike. With that in mind, this solution was the best – of that she was certain. And the security detail attached to her mother and daughter at the house in Ravi had been greatly expanded.

Alice got up to go to the ladies and Faye was left on her own. She caught the eye of a young waiter. He was tall and dark-haired, like an Italian film star.

Since it had been uncovered that she was under surveillance, she'd barely had time to think about men and she interpreted her own covetous glances at him as a sign that she was regaining some degree of balance.

Thanks to Johan, Revenge was safe no matter what happened. She was – at least on paper – no more than a regular employee with a monstrous salary. She could afford to have some fun. Who knew when she'd next have the chance?

Having already checked that the waiter wasn't wearing a wedding ring, she beckoned him over.

'Is everything to your satisfaction?' he asked, dazzling her with his brilliant smile.

She smiled back.

'Not quite.'

He adopted a neutral expression while awaiting further details.

'I'm having a party at my place this evening, but I don't have any guests. So I thought I'd ask if you fancied popping round?'

A flash of uncertainty crossed the handsome face.

'A party?'

'Well, I did buy a new house.'

'So it's a housewarming?'

'I suppose you might say that.'

'Do I need to bring a housewarming gift?'

'That won't be necessary. I've never really been one for vases and that kind of thing.'

He smiled. His confidence had returned. Faye wanted him.

'I get off at six.'

'Give me a note of your address and phone number and I'll send a car to pick you up at eight. What's your name?'

'Philippe.'

'My name's…'

'I know who you are.'

He bowed slightly with a glint in his eye before making his retreat.

Alice returned and sat down again.

'What are you doing tonight?' she said.

Faye smiled at her.

'I've got plans.'

A moment later, Philippe stopped at their table and asked whether they needed anything else. As he bent down to remove their empty glasses, he dropped a piece of paper on the floor next to Faye. She and Alice each ordered another drink.

'Was I seeing things, or did he drop that piece of paper on purpose?'

Alice grabbed the note and read it.

'82 Folkungagatan.'

She looked at Faye in amusement.

'That's just what you need after a week like this,' she said, handing it over to Faye.

'My thoughts exactly.'

The food arrived and as they ate the atmosphere became more relaxed. Alice no longer seemed so worried.

Outside the windows, a crowd of people had begun to form by the main entrance. The hotel staff and some bouncers had set up a cordon with barriers and there were a number of photographers standing there with their cameras raised.

'What's going on?' Faye said.

Alice shrugged.

'I think there's some popstar who's playing at the Avicii Arena tonight staying here. Can't remember who.'

They finished their wine and agreed to go their separate ways. Faye had taken a taxi to the office that morning and was going to ask the doorman to arrange another for her now. She wanted to go home and freshen up ahead of Philippe's visit.

As they moved through the foyer, she heard a voice behind her.

'Faye Adelheim.'

She spun around.

Standing in front of her were two people, a man and a woman. She recognised them as two of the police officers that Secur had shown her photographs of.

'We're from the police. Would you come with us, please.'

The two officers moved to stand either side of Faye, and as they led her out of the building camera shutters clicked and flashes dazzled her, and she heard surprised voices calling out her name.

'Do you want a lawyer present?'

'I don't need a lawyer,' Faye said in a tone of voice that sounded much more confident than she felt.

The two police officers filled the room with their presence. The big policeman was sitting opposite her at the bare table. The policewoman was leaning against the wall, toying with a strand of well-blow-dried hair as she contemplated Faye, a slight smile playing across her lips.

'Very well. Let's start the interview then. Present are Detective Inspector Fred Larsson and Detective Inspector Hanna Bergh.'

DI Fred Larsson's muscles were visible beneath his shirt as he bent forward.

'What do you know about the murder of your ex-husband, Jack Adelheim?'

He took command, but after a quick analysis of their body language, Faye realised that it was DI Bergh who was running the show from the other side of the room. They were playing a game. She just needed to figure out what it was.

Faye shrugged.

'Nothing more than anyone else. As I'm sure you understand, Jack and I weren't in regular contact. I know very little about his life towards the end.'

'Did you hate him?'

DI Larsson suddenly got to his feet and towered over her. He was trying to intimidate her with his size. To some extent, it was working. Her reptilian brain immediately reminded her of the way her father had so often loomed over her like that in those brief moments of terror before the pain followed.

'Of course I hated him,' she said, hopefully without giving away what impact his intrusion into her personal space was having. 'He killed my child.'

'Enough to want to see him dead?'

DI Bergh's voice was gentler than Larsson's. She was studying Faye intently with her arms folded and her back against the wall.

'I think Jack deserves to burn in hell. Does that answer your question? I expect he crossed some line or other in a business context.'

'What do you base that assumption on?' DI Bergh again. Her voice was treacherously soft.

'What I know about Jack. I lived with him for many years. For better and worse. Jack never did know when to quit. And who not to challenge.'

Faye leaned in towards DI Larsson, whose eyes widened before he regained control of his facial expression.

'Why are you asking these questions?' she said. 'Have you found something?'

There was a moment's silence. Then DI Bergh took a step towards her, bent down and spoke in a low voice.

'Yes, we have. We're arresting you on suspicion of murder.'

PART II

Jenny Strömstedt's friendly face and the words coming out of her mouth were in stark contrast to one another. Faye had laughed many times at the popular clip of the time when Jenny had been frying cheesy puffs and had almost set her television studio on fire. She wasn't laughing now. Jenny and her fellow breakfast show anchor Steffo were going through Faye's case step by step.

Faye was squirming on her bunk. There was an impression in the mattress in the shape of her body. She'd been in custody for a long time now. The small grey cell in the Kronoberg Remand Prison where she was being held was as familiar to her as the vast Östermalm apartment in which she had until recently lived.

'This trial really has captured the attention of the Swedish public of late.'

'And it's not just Sweden,' Steffo interjected. 'There's also been huge interest in the international media too.'

'That's right. This trial has been making the front pages both in Sweden and abroad. Faye Adelheim, founder of the multinational beauty empire Revenge, is facing charges for the murder of her ex-husband Jack Adelheim.'

Jenny pronounced these words carefully. Seriously. Faye looked away from the small TV on the bookcase. She had a hard time taking in that it was her they were talking about, that this was about her life.

The media had dispatched legions of journalists to the courtroom and they had all happily reported every single detail. It had been a perfect storm: the enigmatic billionairess, whose daughter had been murdered and who amidst her grief had created the beauty empire Revenge, had avenged her daughter's death by killing the man who was guilty and who – to top it all – was her ex-husband. The public gallery behind the glass in court room 37 on the second floor of the district court building on Scheelegatan had been full to bursting every day.

'Support for Faye Adelheim remains widespread,' Jenny said, and Faye turned back to face the TV. Jenny held up a white t-shirt emblazoned with the words *Free Faye*. 'This t-shirt started appearing a few days ago, while the hashtags "freefaye" and "killemallfaye" are trending across all social media platforms.'

She put down the t-shirt and turned towards a man sitting opposite her.

'But while she may have a lot of backers, it's hard to ignore the evidence, isn't it, Leif G. W. Persson?'

The camera panned across towards Persson, Sweden's most renowned criminologist and one of Faye's favourite authors. He took his time before answering. In a characteristic movement he slowly pushed his glasses up onto his forehead.

'Yes...'

He strung out his words. Jenny and Steffo waited patiently, accustomed to his long pauses given that he was a regular guest on the programme.

'Well ... it doesn't look good for Faye Adelheim. In my view, the prosecutor did a superb job of tying the whole thing together – with a bow on top.'

'Would you say this is a so-called circumstantial case, as her defence lawyer has frequently claimed?'

Jenny leaned forward.

Persson chuckled, making his green jacket rise and fall.

'Well, I suppose I would say that. But the ingenious thing about circumstantial evidence is that if there's enough of it, that constitutes good evidence. The necklace belonging to her that was discovered by a mushroom picker at the site where Jack Adelheim's remains were found is very incriminating in itself. Plus she has a powerful motive for wanting to kill her ex-husband. What's more, her alibi has only been supported by one close friend. I would say things are looking bleak for her.'

'But her defence lawyer said she'd had her car broken into and that the necklace was stolen then, and that she wore the necklace for a long time following Jack Adelheim's disappearance.'

'Well, it hasn't been proven that there actually was a break-in to her car; there wasn't anything to prove that. No one saw the break-in and she might just as well have smashed the window herself. And the strange thing is that nothing else was taken – there was a very expensive handbag full of stuff lying there in the open, and according to her the only thing that went missing was the aforementioned necklace. Besides, no witnesses have been able to testify that Faye Adelheim has worn the item in a long time. Last but not least, only her own fingerprints were found on the necklace and locket. A juicy detail is that the locket actually contained a photo of the accused and her daughter. It seems almost unbelievably careless to drop something like that at a crime scene in the way the prosecutor is alleging she did.'

'But Faye Adelheim can hardly be said to be careless,' Steffo objected. 'She's internationally known for her sharp business brain.'

'Yes, but it's one thing having a business brain and quite another to think smart when you've just murdered someone. Personal emotions and so on come into play and cloud your judgement. And in this case he murdered her daughter. Revenge and hatred. They can cause even the best of us to make mistakes. There are many people with high IQs who are currently under lock and key.'

'Thank you as ever, Leif, for your judicious input.' Jenny looked back to camera. 'The verdict in Faye Adelheim's trial will be handed down today. We'll be live here on TV4 at three o'clock. And now we're welcoming to the studio Lis Evertsson who is going to tell us all about how to make beautiful gifts with things you find in the woods.'

Faye averted her gaze from the screen. She was empty inside. She felt nothing. Not fear; not anger. Now she just wanted to know.

Stockholm, New Year's Eve 1995

I'll never forget the look he gave me as I came into the hotel bar, where he was already sipping a drink. It was as if he hadn't seen me before. I'd never felt more beautiful. The dress sparkled in the dim lighting and the shoes made me some three inches taller. Nevertheless, when Zoran stood up I realised that he was still at least half a head taller than me.

'Milenka, you look ... amazing,' he said.

He drew out a chair for me. I sat down, feigning nonchalance.

'Thanks,' I said, smiling.

He was handsome in his dark suit and with his dark hair combed back.

'What would you like to drink?'

'I'll have what you're having,' I said, pointing to his glass, which was almost empty.

Zoran went to the bar. While waiting for the drinks to be poured, he turned around and contemplated me. I couldn't make head nor tail of that look, because it radiated both love and something wild and untamed. It worried me but also attracted me in a way I'd never experienced before.

It was like a fairytale – a dream. Stockholm was beautiful, exotic, and I'd met a man who was still a stranger yet spoiling me rotten. The war, Zagreb and my toil at the Rose all seemed very distant. I was still on the same continent, but I might as well have been on another planet.

Zoran returned with the drinks, we clinked glasses and I asked him to tell me about Växjö and his life there.

'I work in a restaurant,' he said. 'Although I won't be doing that for much longer.'

'Are you leaving?'

He shook his head with a smile.

'No, I'm going to buy it.'

'The restaurant?'

He nodded enthusiastically.

'The owner is also a Croat. He's moving to Gothenburg. He's letting me have it cheap. I've basically been running the place for the last year, so I know it's got potential.'

I gazed at him wide-eyed. Sweden really did seem to be a place that only got stranger. A country in which a poor boy from Croatia could become a restaurant proprietor after living there for barely three years…

'Things are going to work out for me,' he said, raising his glass into the air again. He sipped the drink without taking his eyes off me. Those green eyes were gazing at me intently. 'Here's to us. I'm going to take care of you, Milenka.'

'I know,' I said in a low voice, raising my glass.

I'd always cherished being as independent as I could be, making my own money, having my own life, but all those dreams were overthrown in that hotel bar. I couldn't bring myself to be strong any longer. I wanted to be taken care of by Zoran. I wanted him to look at me with that covetous gaze every single day for the rest of my life and I wanted him to be my husband.

If he'd asked me to get married to him there and then I would have said yes without hesitation.

We finished our drinks and Zoran settled up. He draped his coat around my shoulders and since the snow was still lying on the ground, white and soft, he carried me on his back over to the cab rank outside the railway station. We got into one, Zoran gave the address to the driver and then the car pulled away. I couldn't help but gaze out of the window. Large expanses of the water had frozen to ice. Festively dressed people were visible everywhere.

'Over there is the palace where the King and Queen of Sweden live,' Zoran said.

It was a beautiful, illuminated palace, but it didn't look like the castles I'd imagined as a little girl.

The car turned off the road and pulled into a big park. There was electronic pop music pumping out of a large building. A long queue of people were stamping their feet in the snow outside. Zoran opened the car door and helped me to get out. The snow had melted here, so I was able to walk on my own with my arm linked into his.

'Is this where we're going?' I asked, pointing to the door.

'No, that's a nightclub. We're going to the restaurant around the corner.'

'What's it called?'

'Operakällaren.'

I tried to imitate the word noiselessly so that he wouldn't hear me, but he noticed and his mouth twitched.

'You'll learn Swedish, no problems,' he said with conviction.

There was an inviting glow from the windows, through which well-dressed people could be seen eating at low-lit tables. He held the door open for me and we stepped into the warmth. The maître d' ticked off Zoran's name on a list and showed us to our table. My nerves only got worse. The other patrons all looked so urbane. I tried to behave like them, mimicking their movements and placing the napkin on my lap.

Zoran ordered a bottle of champagne and then he moved his chair around the small table so that we were sitting close together, side by side. I glanced at the other tables to see whether anyone else had done that, but it was just us.

Zoran seemed completely unfazed. It was as if we were alone there. He opened the menu and pointed to the different dishes, explaining to me what was in them. We settled on steak frites with something called Béarnaise sauce, which he claimed was the most delicious sauce he'd ever tried.

'Do you have this at the restaurant in Växjö?'

'Yes, of course. Although I think it'll be better here. Actually, I'm sure of it. There's still a lot to do to get the restaurant profitable, but I'm not afraid of hard work. We're going to succeed.'

A tingle ran down my spine when I realised he'd said 'we'. That meant we belonged together; that we were a unit.

He looked at me gravely and then placed his big hand over mine.

'Are you worried?'

I shook my head.

'No. I trust you.'

I meant it. There was something invincible about him. He was a man who couldn't be defeated, who took whatever he wanted. This scared me but it also left me weak at the knees.

'There's our food.'

The sauce really was exquisite, just like the rest of the dish. I'd never eaten anything as delicious. Zoran had ordered a bottle of red wine and as we drank I felt the alcohol begin to take effect.

The conversation never faltered. Zoran told me about Sweden, about his difficult beginnings, about how lonely he'd felt. I had thousands of questions that he patiently answered with a smile.

He pressed dessert upon me and I opted for the crème brûlée.

The time was getting away from us. I could see from Zoran's wristwatch that it was already gone eleven.

'I thought we'd go and watch the fireworks down by the Palace,' he said.

I shook my head.

'Let's go to the hotel.'

He furrowed his brow.

'Are you tired after your journey?'

'Yes, but I don't want to sleep.'

He looked at me askance and I responded to his gaze without blinking. He summoned a waiter to request the bill. When it came, he produced a money clip and deposited two red banknotes on the table before getting to his feet.

When we emerged into the cold, I was surprised that he didn't offer me his coat. I wondered if I'd done something wrong; if he was disappointed in me. But as soon as we had turned the corner, he stopped. He unfolded the coat and draped it over my shoulders. I spotted that he was holding something. It was a bottle of champagne.

'We need something to toast the arrival of 1996.'

I tucked my cold hands into the coat pockets and found something hard in them. He'd brought the glasses with him too. I couldn't help but smile.

Zoran flagged down a taxi, opened the door for me and we got in. He handed me the glasses, opened the bottle and poured. From time to time there was the sound of firecrackers. Everything felt unreal.

There were more people in the streets now; big groups were moving about, presumably seeking spots from which to view the fireworks that were going to illuminate the dark sky to welcome in the new year.

The taxi stopped outside the hotel and we entered through the glass doors. When we got out of the lift on our floor, there was suddenly an air of seriousness about us. We'd stopped talking to one another.

He took my hand and led me to his room. He unlocked the door and let me in. The room was meticulously tidy, the bed made. There was the faint smell of his cologne. I shrugged off the coat and helped him to take off his jacket. Then it was me who took him by the hand, led him to the bed and told him to sit down. I'm not really sure where my audacity came from.

I loosened his tie and undid his shirt and pulled it off him. Then my hands moved to my shoulder straps and the black dress fell to the floor. He stared as I took off my bra and panties.

I pressed his chest, causing him to fall backwards onto the bed, and then I straddled him. I moved back and forth on top of him; I could feel he was hard.

The sky exploded above us. I reached out for the bottle of champagne he was clutching, raised the heavy bottle and drank greedily from it. I pressed myself down against him even harder.

'I'm yours,' I whispered. 'Do whatever you want with me.'

It was an unusually cold morning. On the news they'd said that February hadn't got off to this cold a start in years. Outside the window, the snow was falling onto the frost-covered birch trees.

Faye thought it would have been beautiful were it not for the high fences topped with barbed wire that surrounded the prison. It was still dark as she pulled on her drab and shapeless prison clothes. She'd arrived at Stenakull Prison the night before; the prisoner transport had been delayed by snow.

She'd been convicted of the murder of her ex-husband Jack. She was now regarded as one of Sweden's most dangerous women, and as such there had been no option for her but Stenakull.

Neither the District Court nor the Court of Appeal had paid any heed to the many women who had gathered outside the courts with placards as they shouted loudly for justice for Faye. She'd been handed a life sentence. They'd swallowed the assorted pieces of circumstantial evidence, topped off by her necklace being discovered close to the burnt-out house where Jack's body had been found. Just as Leif G. W. Persson had predicted.

Clearly, someone who wished her harm had framed her. The necklace had disappeared from her car and been planted at the murder scene after the murder took place. Faye was convinced that her father was mixed up in it somehow. And she couldn't help worrying that a worse fate than that awaited her in this prison. She would have to be vigilant – constantly ready to defend herself.

She went into the small bathroom and splashed water on her face. When she had arrived here the evening before, she'd been surprised to find that the inmates had ensuites with toilets and showers in their cells. Having watched far too many movies and TV shows about women's prisons, she'd been picturing a rusty bucket in a corner and communal showers.

Faye stood by the cell door which was going to be unlocked soon, and stretched her aching back. The narrow bunk comprised a wooden base with a thin mattress on top.

On the table there was a set of cutlery made from hard plastic. She guessed she was supposed to take them with her, so she picked them up to be ready.

The door was unlocked and she set off for the dining room where the inmates ate breakfast together. There were twelve women in her wing. Shortly after Faye entered the anonymous dining room, a young woman with brushed-back black hair and wearing a tracksuit appeared and stood by the serving counter. She nodded at Faye. A woman in her sixties slouched in behind her. The older woman came up to Faye and introduced herself.

'Louise Axén,' she said.

'My name's—'

'Faye. Everyone in here knows. We've been following the trial. Both in the District Court and at the Court of Appeal. Obviously we wanted you to be acquitted, although there were a few of us who were hoping you'd end up here if you went down.'

She smiled and the woman in the tracksuit turned towards Faye.

'Hey, celeb, you gonna help out or what?'

Faye hurried to do as she was told. She noticed that Louise

and the young woman in the tracksuit were bickering, almost as if they were mother and daughter. She realised that she liked listening to them as she stirred the big pot of rice pudding.

More women arrived. Sleepy, their hair dishevelled, they trudged in and sat down at the tables. Some came over and greeted her, while others didn't.

Faye watched them carefully without staring, fearing she might provoke them. She noticed that one of the women was pregnant. The conversations she caught snippets of were about visits from children and relatives. She wouldn't be receiving any visitors of her own for a while. She'd told Kerstin, Alice and Ylva that it would be for the best if they didn't come to see her for the foreseeable future.

When memories of Julienne came to mind, her blonde hair flowing behind her in the wind as she ran to the pool or her breathing when she had just fallen asleep, Faye was hit so hard by the sense of longing that her body ached and a knot formed in her stomach. She hoped that her mother was giving her granddaughter all the love and security she needed in Ravi. And she hoped they were safe.

The older woman, Louise, came over and put a hand on Faye's shoulder.

'If there's anything you need, you come to me. I've been here a while.'

Faye forced herself not to ask what *a while* meant.

'Thank you. I appreciate it.'

They sat down at a table. A male prison officer, or a 'screw' as Louise referred to him, came in and wished them a good morning. The women listlessly returned the salutation. Once he'd turned around and left, they went back to their conversations.

Louise poured fruit sauce onto her rice pudding.

'I'm training to be a welder. There are quite a lot of us who are. Have you decided what you're going to do?'

All around them, women were stuffing themselves with rice pudding. Their table manners were definitely so-so at best.

'Yes, I'm going to sew,' Faye said.

'Then you'll be making clothes for every prisoner in Sweden – you'll be a hit.'

The girl in the tracksuit, whose name Faye still didn't know, leaned forward.

'Can you make the tops a bit tighter? Preferably with a proper neckline.' She clasped her voluminous bust. 'My bae paid fifty grand for these puppies.'

Faye laughed.

'I promise to give it some thought. What's your name?'

'Miryam.'

She offered her hand to Faye, who shook it.

Once breakfast had been eaten, some of the women rinsed their cutlery and then left for their cells, while others lingered by the sofas.

Faye helped Louise and Miryam with the washing up.

'Fuck it, I really hate weekends. Nothing happens,' Miryam said.

'What do you do during the week?' Faye said.

'I'm a welder.'

'Is it fun?'

'I mean it's not Gröna Lund, but it's okay.'

Two women were standing outside the phone booth clutching phone cards, waiting their turn to make calls. The screw who had greeted them earlier was standing by the door with his thumbs in his belt. He was in his forties and his posture showed that he thought he was good looking.

'That's Arvid,' said Louise. 'He's—'

'Arvid's a ballbag,' Miryam interjected.

Louise gave her a sharp look and Miryam held up her palms.

'How come?' Faye said.

'Let's save that for another time,' Louise said. 'We just call him the Ballbag. According to reliable sources, that's because he's only got one testicle.'

Miryam went back to rinsing mugs before putting them in the dishwasher.

'Hey, Faye, how rich are you?' she said.

'Very.'

Miryam straightened up.

'So what happens to your money now?'

Faye shrugged.

'It's invested in funds, where hopefully it's growing.'

'Can you teach me how to make money grow?'

Faye set to work on the large pot that had contained the rice pudding.

'Of course.'

Miryam closed the dishwasher with a slam.

'You're doing life,' she said. 'Say you do twenty years. Maybe they will have come up with a way to stop ageing by then, so you won't be an old hag when you get out. Then it won't really matter if you're rich or a tramp like me, just as long as you're young and beautiful, right?'

Faye laughed.

'How long are you in for?'

'Another seven years. I'll be thirty when I get out,' said Miryam.

A woman that Faye had noticed while they were eating sat down on the sofa. She thought she recognised her from somewhere. She'd immediately noticed the way the other women behaved towards her and the respect in their eyes. She hadn't come up to say hello to Faye and she'd been silent throughout breakfast. Nor had anyone else addressed her. The inmate who had been watching the TV immediately passed her the remote. The woman was in her thirties, with brown hair and big, dark eyes.

'Who's that?' Faye asked Miryam in a low voice.

'Ines,' Miryam whispered back to her.

At that moment, it dawned on Faye why she knew her. Two years ago, there had been extensive tabloid coverage of a story about a gang bust in Rinkeby that had broken up a network involved in everything from drug smuggling to fraud. Ines Makhrabi had been one of the kingpins and the only woman to be convicted in the case. Because the case was so remarkable, the press had unusually published her name and picture. The journalists had been fascinated by this beautiful, taciturn young woman with her dark eyes.

It also seemed as if she held significant sway over the other inmates, without making much of a fuss. Maybe they were afraid of her? Faye resolved to be careful in Ines's vicinity.

She rinsed her cutlery under the tap.

'How come we keep the cutlery in our cells?' she asked Miryam.

'They always went missing before, so there was never anything for us to use at mealtimes. This way, the screws can keep an eye on them to make sure we're not grinding them down into shivs. Even though they're only plastic, they can get really sharp.'

'Does that sort of thing really happen?'

Faye made an effort not to sound anxious. The feeling that she'd had of being watched in the weeks before her arrest suddenly returned with full force.

'Sometimes. But don't worry. I've got your back.'

The sewing machine felt like an alien object under her hands. Faye hadn't done any sewing since her high school textiles class. But she'd been allowed to start on easy jobs. Straight seams, up and down, up and down.

The monotony of the work was strangely soothing. It was so different from her usual working environment, where no day was like another and new crises and issues were constantly coming her way for her to resolve. She loved that. But she couldn't allow herself to miss it. If she gave in to the sense of loss then she'd fall to pieces. Right now, she let herself be lulled by the monotony of straight lines on green fabric.

The machine made an odd sound and Faye swore. The thread had got tangled. She gazed despondently at the mess. A voice behind her made her jump.

'Do you need help?'

Louise was standing behind her. Faye smiled gratefully and moved aside. Louise took her place and began to quickly and deftly adjust the thread in the machine.

'I was on sewing before. I can do this in my sleep. You just have to make sure that you're careful when you're threading it. And keep the material nice and taut as you sew.'

Louise finished the row for her before getting back to her feet.

'*Voilà.*'

'Thank you. I really have no idea what I'm doing.'

'You'll soon learn.'

Louise patted her on the shoulder and went off towards another of the women. There was a radio on at low volume and Faye found herself humming along to the music as she picked up a new piece of fabric, which she carefully positioned underneath the presser foot.

'Dreams of silver, dreams of gold...'

It was a golden oldie that Faye remembered her mum had often sung when she was little.

'No dreams of silver or gold in here. Only dreams of bronze. The worst kind,' Louise called out to her from the door before leaving the room.

Faye smiled, but she felt her heart aching. Louise was right. All she had left were dreams of bronze.

It was mid-February. The snow was thickly layered on the rooftops as Faye and Miryam strolled around the exercise yard. They were entitled to an hour outdoors every day. The days were dragging. Faye was trying to adapt to the monotonous life at Stenakull. In those moments when the realisation hit her that she would be in here for years and never be able to receive visits from her daughter, she struggled to breathe for minutes at a time, gasping for air. She had to force herself not to get hung up on her longing; if she did then she wouldn't survive in here.

While Stenakull seemed calm on the surface, she had noticed that there were deep underlying machinations and serious conflicts between the women.

Miryam was more than happy to tell her who were in relationships, who had broken up and who was screwing which screw.

One night Faye had woken to the roar of vehicle engines. She'd climbed out of bed, gone to the window and sat down on her desk to stare into the darkness. Over the past week, she had been so focused on finding her place among the others that she had almost forgotten about the outside world. The roaring of engines – probably from some drag race somewhere on the far side of the woods – was a reminder that life was continuing as normal in the world beyond the high fences.

At the same time, she tried to deliberately shut out the world by not responding when people got in touch. Only today she'd received a letter from Alice in which she explained that all the major newspapers, online outlets and TV channels in Scandinavia, several other European countries and even the *New York Times* wanted to bag the first, exclusive interview with the billionairess who had taken revenge on her husband by murdering him. Was she interested, Alice asked.

Faye knew she wasn't going to reply. She also knew that she needed to get out of there – and not just because of her purely physical need to get to Julienne and be her mum. She was vulnerable inside Stenakull Prison – she was a soft target if her father somehow managed to reach her in here.

She slowed down and lowered her voice.

'Has anyone escaped from here?' she asked Miryam, who was blowing on her hands before rubbing them together.

'Not for a while. But it's possible.'

'How?'

Miryam ran a hand through her hair and then looked at her.

'The screws. You take their keys.'

'How do you do that?'

'By sucking dick or eating pussy. If you'll pardon my French.'

Faye grinned. She spotted Ines walking not far away, alone as always.

Miryam continued:

'The problem isn't how to escape, the problem is how to keep your head down. I've been inside for four years and I'm not really sure what I'd do on the outside. And keeping clear of the pigs is way harder than you think.'

'But you told me on my first day here that you wanted to get out…'

Miryam laughed.

'Talk's easy. The truth is, you get comfortable in here. I'm shit scared of getting out. And I don't think I'm the only one.'

They turned around and began to walk back again.

'Do you mind me asking why you're here?'

Miryam coughed, the moisture in her breath forming a white cloud that quickly dissolved.

'Same as you. I killed someone.'

Faye waited; she didn't want to pressure Miryam. They walked on in silence. Eventually, Miryam seemed to make up her mind to tell her story after all.

'When I was eighteen, I met a guy,' she said. 'He was older than me, and very rich. I fell in love. Maybe with him, maybe with the money. The comfort. I grew up with a single mum, see. My old man legged it when my baby sister was born. She bust a gut to provide for me and my two sisters, but it just wasn't enough. The money would run out on the twentieth of every month and there was never any grub at home. I'd inherit my big sister's clothes. It wasn't so bad. My baby sister inherited mine. That was worse. Those rags had been through two generations by then.'

Miryam laughed.

'But then I met this guy – Olof – in a bar. He treated me like a princess. We went travelling. Italy, Dubai, Paris, Miami. I got to see things I'd only ever dreamed of. He was kind to my mum and my sisters too. I was worried about what he'd think of them. We came from Hagsätra, see, while he was from Djursholm.'

She snuffled and Faye didn't know whether it was because of the cold or the memories that were being forced to the surface.

'We went to a bunch of parties and did a bunch of drugs. You know what they're like in those circles. You do a line every now and then. Whenever there's a party, it's all part of the ritual. Because they're rich, they don't see themselves as addicts. But Olof... He started to... Let's sit down.'

They sat down on a bench beneath the solitary tree in the exercise yard. It took a while before Miryam carried on.

'He was addicted. I noticed that. He couldn't think about anything else. And I also noticed that I wanted more and more coke. First thing in the morning when I woke up. As soon as I drank anything, I wanted some. Everything started to be about drugs. I realised I had to get away from Olof.'

'What happened?' Faye said gently.

Miryam sighed and then swallowed a few times.

'I'd noticed that he was jealous of me, but I didn't realise how bad it was. One night when we were at home, I told him I wanted to leave. That I wanted to stop. That we'd die if we carried on. I could see the fire in his eyes. He went all silent and then he went out. I went to bed. My thoughts were still all over the place and I couldn't sleep. But finally I did. Then I had terrible nightmares. When I woke up, I found him on top of me, choking me. He was strangling me and his eyes were totally insane.'

Miryam stared blankly at the wall. Faye didn't know what to say.

Ines passed nearby, walking quickly with her fists clenched.

'I'd been drinking wine in bed before I'd settled down for the night. The bottle was still on my bedside table but I couldn't reach it. I could reach the corkscrew though. I was desperate. I knew I might pass out at any moment. I stabbed him in the throat with it.'

Miryam coughed.

'He died, and I ended up in here.'

Faye nodded.

Many years ago, she had also clutched a shard of glass between her hands. A jagged, green piece of glass. She'd hidden it behind a piece of broken skirting board in her bedroom in the draughty house in Fjällbacka. She'd fantasised about using it against her big brother, Sebastian, who paid her visits in the night. Who raped her. It was probably still lying there, unused.

She'd bought the house and it was now standing empty.

She'd never had it in her to sell it – perhaps because she wanted to preserve those memories. To keep control over them. How many times had she fantasised about thrusting that long, sharp piece of glass into her big brother's throat during those long, terrible nights?

'You had your reasons,' she said briefly. 'Otherwise you would have been dead.'

'We all have our reasons,' Miryam said. 'Fuck it, I'm going back inside. I'm freezing.'

'I'm going to stay out here for a bit longer. I like the fresh air.'

'Get you, Mrs Health Nut.'

With a shiver, Miryam headed for the door, hugging herself.

Out of the corner of her eye, Faye could see that Ines was rapidly approaching. She started to walk but kept her pace steady so that Ines would soon catch up. When she came alongside her, Faye picked up her pace to walk in step with her.

'Faye Adelheim. I'm new here.'

'I know who you are,' Ines answered without looking at her.

'Always nice to get a bit of fresh air, isn't it?'

'I like to walk alone.' Her voice was harsh. Or clear, as Kerstin might have said.

'Sorry, I didn't mean to...'

Ines sped up, leaving Faye in her wake. The woman had a kind of magnetism that intrigued Faye. She looked at the clock on the wall. There was still half an hour left until lunch. She headed back inside, enjoying the heat in her cheeks as she entered the warmth.

The library was on a corridor to the right of the exercise yard. She'd already been there once and checked out some books for her cell, so Bibbi the librarian nodded to her in recognition when she entered.

'The newspaper archive?'

'The computer at the far end on the left.'

The short blonde woman pointed towards a big, antiquated-looking computer in a corner. It didn't have an internet connection, but there was access to newspapers.

After running a few searches, Faye found what she was looking for: articles on Ines. She started to read. Something told her that she ought to learn as much as possible about Ines before she approached her again.

Faye remained vigilant, although she pretended when mixing with other inmates that she was open bordering on naïve. She lived in constant worry that her father would somehow get to her inside Stenakull. The fear kept her awake at night. She was certain that it was he who had broken into the Porsche, taken the necklace and planted it at the house where Jack had been found dead. That must have been the first part of his plan: putting her in prison where he'd have her in check and know where she was. The next step was to kill her on the inside – presumably through another inmate.

Her work in the sewing room was monotonous, but at least it helped to make the time pass more quickly. After work was over, Faye would hit the sports hall. She hated exercise, but realised it was imperative she keep her body strong. She couldn't go downhill, not now.

After a couple of weeks, she actually began to notice the effects. The stiffness from the nights spent on a hard bunk disappeared. She felt more alert, her mind was clearer and she was able to lift heavier and heavier weights.

One Saturday afternoon in the sports hall, Faye was interval training along with Miryam, who had become her constant companion. Inmates from the other wings were spread out across the room. Not far from them, Ines was sitting on a thick mat on the floor, apparently in a state of deep concentration. The female gang leader remained an enigma to Faye. But she understood that nothing happened in her wing without Ines having a hand in it.

She was the mistress. The queen. And she exerted her power in an unobtrusive manner that impressed Faye.

A couple of inmates from another wing were playing volleyball and when the ball came flying towards Faye she caught it.

'What you doing, cunt?'

A woman in her thirties with yellow teeth and an erratic gaze was staring at Faye. A moment later, she tried to snatch the ball from her grip. Faye resisted, knowing the attention of everyone in the sports hall was trained on them. Her impulse was to return the ball, but she knew she had to prove that she could stand up for herself or she'd end up becoming a doormat.

'What did you call me?' she said in a voice she hoped sounded quietly confident.

'Cunt. Little rich man's cunt. That's what you are.'

Faye smiled.

She made a sudden movement, causing the other woman to lose her grip. Faye hurled the ball with full force at her face and it hit her hard on the nose. The woman staggered backwards and lost her balance. She ended up on her rear end, hands to her nose as blood seeped between her fingers. The screw came running and grabbed Faye's arm while yelling for reinforcements.

'Why'd you do that?' he roared.

'What do you mean? She said she wanted her ball back,' Faye said with a smile, not taking her eyes off the woman.

She knew Ines was watching this spectacle.

'If there's anyone else who wants to play ball with this rich man's cunt, just say the word,' she said loudly.

Another screw came running and crouched down beside the injured woman.

'Jesus Christ, you're bleeding a lot, Regina!'

The woman – Regina apparently – batted his hand away and got to her feet, cursing as she almost slipped on her own blood. She didn't look at anyone as she left the sports hall.

Faye was escorted back to her wing together with Miryam and Ines. They didn't say a word to each other, but she could tell that Ines was seeing her in a new light.

Växjö, 1996

By July I was six months pregnant and Zoran and I were spending almost all our waking hours getting Ristorante Napoli – now owned by Zoran – into the black. Although the working days were long and tiring, I was happy. We were madly in love and had married in March in the town hall. Unfortunately, none of our relatives had been able to come, but Zoran had promised that we would do it all over again – except on a grander scale – in a church some day and then every single person we knew would be invited. I was content with that; it wasn't of any great importance to me. My focus was on getting the restaurant into a state to support us and the small family that we were about to create.

I learned Swedish surprisingly quickly. Those guttural sounds which had initially been no more than animal-like noises began to make sense. I had no alternative, after all. Zoran and I waited tables, processed payments, and cleaned the place, and we had an Italian chef by the name of Giuseppe. Our evening sittings were frequented by an increasing number of patrons, our cashflow improved and we were soon able to hire a waitress by the name of Stina – a local blonde with a pretty smile.

Late one Friday evening when I was in the small office off

the kitchen cashing up, Zoran came in. The last patrons had departed and it was half past eleven. He sat down, lit a cigarette and gazed at me adoringly.

'How did we do?'

I put down the last banknote and scribbled the total.

'14,500 kronor.'

He laughed.

'A new record.'

I wafted the cigarette smoke away and stood up to stretch my back.

'Yes.'

He undid his top shirt button.

'How's my son doing?'

I placed a hand on my belly.

'How do you know it's a boy?'

'Men make men,' he said cockily, grinning at me.

He got to his feet, hugged me and kissed me tenderly on the cheek.

'Shall we go home?' I said.

We lived in a small flat in the Araby neighbourhood, so we didn't have far to go, but since Zoran didn't like to stroll around with the night's takings we had the car. I was grateful for that. My feet and back were aching atrociously because I'd spent the whole evening on my feet.

'Can we wait a little?'

'Why?'

'There are a few things I'd like to talk about.'

He turned on his heel and went back out into the restaurant. I didn't protest even though all I wanted was to go home. I sank back down onto my chair and contemplated the framed photo of Zivko that I kept on the desk.

The war was over but Zivko was still in Croatia helping Mum. Dad had recently died. He'd been left disabled after losing both his legs in the rocket attacks in May the year before. Since then, he'd just spent his days at home in front of TV, slowly fading away. One day Mum had found him dead in his wheelchair when she came home. It had probably been a heart attack. I never thought about him; didn't mourn him. I'd never got my apology. When I'd said my goodbyes in December before leaving for Sweden, he'd barely even looked my way. Mum had come with me to the bus station.

I could hear Zoran saying goodbye to Stina out in the restaurant before locking the front door. After a while, he came back carrying a bottle of vodka and a Pepsi and two glasses filled with ice. He put them down on the desk, pulled a bottle opener out of his pocket, popped the cap off the fizzy drink and poured it for me. Then he poured a vodka for himself before sitting down again.

'The unit next door is coming onto the market,' he said, gesturing with his thumb. 'I had a word with the owner today.'

I sipped the Pepsi, biding my time as I pictured the owner's kindly face in my mind's eye. His name was Lennart and he ran a café.

'The lease is ours for forty thousand.'

I raised my eyebrows.

'We can't afford that. And who's going to work there? I'm due in three months' time. What are we going to do with the space?'

He waved his hand, took a generous mouthful of vodka and lit a fresh cigarette.

'Ivan's going to lend us the money.'

Ivan Vladic was a man in his fifties who lived in Stockholm; he was a Croat but had arrived in Sweden in the mid-eighties and done well in his adopted country. In February, Zoran and I had visited him in his huge house by the water in the suburb of Botkyrka. Zoran had walked around the place with desire in his eyes and something akin to envy.

'It would solve our financial problems and we'd be able to pay ourselves a decent wage.'

'But it won't solve the problem of who's going to run the café.'

Zoran leaned over the table.

'It's not going to be a café – it's going to be a nightclub. Upstairs. I popped round and looked the place over earlier today. There's a big basement too.'

'What do you need that for?'

'To build a bigger nightclub. A downstairs. It's going to be the place that people come to from miles around to party.'

I was tired; I just wanted to go home. Besides, I trusted Zoran. I had no other choice, because I didn't know anyone else here. I was longing to be asleep in my bed, but I still couldn't understand how he was making it all stack up. One of us had to be at Napoli at all times to make sure things were running as they should. Zoran wanted it that way. So who would oversee the nightclub?

'I can't run a nightclub, not with a baby,' I said.

'You're not going to, sweetie. I am.'

'What about the restaurant? Stina's too young. We don't even know if she'll be staying after the summer.'

'He is.'

Zoran smiled and pointed to the photograph of Zivko.

My gaze shifted between Zoran's smiling face and the photograph of Zivko.

'What do you mean?'

'I spoke to him on the phone earlier today. You wanted him to come to Sweden, and now he's got a job to come to.'

'Did he want to come?'

'Yes, of course. There is nothing for him in Croatia. We'll train him and then he'll be in charge of Napoli. You've said he's a smart guy – so he'll be able to handle it, right?'

'Of course he will. And we can trust him. He'd never let us down.'

I stood up and moved around the small desk. Zoran held out his arms and I sank onto his lap. I was so grateful – so in love with him. He loved me so much that he was bringing my little brother to Sweden to make me happy.

'Thank you. I love you.'

'And I love you.'

He tucked the cigarette into the corner of his mouth and ran his hand tenderly over my round belly.

'You'll want for nothing, my boy.'

I kissed him on the cheek.

'What do you think about calling him Luka?' he said.

I liked the name.

'Sure. But what if it's a girl? Will we call her Luka anyway?'

'I know it's a boy. But if it's a girl then you can pick.'

'Then I'd like her to be called Aleksandra, like Mum.'

'I like that.'

Zoran reached for the glass of vodka and tapped it gently against my stomach.

'Cheers, Luka or Aleksandra. Whichever one it is, I'm going to love you a lot. Time for your mum and me to go home and sleep. Then we're going to open a nightclub.'

With a tilt of his head, he knocked back the full glass.

Following their brief encounter in the exercise yard, Faye hadn't exchanged a single word with Ines. She knew she would only have one chance to say her piece, and after what had happened in the sports hall she'd decided to go onto the offensive. From her conversations with Miryam, she'd got a pretty clear idea of Ines's background and she'd done her research on Ines's trial by reading through old newspaper articles on the computer in the prison library.

On Tuesdays, Ines was responsible for cooking. Together with another woman – Katya, an Estonian sex worker serving a sentence after being caught smuggling large quantities of amphetamines in her vagina – she was responsible for providing them all with breakfast, lunch and dinner. But Faye had noticed that it was Katya who did everything while Ines would sit quietly reading a book on the sofa.

On the Tuesday morning three days after she'd hurled the ball into Regina's face, Faye was ready. As soon as her cell door was unlocked, she picked up her cutlery and hurried along the corridor.

Katya was standing by the sink preparing the breakfast. Ines was already in her usual spot with her book, and Faye settled down next to her. Ines didn't look up and pretended not to notice Faye.

'You didn't have to be here. You could have walked and never been convicted,' said Faye.

Ines looked up from her book and gave Faye a searching look, but said nothing.

Faye had to bite her lip to ensure she didn't keep going – she just hoped she'd aroused Ines's interest. She got up, went over to the counter, filled a mug with coffee and then returned.

Ines had gone back to reading.

The seats around the tables were beginning to fill up. Some of the women were chatting, while others were staring into space with vacant, sleepy eyes.

Miryam, who was a morning person, turned towards Faye.

'There are two new girls coming onto the wing,' she said.

'How do you know that?'

'Ballbag told Katya. That guy really likes to wag his tongue in more ways than one, as you know.'

Naturally, sexual relations between the screws and the inmates were forbidden, but they happened nonetheless. Just as they did between the female inmates. On more than one occasion, Faye had happened upon fellow prisoners with their hands down each other's trousers. According to Miryam, Ballbag's cover had almost been blown a year or two earlier when he'd got someone pregnant in another wing of the prison. It had all been hushed up and Arvid had kept his job. That he and Katya sometimes slipped away together was common knowledge.

Most of the women had someone they'd become extra close to, but so far as Faye knew Ines was one of the few there who tended to her own needs single-handedly.

'What did they do? The newbies, I mean.'

'Don't know.'

This was the first time since Faye's own arrival at Stenakull that new inmates were coming into the wing. For some reason, this made her nervous. They were going to pierce a hole in the protective bubble. It was as if she had already forgotten that there was life beyond the barbed wire where every single hour wasn't meticulously planned and where every single step wasn't supervised. Humans really could get used to anything.

Faye looked around. The others were hunched over their breakfasts as usual, wolfing down the food. Her thoughts were drawn to Alice. She would have been astonished by their table manners. Her years with Jack and mixing with the upper classes meant that sitting up straight with her elbows at her side came naturally to Faye, and she always handled her cutlery elegantly while inserting her food into her mouth in small, refined movements. The same was true on the inside. But it hadn't always been like that. Growing up in Fjällbacka, back when she'd been called Matilda, no one would have cared if she'd eaten with her hands.

It was possible to learn how to eat demurely.

That gave her an idea, which would either boost her reputation on the wing – or get her killed.

Ines stood up from her table and went back to the sofa. One of the women immediately handed the remote control to her. Ines took it, switched off the TV and went back to reading her book.

Faye needed Ines. And if Ines wouldn't be her friend then Faye would have to topple her from her throne. She hoped she wouldn't have to try, because she wasn't sure of success, but in the end it would be inescapable.

It had been a week since Faye spoke to Ines at breakfast. She continued to be hounded by dreams of Julienne at night, and it would often take her hours to shake off the feelings of sadness and melancholy they left her with. The cold air made her gasp sharply as she emerged into the exercise yard.

There were fewer women outside than usual. The walls around the exercise yard meant the area was partly sheltered, but the snow was swirling around them. A fresh snowstorm had blown in from the west. Faye and Miryam were among the few who still insisted on making use of their hour outdoors to get some fresh air. They had their hands shoved deep inside the pockets of their prison coats as they did their usual beat around the yard, hunched forward against the cold. There were only fifteen minutes left until they would be ordered back inside when Ines suddenly approached them.

'We need to talk,' she abruptly said to Faye.

Miryam left without saying a word. Faye began to walk again, forcing Ines to walk in step with her.

Faye didn't say a word. Ines had come to her. She couldn't capitulate in her eagerness to connect with Ines.

In the end, however, Ines couldn't contain herself.

'You said I didn't have to be here,' she said. 'What did you mean by that?'

Faye scrutinised Ines's face. It was obvious that it went against the grain for her to turn to someone else.

'You did it all wrong. I've read about the trial and your frauds.'

Ines looked surprised, but there was an interested twinkle in her eye.

'So what should we have done?'

Faye sighed in relief. She'd managed to capture her. She didn't look at Ines, but she knew she was trapped.

'AI.'

'Are you serious?'

Faye nodded.

'You got caught because you used kids as fraudsters. You told them what to say, which meant it was easy for you to be found out. You gave them orders. And people tend to screw up, and they cost money.'

They turned back towards the sports hall and continued walking.

'What difference does AI make?'

'It's not been tested legally, as far as I know. It's hard to control artificial intelligence, even harder to prove to a prosecutor that someone tried to. And you would have been spared your personnel costs. Not to mention the absence of any witnesses who could claim you were behind the whole thing.'

Ines nodded.

'Go on.'

'How long did one of your scam calls take?'

'A minute, maybe?'

'Instead of making *one* call in Sweden, the AI could have been making at least three hundred calls a minute across every country in the world. For instance, to countries that don't cooperate with Swedish law enforcement…'

Faye shivered. The snow was settling on the two of them even though they were still moving.

'Even if you had been caught, the police would have had

to prove you'd given orders to the AI. Your defence could have been that the AI had followed its own initiative or that someone else had manipulated it.'

For the first time during their conversation, Faye dared to glance sidelong at Ines.

She was incredibly beautiful. Had they not been in a prison, she would never have believed that this young woman was a remorseless and dangerous criminal. Faye suddenly realised that she wanted to know more about her, not just to exploit her as a springboard to rise in the prison hierarchy but because she was genuinely intrigued by Ines as a person.

'I've had an idea,' Faye said.

A short distance away, she saw Regina glowering at them as she slowly paced around the exercise yard with her shoulders hunched and her hands in her pockets. Her nose still looked a little swollen. Faye didn't like the way she was looking at them, but there wasn't much she could do about that. However, she intended to be extra vigilant.

Ines looked askance at Faye, so she continued:

'I want to give the girls some courses.'

Ines raised her dark eyebrows.

'Courses in what?'

'Behaviour and etiquette. I'm sick of watching them eat like pigs. And I think it might help when they eventually get out.'

'Can that sort of thing be taught? And what use do you think it will be to them?'

'I learned it when I was twenty-five. I wasn't born into money. But I did learn the rules of the upper classes and I played their game to take their money.'

'How so?'

'Because they only trust their own. They don't trust a hungry, ambitious girl from Fjällbacka or a young, beautiful girl from...'

She pretended not to know where Ines was from.

'...Husby,' Ines supplied.

Faye nodded.

'You've got rules in Husby too. You've had those since you were a kid. If you join a club, you have to learn its rules – doesn't matter whether that club is the Swedish upper crust or Stenakull Prison. If the women here learn it, then they'll have an edge. You can think it's silly for all I care, but if you think about it you'll see the value in it. It might be … extremely valuable.'

Faye didn't know exactly what convinced Ines, but at any rate she spoke to the other inmates on the wing. The governor had given the thumbs up, so a week after Faye had told Ines about her plans it was time for the first etiquette lesson. Everyone on the wing was there, apart from Ines, who was on the sofa with a book.

They started with table posture.

'Miryam,' Faye instructed. 'Keep your arms closer to your body, like the wings on a chicken.'

'It's hard with these tits,' Miryam said, squeezing her ample bosom.

The other women laughed.

Faye shook her head. She stood behind Miryam and pressed her palms against her elbows to bring them in to her sides.

'That's better. And don't forget your back. It needs to be straight, rather than ready for... reproduction.'

Miryam arched her back inwards even more, and was rewarded with yet more laughter.

Faye squeezed her shoulders gently.

'You'll be doing that afterwards,' she said. 'I can teach you a thing or two there as well. But that's a very different course.'

The other women roared with laughter.

The young woman next to Miryam laughed unexpectedly loudly. Faye didn't know much about her other than that she was called Marissa and she'd come to Stenakull six months before Faye. She was in her twenties and usually kept herself to herself. She was very beautiful and clearly perfectly aware of that fact. Faye was pleasantly surprised that she'd come, but perhaps it was because she was keen to behave in a manner that matched her beauty.

Faye continued by telling them about different types of toast.

'This is a full table toast. Look at the person who proposes the toast – that's me in this case – then at the person on your left. Then you look at the person on your right and then finally back to me, since it was me who proposed it in the first place. Then you drink.'

The ten women sitting around the tables raised their small glasses over and over while giggling. Occasionally, Ines glanced towards her with curiosity from the sofa, observing each new step that Faye described. Sometimes it seemed to Faye that there might be a smile tugging at the corners of her mouth. She assumed that it was the course that was cheering Ines up, given that she was reading Ulf Lundell's snoozefest *Vardagar 2*.

'Now let's move onto the food. The most important thing is the size of your mouthfuls,' said Faye. 'You mustn't look like this is the final bite of food you're ever going to eat.'

'That's cos the rich can afford to wait,' said one of the girls, who was called Sumeya. 'I grew up with seven siblings. They were like dogs. If you didn't eat quick enough then they'd scoff it all.'

'Doesn't matter,' Faye said. 'You're not in the kitchen back home now. Imagine that you're at the Nobel Banquet.'

'Is the King here?'

Faye laughed.

'Yes, he's here. And Queen Silvia too – she's over there on the sofa, just like always. And the man next to you is a billionaire and is wearing a Rolex that you'd like to take off him.'

'Oh right, so I'm nicking it? That's okay then?'

'How do you think he got rich in the first place? He's done his fair share of nicking. But to get it off him, you want his eyes on your boobs, so he's not concentrating on your right hand that's holding a knife as if you're planning to stab him in the spleen.'

Sumeya laughed and adjusted her grip on the knife. Faye nodded at her.

'There we are. Much better. Now you're almost ready to eat with the king.'

Faye stretched. She had been hunched over her sewing machine all morning and had barely noticed what had been going on around her, but something had made her react. Something different from the hum of the sewing machines.

Faye looked around the room of women bent over their own machines. She pricked up her ears. Was that crying she could hear? She got up, grimaced at her stiff knees and headed towards the toilets.

When she opened the door to an unlocked cubicle, she found Marissa sitting on the lid sobbing.

'What's the matter?' Faye exclaimed.

Marissa didn't answer, but Faye could see that her eyes were red and swollen with tears. She gently pulled her up, wrapped her arms around her and held the shaking woman close.

'There, there. It'll be all right. Whatever it is, it'll be all right.'

She caressed Marissa's hair, which was soft and smelled pleasantly of shampoo.

'I miss her,' Marissa sobbed.

'Who?'

'Sara.'

Faye stroked her back.

The etiquette course had enhanced her reputation on the wing. Following some initial doubts and a fair share of laughter and mockery, they had slowly started to listen to her when she argued that it might be a good idea to be able to comport themselves properly in more refined company. These gatherings also provided them with a new source of unity, and offered a welcome interruption to the monotony of daily life. Slowly, the women began to relax. They began to share the stores of secrets and childhood experiences that they carried with them. Just as they were starting to see Faye with different eyes, she too was beginning to see them in a different light. She discovered that their backgrounds all shared something in common. Almost all of them had seen their lives smashed to pieces by men, or at the very least men had knocked them off balance through long-term physical or psychological abuse, or both. Not infrequently this had led to addiction.

Louise, who was the first person to have shown Faye kindness on her first day at Stenakull, had told her about how as a fourteen-year-old she had been sexually abused by her mother's new boyfriend until she had run away from home. Many of the younger women had been exploited as drugs mules until they'd been caught. They'd either done it out of love or in return for payments to provide for their young children or younger siblings.

'Is Sara your mum?' Faye said after a while.

Marissa shook her head, blowing her nose into some toilet paper that Faye had handed her.

'No. My daughter. She's five years old.'

'Where is she?'

'She's staying with my family. I'm so scared she'll forget me.'

Marissa sobbed loudly.

'She won't forget you. You never forget your mum.'

'Do you promise?' she said faintly.

'I promise.'

Faye hugged Marissa tighter until she had stopped trembling.

'Are you ready to go back out there? Think of the thirteen kronor an hour they're paying you. You've been gone for half an hour, so someone really should knock six fifty off your wages.'

Marissa laughed and Faye patted her arm.

'Come on, let's go.'

The air was cold when Faye and Miryam emerged into the exercise yard. The sun had already set.

'What do you know about Marissa?' Faye said.

'Why do you ask?'

Faye didn't want to tell her about what had happened in the toilets. It wasn't that she didn't trust Miryam, but it felt like a betrayal of Marissa.

'Because she's one of the few girls in here that I've not managed to figure out.'

Miryam looked behind her to check that no one could overhear them.

'Marissa is Zoran Rakitic's girlfriend.'

Faye was startled.

'The gangster? The one behind the shooting of that other kingpin?'

'That's the one. Absolutely deadly. Married to someone else, of course. But they've been together for seven years, since Marissa was eighteen. She was working as a waitress in one of his restaurants when she caught his eye.'

'How did she end up in here?'

'From what I've heard, she went down for Dragan Maric – one of Zoran's lieutenants. Zoran was already inside and Marissa had just given birth to his daughter. They were caught up in a stop and search and they found two grams of cocaine in the car. It was Dragan who had left it in the pocket of his coat in the boot. But she said it was hers and that he didn't know anything. Probably on Zoran's direct orders. I guess Dragan was more valuable to him than Marissa.'

Faye shook her head in resignation. This constant exploitation of women who were in vulnerable positions!

After a while, they walked back towards the door. Marissa too was in here because she loved a man. And somewhere out there was another girl missing her mum.

Växjö, 1998

In November Luka turned two, and six months earlier we had welcomed our second son, Marko. Zoran now owned both Ristorante Napoli and The Palace, as he had christened the nightclub. We had moved to a detached house in the suburbs because we had plenty of money – sometimes, at least.

It was half past eleven and I was in the kitchen, having just finished my lunch. Marko was asleep in his crib and Luka was at nursery when the doorbell rang. I got up and opened the front door. Zivko was standing there. I hugged him and asked him what he was doing there.

Zivko lived in our old flat in Araby, but he – like Zoran – was fully occupied by business. I regretted that we didn't get to see more of him. I felt alone, as if I were on the outside. My whole world was devoted to caring for Luka and Marko. I loved them above all else, but I wanted to do more than just change nappies and push the pram along the deserted streets of Växjö during the daytime. Zoran's absences had become longer and longer – sometimes he'd be gone for three or four days and when he came home he'd explain that he'd had to go to Stockholm on various errands.

'I just stopped by to visit my big sister,' Zivko said with a wry smile.

'Come in – but Marko's asleep, so keep your voice down.'

Zivko nodded, took his shoes off in the hall and followed me into the kitchen. He sat down at the kitchen table.

'Coffee? I'm afraid I haven't got any food to offer you.'

He said yes and told me that was fine. I started the coffee maker before sitting down.

'How's it going at Napoli?' I said, trying to recall when I had last been in. It must have been sometime in the spring, when Marko was still in my belly. My God, time was flying by.

'Totally okay; we're keeping afloat.'

'And The Palace?'

The nightclub was the talk of Växjö, although unfortunately not always in the right way. There were often pieces in the local paper about fights and unrest. There had also been complaints from the neighbours about the loud noise and drunkenness in the street outside. Whenever I asked Zoran about that, he merely waved away my concern and said that it was the police and reporters harassing him. He thought they were jealous and couldn't tolerate the fact that a foreigner was making a success of himself.

'The Palace is The Palace,' Zivko said with a shrug. 'Zoran's doing his best, but that might not be enough.'

I raised my eyebrows in surprise. That wasn't quite what Zoran had told me.

'Can't we talk about something else?' Zivko said when he noticed my reaction. Perhaps he realised that Zoran didn't want me to know exactly what the situation was.

But I ignored his objection.

'I thought things were going well? Isn't the place full every Wednesday, Friday and Saturday?'

'Oh yes, it is. Forget I said anything.'

He stood up, opened the cupboard where we kept the coffee cups and poured for both of us.

'How can it be going badly if it's full? I want to know the truth – this is about my family.'

Zivko sighed and then held his hands out in resignation.

'Because as you know, Zoran took big loans from Ivan. He hasn't managed to pay them back yet, so right now all our profits are going on servicing the interest.'

He blew on his coffee.

I knew what he was saying was true. Zoran had been stressed and exhausted in recent months. At times he'd almost seemed afraid. He'd been smiling less, and when he did it wasn't in the same carefree way as before.

I took a deep breath. Ivan was dangerous. Zoran had to repay the money, otherwise we'd be in trouble. I didn't doubt for a second that Ivan would hurt Zoran. The thought of it left me petrified with fear.

I heard Marko start to whimper in the bedroom and I went to fetch him. I picked him up from his crib and returned to the kitchen.

Zivko came over and kissed the baby on the forehead before hurrying towards the front door.

'Going already?'

'I've got to get back to the restaurant.'

I came with him to the front door, disappointed, and watched as he put his shoes back on.

'Please don't tell Zoran that I said anything,' he said.

'Why not?'

'Please, just don't. He's obviously going to figure this out. He doesn't want you to worry.'

Two weeks later, I was at home alone with the boys as usual. It was just after ten o'clock on a rainy, windy Thursday night and the kids were both fast asleep. Zoran had told me that morning that he was going to Stockholm and would be back on Friday afternoon. I'd kept my promise to Zivko and not mentioned our financial problems, even though I'd had to bite my tongue on several occasions.

I was dead tired but I was still stuck in front of TV when

the doorbell rang. Was it Zivko? Because if Zoran had decided to come home early then it was weird that he didn't open the door with his own set of keys.

I stood up and went to the front door. Through the peephole, I could see two burly men whom I didn't recognise. I hesitated. The prospect of letting them in made me uneasy.

'Open up,' said one of them in Croatian.

Now I was worried. Something might have happened to Zoran. I unlocked the door and opened it.

'Who are you?' I said.

They barged into the hall and quickly shut the door behind them. Both were wearing long leather jackets.

'Is he here?' said the stockier of the two.

I folded my arms. I didn't want to show them how worried I was.

'First of all, I want to know your names and what you are doing here.'

The man stared at me in surprise.

'I'm Dragan and this is Mirko,' he said, gesturing to his companion. 'We're looking for your husband. Is Zoran at home?'

'How come?'

'We'd like a word with him.'

Thoughts were racing through my head. I decided to tell the truth.

'I don't know where my husband is. Do your wives know where you are at every waking moment? Zoran doesn't tell me where he's going of an evening and I take it you don't tell your wives either. I mean, do they know that you're here right now?'

'When was the last time he was at home?' Dragan said without acknowledging my small outburst.

'This morning,' I said. 'He left in the car at about nine o'clock. Have you tried calling his mobile?'

'Yes, but he's not answering.'

Dragan pointed at the landline phone which was on top of a hall console.

'Call him now.'

I hesitated.

'You said he wasn't answering,' I said.

'Not when we call, but perhaps he will when her indoors rings him up.'

He went over to the phone, picked up the receiver and held it up towards me. His shoes left wet footprints on the parquet.

I just wanted to get rid of them. While they weren't being overtly threatening, they clearly weren't to be messed around with. I didn't want them in the same house that my sons were asleep in.

I took the receiver from Dragan and tapped out the number on the keypad. Zoran picked up after three rings.

'Yes?'

He sounded annoyed.

Before I could say a word, Dragan took the receiver from me.

'Good evening, Zoran,' he said in Croatian. 'We've been looking for you. Your wife doesn't know where you are and got worried.'

I didn't hear Zoran's reply, but Dragan nodded several times before speaking again.

'Good,' he said. 'That would be for the best, otherwise we'll have to stay here and take a look around the house. We'd really rather not wake up Luka and Marko. Your wife is very beautiful, but she looks tired.'

I shuddered when my sons' names passed his lips. The way he said them terrified me. There was no doubt whatsoever that it was a threat.

He handed the receiver back to me, but when I raised it to my ear, Zoran had already rung off.

Dragan and Mirko nodded to me before opening the front door.

'How much does he owe Ivan?' I said.

Dragan gazed at me, his eyes wide with surprise. He opened his mouth as if to say something, but then he shook his head and cast his gaze down.

Mirko looked at me.

'You'll have to ask your husband that,' he said.

'Well, I'm asking you. You're here and he's not, as you might have noticed.'

A flash of pity crossed Mirko's face.

'You'll have to ask him,' he said again.

Mirko and Dragan turned on their heels and stepped out into the rain. I stood at the window watching them go down towards the front gate.

Once they had vanished down the street, I went back to the phone and tried calling Zoran back, but he didn't pick up.

On Fridays, they were spared the early lock-up. 'Time for some Friday hanging-out,' as Louise would put it. Faye was sitting next to Ines on the sofa in front of the TV, where *The Masked Singer* was about to start. Ines had already changed channels from the news and weather forecast so as not to miss anything. The women loved the show and spent all week talking about it. Many of them had children and knew their kids would be watching the show at home at the same time as they were. Louise's daughter Paula had twins who were hooked on the programme. There was something both tragic and beautiful about their attempts to create a sense of community with their families despite the fences and the distance that separated them, Faye reflected.

Personally, she was struggling to let go of the main headline from the news bulletin. Yet another shooting. Someone else from Zoran Rakitic's gang gunned down. And Rakitic was apparently Marissa's boyfriend. The guy in Hall Prison. That was the same prison that her own father was on the run from. These most recent killings appeared to be connected, according to the police, but they weren't willing to go into any further details about what that connection might be.

Her thoughts were moving in different directions and forming patterns that Faye wasn't yet sure she understood. Her stomach felt uneasy and her arms had come up in goosebumps.

'You should do more courses,' Ines said, and Faye started. For a moment, she had forgotten about the beautiful woman next to her.

'What did you have in mind?'

'Well, it's good to teach the girls how to hold a knife and fork, and it's probably important sometimes, but it's only a marginal help once they're on the outside.'

'So what would help them?'

'Teach them how to make money.'

Faye met Ines's intelligent gaze and realised where she was going with this.

'Yeah, I suppose so.'

'Give them a course on entrepreneurship. Teach them how to build companies. Basic stuff. Tax and shit like that. No one's going to hire them once they get out. They're marked for life but they need to be able to make money legally, otherwise they're done for. No matter how good their table manners are.'

Faye nodded and Ines looked pleased with herself.

'I'll think about it.'

Ines was right. Admittedly, some of the women in here were working on getting their grades up or doing professional training, but telling prospective employers you'd done time often scared them off. Faye wondered whether she would have had the courage to employ someone with a record. Of course that was before she'd wound up in this notorious women's prison outside Gothenburg. The answer was probably yes, but then again she was different to most other business leaders and she knew that all too well.

She immediately set to thinking what she should include in the course. What would she teach them? Accounting? No, that felt wrong. Practical things to do if you wanted to start your own business? No: perhaps the most important thing was to teach them to believe in themselves and their dreams. Even if they were dreams of bronze.

These were women who generally lacked trust in the world around them, but that state of affairs had surely begun with a lack of self-confidence, she thought. There was nothing wrong with their brains. In the right environment and with the right education, almost any one of them could go far – of that much she was certain. Maybe the course shouldn't just be for the women in their own wing? There might be more people who needed help.

Ines cleared her throat and Faye realised she had been lost in her own thoughts.

'What did you say?' she said.

'I asked whether you were cold.'

Without waiting for an answer, Ines spread the blanket she'd been under across Faye's legs too.

'Fuck, I'd let him do whatever he wanted with me,' Miryam exclaimed when the host David Hellenius appeared on screen.

'Have you seen his wife?' Louise chortled. 'You don't stand a chance against her!'

Several more of the women laughed but Faye wasn't listening anymore. She was sitting completely still and holding her breath. Under cover of the blanket, Ines's hand had found its way past the waistband of her trousers and was moving downwards, painfully slowly. Faye clenched her jaw so as not to moan out loud when Ines's fingers carefully made their way inside her underwear and began to stroke her with soft, slow movements. She discreetly spread her legs. Ines worked away with small, precise movements.

Faye trembled slightly when the orgasm followed. Moments later, Ines's hand disappeared. In the green and white glow of the TV, Faye thought she could see a smile out of the corner of her eye.

She leaned back and gazed up at the ceiling. She needed more. Now.

Right away.

She got up and made for her cell. When she got there, she

went inside, leaving the door open. After a short time, she heard footsteps coming along the corridor.

Faye shut the door once Ines had come inside. They looked at each other in silence and then Faye grabbed Ines's shoulders and pushed her against the bare wall. Ines, who was always outwardly dominant, submitted to Faye, who tugged down her trousers and underwear with urgency.

Kneeling, she teased her pubic mound and the insides of her thighs with the tip of her tongue. Ines leaned back against the wall and moaned, grabbing hold of Faye's hair and pushing her head towards her sex. Faye gripped her wrists and held them fast so that Ines couldn't move, then began to lick her hard. Ines tore her hands free and used them to support herself against the wall, dragging her nails back and forth as she began to quiver intensely.

Once she'd come, they lay quietly on the bunk holding each other. Faye was panting as she looked up at the ceiling. She knew this wasn't love; it was something else. But she'd never felt anything close to the emotional intimacy that she was sharing with Ines right now. Perhaps it was because they were locked up and surrounded by barbed wire fences. Perhaps it was because Ines was a woman.

'I've wanted to do that since the very first time I saw you,' Ines whispered.

After a while, she got up, pulled on her clothes and left Faye's cell without saying another word.

Faye continued to stare up at the ceiling and couldn't help but smile to herself.

Faye was lying on the bunk in her cell reading. It was one of the things she actually appreciated about life at Stenakull; she had started to enjoy novels again. While growing up in Fjällbacka, books had been an escape for her. Without them, she wasn't sure she would have made it. Without them, she might have perished. They were what had made her dream of another world, of a way out. And they were what had got her to keep believing in the future even when everything felt hopeless.

Faye still didn't know where her father was. Whether he was close to finding her mother and Julienne, or whether he could get to her in prison somehow. But she couldn't allow herself to become too engrossed in these thoughts – she wouldn't be able to bear it if she did.

There was the sound of footsteps in the corridor. It was only around half past six in the evening and it wasn't yet time for lock-up. Most of the women were still in the common area watching TV or playing cards.

Faye was trying to concentrate on her reading. She'd borrowed *The Life and Loves of a She-Devil* by Fay Weldon from the library; it was a favourite that she'd reread several times since first reading it as a thirteen-year-old.

Suddenly she felt certain that someone was watching her. She lowered the book to find Regina in the doorway with her ferocious gaze fixed on her.

Her pulse began to race so fast that her ears were whistling.

Regina took a step into the cell, her right hand hidden behind her back. Was she holding something in it?

'Faye.'

That was Ines's voice coming from the corridor. Regina stopped where she was, halfway across the floor. Ines came in behind her and looked from one to the other.

'What are you doing here?'

Regina opened her mouth to answer but then settled for licking her lips.

'Beat it,' Ines said sharply.

Regina immediately left the cell.

Ines came over and sat down on the edge of Faye's bunk. Faye put a hand to her chest. She took long, deep breaths to try to bring her pulse back under control.

'What did she want?' Ines said.

Faye shook her head.

'I don't know,' she whispered. 'But I challenged her. You know how that goes. Someone has to back down.'

Ines took Faye's hand while she waited for her to recover. After a while, Faye felt calmer. She settled up against the wall and pulled Ines close.

'Is something up?' Ines asked gently. Her beautiful eyes gazed deep into Faye's.

She was overcome by a strong urge to tell her everything. About her father, about how Julienne and her mother were secretly living in Italy. For the last month it had all felt distant – Stenakull had almost been a sanctuary, a protective shell that only her longing for Julienne could penetrate.

But Faye reminded herself that she was more vulnerable than ever. Her father knew where she was. She was stuck in a routine and surrounded by convicted murderers and other criminals. Just how far did his contacts extend? He wouldn't be satisfied until she was dead. Maybe there was already someone on the wing who had been tasked with killing her. Maybe it was Regina. Maybe it was one of the others.

'There's a man who wants to hurt me. He won't give up until I'm dead.'

'Who?'

'My father.'

She gave Ines a modified and touched up version of the truth. Of course, she omitted the most important point: that Julienne and her mother were alive. That truth was too much. She didn't know Ines that well yet.

Once she had finished, there was a period of silence.

'So you killed him then? Your ex-husband? Jack?'

'Yes.'

She didn't hesitate to say that, at least.

Ines nodded slowly, not taking her gaze off Faye.

'I would have done the same thing if someone had killed my kid or someone in my family.'

'I don't regret any of it.' Faye's voice was steady.

'Does your dad have someone helping him? On the outside?'

Faye paused for a few seconds before she answered Ines's question. She'd been wondering the same thing.

'I don't know. As far as I know, he doesn't have any friends from before. But I've no idea what contacts he might have made in prison. There's been a lot of stuff on the news about Zoran Rakitic, who's apparently still active from his cell at Hall. It did cross my mind that they might have come to an arrangement, since they were in the same prison. And that scares me. But what scares me even more is that I don't really know anything at all. All I've got is speculation and guesswork.'

Ines placed her hand over Faye's. Faye was overcome by a wave of fatigue. She leaned her head against Ines's shoulder. When Ines began to stroke her hair, she could no longer fight the exhaustion and she slipped into merciful sleep. And for once she didn't dream about Julienne.

When Faye entered the sewing room, she saw Marissa sitting in the seat next to hers. The young woman was staring irresolutely at the machine in front of her.

'Never sewn before?' Faye sat down in her spot and moved closer to her.

Marissa shook her head.

'It's easy – I can teach you.'

Faye deftly threaded the machine while explaining each step to Marissa as informatively as she could. Then she picked up one of the green pieces of fabric and patiently instructed her on how to achieve a straight-line stitch.

'You're doing really well!' she said as Marissa sewed.

'Thanks. I didn't even know where to start. My mum knew how to sew, but she never taught me. Which is a pity because I'd like to be able to sew so that I can make my own clothes for Sara. Mum did that for me, so it's always felt like something you're supposed to do as a good mother.'

Marissa shrugged and looked embarrassed.

'I'd barely sewn anything before I arrived here either,' Faye said, threading her own machine. 'And I definitely hadn't made any clothes for my daughter.'

'How old's your daughter?'

Faye hesitated. She regretted mentioning Julienne. Talking about her still felt like a raw, open wound. What would happen if she accidentally let the cat out of the bag? What if Marissa realised that Julienne was alive? But she was the one who had opened Pandora's box. Marissa was just showing interest and looking for a connection: two mothers talking about their daughters.

'Julienne's not with us anymore.'

'Oh, I'm sorry!' Marissa put a hand over her mouth and looked distraught. 'I knew that, actually. I just forgot. I guess it was her dad who … sorry.'

'Don't sweat it,' Faye said soothingly.

'I mean, it's my biggest fear,' Marissa said, brushing a tear off her cheek. 'That the same thing could happen to me. You never know with my husband how…'

She bit her lip and faltered.

Faye leaned in close.

'Was your husband … was he violent?'

Marissa nodded.

'Never towards Sara. But who knows what'll happen when I'm not there to protect her? She doesn't live with Zoran. That's his name. He's met her before, but he's inside now. Him too.'

Marissa laughed bitterly, brushing away another tear.

'I know he's still keeping tabs on Sara through his mates. He's … he's not a good person. And the people he knows are just as violent as he is.'

'You said "my husband". Were you married?'

'No, it's just what I say. I mean, that's how I saw him. My husband. But, no. He's married to a woman called Milenka. They've been married for years and have kids together. I was… she didn't know about me. And she doesn't know about Sara.'

Faye saw the beautiful Milenka pictured in *Aftonbladet* in her mind's eye. What would she say if she heard about Marissa? And about Sara?

'You said he was keeping tabs on your daughter from inside. Is there anything else he's keeping tabs on?'

Marissa shivered.

'I dare say he's keeping tabs on his entire operation. His men are loyal. And his wife... Milenka... I think she's probably in on it too. Well, except for me.'

The goosebumps on her arms were back. Could it possibly be that her father and Zoran Rakitic had embarked upon some form of collaboration? And if so, what shape did that take? What was in it for Zoran if he helped her father out? And what was her father doing in return for Zoran?

A shiver ran down Faye's spine.

Marissa had stopped crying altogether.

They sat in silence for a while. Perhaps both of them were thinking about the paths that life had taken them down, and the men who had led them there.

Växjö, 1998

I had started to see through Zoran. Or rather, I'd started to see who he really was. Maybe it was my own fault. During our first three years together, I had idealised him, built up a romantic and unrealistic image of a man that no person could live up to. But now our relationship was under real strain.

Zoran came home on Friday as he had promised. I was still shaken following Dragan and Mirko's threatening visit to the house. He barely greeted me or our boys, instead going straight to the study that I had set up for him upstairs. I followed with Marko in my arms and Luka clinging to my leg.

Zoran was sitting at his desk cradling a glass of whisky. He glared at us in vexation as we entered, as if we were disturbing him.

'What is it? I've got to work,' he said.

Luka went around the desk and tried to clamber onto his lap, but Zoran ignored him.

Luka came back to me confused and crushed. My heart ached. Zoran often spoke of the family and how important it was, but love always had to be on his terms.

'We need to talk,' I said.

'Now? I don't have time. I've got to work.'

I looked from him to the whisky glass and had to bite my tongue to avoid pointing out the obvious.

'The two men who came here scared me. Zoran, I'm afraid,' I said.

He refused to meet my gaze, keeping it fixed on his glass.

'I'll take care of it.'

'How?'

'You don't need to know. Just trust me. This is no business for women.'

Marko whimpered gently. While wondering how to approach Zoran, I rocked the boy back and forth. I realised I couldn't let that home visit slide. It had crossed the line in every sense. And it told me that this was about more than chicken feed; Zoran must owe Ivan a lot of money.

'When two goons come round to a family home where there are kids asleep, that makes it a concern for the whole family. How much do you owe Ivan?'

Zoran muttered something and drained the last of his whisky.

'What did you say?' I said.

He stood up so quickly that his chair tipped over. He grasped the glass and hurled it at the wall, where it shattered, sending shards of glass and drops of whisky flying in every direction. I stood there, dumbfounded, pressing Marko close while Luka hid behind my legs.

'I told you to get out of here. Otherwise I'll throw you out.'

'No.'

I refused to avert my gaze. Zoran was the same. He approached slowly. I stood still, my heart pounding.

He stopped in front of me.

'You refuse to obey me?'

'I didn't realise you were the boss of me.'

He raised his arm quickly; I never even saw the blow coming. All I felt was the stinging pain on my cheek.

I stumbled but didn't drop Marko.

'Now you know.'

Luka began to cry. My eyes filled with tears – of pain, humiliation and sorrow.

Zoran shoved us out of the study and I didn't resist.

I took Marko and Luka down to the living room. I had to rock Marko back and forth for a long time before I was finally able to put him to bed. I picked Luka up and sat down on the sofa with him.

'Daddy hit you,' he said. There were so many emotions writ across his face. Anger, sadness, surprise.

'Yes, he did. But he didn't mean to.'

I pressed his body close to mine and felt his breathing become calmer.

'I need to talk to Daddy,' I said.

Luka looked up at me anxiously, but I smiled at him.

'Don't worry.'

I got up, turned on the TV, inserted a video of cartoons into the VHS player, and then fetched a glass of milk and a bun for Luka, who had curled up on the sofa.

'I won't be long,' I said, before going back upstairs.

I entered the study without knocking. Zoran had poured another whisky. He refused to meet my gaze when I stood in front of the desk again. I hoped it was out of shame, but I wasn't sure. I was making an effort not to tremble, but I was afraid. And hurt. But I had to be strong for the boys' sake. Zoran's slap was the least of our problems. Ivan and his goons were a threat to our family. I'd have to solve that first.

'How much do you owe Ivan?'

He raised his head and looked at me wearily.

'One point two million.'

I gasped. I took a deep breath. I wanted to tell him off, to shout at him, to hit him. But that wouldn't help. I'd protested when he'd insisted on refurbishing The Palace with expensive materials and exclusive furniture, but Zoran had merely waved me away and told me it was all under control; there was nothing for me to worry about.

'How much do Napoli and The Palace bring in each week?'
'About a hundred grand.'
'And the profit?'
'Ten grand. Sometimes a little more. Fifteen, maybe.'

I nodded. At the current rate we'd never be able to pay it back.

'What are you doing with the basement?'
'It's a nightclub. You know that.'
'Not the one at The Palace. The one at Ristorante Napoli.'

He raised his eyebrows.

'Well, it's a storeroom, isn't it?'

In my mind's eye, I was picturing the dark gambling dens of Zagreb, where family breadwinners would gamble away their pay packets, bringing ruin and misfortune upon their families. There was nowhere like that in Växjö. I knew how lucrative they were and how much you could make running one. What I was about to suggest wasn't pretty and it went against everything I stood for, but we needed to clear our debt to Ivan. Otherwise his goons were going to kill us.

'Turn the basement into a casino. But the gamblers aren't to come in through the front door off the street. They'll have to come through the courtyard at the back, through the kitchen and straight down the stairs. That way we won't disturb the diners in the restaurant. And while the police are busy with all the fighting at The Palace, our gambling den will be left alone. The Palace will be a decoy to keep them away from our real source of income.'

Zoran stared at me, then he smiled.

'That might just work,' he said.

My face remained blank. I had no intention of forgetting that he'd hit me. Never again would I allow that smile to manipulate me.

'It will,' I said. 'I know what you men are like.'

I turned around and left the room.

March had got off to a somewhat milder start. The entrepreneurship course would be starting in about a week. When word had got out on the other wings, interest had been so great that the governor had decided to let her use the sports hall. Eighty-eight of the one hundred and twenty women at Stenakull wanted to listen to her. Everyone from Faye's wing was going to join in again.

Faye had decided it was time to start communicating with the outside world again. For the first time, she bought a phone card and made a call from the booth.

Alice sounded surprised when she picked up.

'Faye?'

That bright, almost girlish voice.

Faye smiled. She'd missed her friend; had forced herself to keep her out of her thoughts. Alice hadn't sent any more letters after the first one that had come in February.

'How are you doing, Alice?'

'Fine, but how are *you*?'

Faye smiled again.

'It's not so bad – better than you'd think, actually. Most of the girls in here are good people. You'd like it.'

Alice snorted.

'I sincerely doubt it. Why haven't you been in touch?'

Faye gazed at the graffiti inside the phone booth: the names of men and women who must have meant a lot to someone, some of them probably decades ago.

'I needed to do some thinking and make some decisions.'

'Okay... and what have you decided?'

Faye didn't know whether the phones were bugged, but there was a risk that they were.

'Could you come and visit?'

'Does my new boob job mean I have to sleep on my back? Sure thing! Whenever you want.'

'There's a form winging its way to you that you have to fill in. Then you should be able to make a request and get here as soon as possible. I miss you so much, but I've had to isolate for my own sake. This place changes you – for better and for worse. And you have to constantly stay in the here and now to avoid being consumed.'

'I get it. I miss you. We all do.'

A brief silence ensued. Faye tried not to picture the people closest to her – it was easiest just to push them away.

'I need a favour,' she said after a while. 'Are you at the office?'

'Yes.'

'Could you check with PR on those interview requests that you mentioned in your letter?'

'Which you didn't reply to.'

'Sorry.'

There was a slight exhalation on the other end of the line.

'You don't have to apologise for anything, Faye. On my way.'

Faye heard her heels clacking on the floor as she walked down the corridor.

She could see Alice now. It seemed almost unreal that there was a regular world out there. A world that worked and kept on spinning and where people could move about as they pleased.

'What I can tell you is that they haven't stopped coming. We're getting at least ten requests a day,' Alice said.

Faye laughed in surprise. Unbelievable.

'Right, I'm here. The *New York Times* wants to meet you. SVT. *Le Monde*. The *Daily Mail*. You're little Miss Popular, as you can probably tell. All you have to do is pick and choose.'

Faye thought for a moment.

'Has anyone from *Strömstads Tidning* asked to see me?'

It was the local newspaper that everyone in Fjällbacka read, and she remembered sitting at the kitchen table as a child and ploughing through the articles. There was a certain appeal in her old local paper getting the world scoop. It didn't matter where she spoke out; she knew it would be disseminated to the other media outlets anyway.

'You're kidding?'

'No.'

Faye heard Alice clear her throat. Then she exclaimed.

'Yes! Here it is! There's an Agneta Persson who submitted a request.'

'Tell her she can have her interview provided she can do it by next week. I'll request a meeting with the governor, but she'll also have to contact him to expedite things. I don't think there will be any problems getting permission.'

'I'll let her know right away.'

After they'd hung up, Faye couldn't help but feel deflated and gloomy. The conversation with Alice had been a relentless reminder that there was a world beyond the prison walls. A world that was carrying on in her absence. She had to get back out into it.

The interview with Agneta Persson of *Strömstads Tidning* would be her first step towards freedom.

On the same day that Faye was due to deliver the first part of her entrepreneurship course, she received a visit from the *Strömstads Tidning* reporter, Agneta Persson. She turned out to be one of Faye's old classmates. At high school, she'd been called Agneta Boman and had been a quiet but kindly bookworm who didn't make much of a fuss about anything. Faye dimly remembered her and thought she still seemed the same in many respects – she acted as if she were somehow diminished, although that might have been the prison setting.

Faye met her in a bare room that was reminiscent of the interview room at Kronoberg Remand Prison where she'd spent hour upon hour with the police questioning her.

They had been promised an hour in the visiting room, and then Agneta had been given permission to follow Faye for the day, which was going to wrap up with a talk on entrepreneurship in the sports hall.

'I have to say that I'm a little surprised that out of everyone, you chose to invite our newspaper,' Agneta said.

'Oh, how come?' Faye said, with feigned surprise. It was obviously nothing short of bizarre.

'There are so many people who want to talk to you – major newspapers and TV shows both in Sweden and abroad.'

Faye sipped her coffee.

'I'm from Fjällbacka – it'll always be my place on Earth.

That's why I wanted to talk to you, since you understand where I come from.'

Agneta smiled shyly.

'How's life at Stenakull?'

Faye paused for a moment's thought before she answered.

'Humdrum and monotonous. But I'm surrounded by amazing people. Women who made bad decisions and ended up here. Sometimes justly, sometimes downright unjustly.'

Agneta nodded gravely.

'And what about you? You've been convicted of the murder of your ex-husband and given a life sentence.'

'Convicted, yes. Guilty, no.'

A brief silence ensued. Agneta seemed hesitant as to how to proceed. Faye pursed her lips and at last the reporter found the right words.

'You still deny it? Just like you did during the trial?'

Faye shrugged.

'Yes, of course. I'm innocent – although God knows I had reason to want him dead. He murdered our daughter – my only child.'

'Do you think about her often?'

Faye replied quick as a flash and truthfully:

'All the time. Every single second.'

Her throat constricted and Faye tried to push the image of Julienne's smile from her mind's eye. She couldn't break down now.

Agneta pulled out her camera and took some pictures. Faye reached out for her glass of water and took a few sips.

'If you didn't kill Jack, then who did?' Agneta said once Faye had set down her glass with a trembling hand.

'I don't know.'

'Your necklace was found close to where … the remains of his burnt body were discovered.'

'Yes.'

'What do you have to say to that?'

'That it's strange, especially since it wasn't there when the police were at the summer house the first time. Despite the fact that they searched that very location with dogs. It's even stranger when you consider that my car was broken into just a couple of days before it was found. The necklace was stolen but they didn't touch my expensive handbag, my credit cards or anything else.'

'You mean to say that...?'

Faye interrupted her.

'Someone framed me. Absolutely. I've pissed a lot of people off – especially men. Successful women have a tendency to do that.'

'You've never been to the scene of the murder?'

Faye shook her head.

'Never.'

Agneta looked down at her notes. She seemed to be content with that.

'Tell me what your days are like here,' she said instead.

The change of subject was a relief to Faye.

'They're all the same. Doors open at a quarter to eight and then breakfast. We get to work or start our studies at half past eight. I work – I make clothes.'

'Do you like it?'

'I do – a lot,' Faye said. 'Then it's lunch at half past eleven. After that we've got an hour's break before returning to work. Dinner at five. Then we have some down time in the wing. We watch TV, play cards or just talk. Like a big family. They lock us up for the night at eight.'

'Aren't you ever afraid?'

'Of what?'

'The other inmates?'

'No, not at all. I'm never afraid.'

Faye smiled. She kept her body from trembling at the mere thought of Regina and the look she'd had on her face as she came into Faye's cell with her hand behind her back.

'What's the hardest thing about being incarcerated,' Agneta said, interrupting her train of thought.

'Being deprived of my liberty. Being constantly told what to do.'

'Is there anything about it that's ... good?'

'I was actually thinking about that just the other day. I'm doing a lot of reading in here, like when I was a kid. And some of the girls have quickly become sisters to me. They're some of the best, most loyal people I've ever met. I think we'll always be friends, even if some of them make it out to freedom before me.'

'Have you made any enemies?'

Faye shrugged. Once again, she pushed aside the image of Regina with her hand behind her back.

'Don't we always? Being a woman doesn't mean you're a good person. Sisterhood doesn't automatically mean "back all women". There are all kinds of women. Just like with men. But I'll say this: throughout my life I've found far more women than men whom I've been able to trust.'

Following the interview, Faye showed Agneta around her wing while two screws ambled along behind them. She showed her to her cell and was photographed lying on the bunk with her books next to her. Then they went to the common room where Agneta took some more pictures.

'Don't you ever get angry about being behind bars, given that you consider yourself to be innocent?' Agneta said as Faye showed her the kitchen rota on the wall.

'There are worse things that can happen. My life hasn't always been a bed of roses, but life in here makes you humble. There are women here who have been through terrible things – who never even had a chance. And do you know what? Almost every single time it all started and ended with a man. A man who couldn't behave, who exploited, hit or raped her.'

They moved on into the exercise yard where the inmates

would take their walks. Faye inhaled the fresh air, the oxygen rejuvenating her brain.

'The surroundings are actually quite beautiful, even if you can't see much of them,' Faye said. 'And it's obviously not as beautiful as Fjällbacka. But then again, there's nowhere on Earth that is.'

Agneta smiled at her.

'Do you miss Fjällbacka?'

Faye stopped and gazed up into the sky.

'Every day. It'll always be my home and one day I'm going to go back.'

'When do you think that will be?'

'I've got a life sentence, but as you know, that's not how it works in Sweden. I'm going to keep my head down in here and do the best I can to get released as soon as possible. I have no crime to atone for. I'm being robbed of the best years of my life, but I'm not going to let that make me bitter. That would be punishment twice over, meted out both by the judicial system and by me. My daughter never got the chance to grow up; it would be an insult to her if I let myself be embittered. I intend to honour her memory by living my life authentically, wherever I may be. Whether that's in Stenakull Prison or in Fjällbacka. Or in Stockholm.'

A couple of hours later, Faye stepped onto a makeshift stage consisting of a rock-hard gym mat in front of almost one hundred assembled inmates in the sports hall.

She gazed at them and felt almost moved. Ines and Miryam were sitting at the very front and smiled at her. They were two women who in the space of a month had got closer to her than she had thought possible.

'I've stood on a lot of stages and talked about how to build a company, but I can't help wondering whether this might be the best one yet.'

She jumped up and down on the temporary stage and the

women laughed cheerfully. Agneta eagerly snapped shot upon shot.

'I usually begin by explaining one thing to my audience: being born a woman means the odds are against you. You have to fight twice as hard as a man. But I don't have to tell you lot that. There's no one on Earth who knows that fact better than you.'

She paused.

'Women in Sweden today earn less than men for doing the same or better work. That's what the system is like. It's rigged against us. What's more, we shoulder most of the responsibility in the home.'

She met Ines's gaze. It felt as if her beautiful eyes contained embers, as if she might ignite the whole world with that spark – change it.

'That's why I have this to say to the system: fuck you. I realised early on that if you fight the system you can actually win. No system is unbeatable. But it takes time. You have to build your own system – your own universe. I created Revenge. A company by women, for women. With products for us, by us. I was sick of seeing the same old codgers making the rules for female beauty products. What do they know about us and what we need?'

She took a deep breath. It felt as if the air itself were quivering, as if everyone were holding their breath and soaking up every word she had to say.

'Each and every one of you has your own story, your own energy that you can use to create your own Revenge. Not everyone will succeed – but at least you'll die knowing you tried. Don't let these walls hold you back. Use your time in here to dream, to read up and to figure out what your universe is.'

She gazed towards the back rows.

'But what about the money, I hear you asking? Don't you need money to start a company? Well yes, you do. That's why

I'm launching a foundation for people to apply to for grants to start their own businesses. Quick loans, no interest.'

Louise stood up with a roar and several other women followed her example. Before long, everyone in the room was on their feet clapping, whistling and cheering. Ines was smiling at Faye and Faye realised that all she wanted to do was kiss her.

Once the jubilation had died down and the women were back in their seats, Faye moved on to the more practical details. She explained how they could go about it and gave them advice on what to consider. She mentioned the different types of company that existed and the rules that applied to each, telling them how she had started out as a sole proprietor when she was a dog walker.

'Any questions?'

Louise raised her hand.

'How do you know what to do? What to sell?'

A few of the women in the audience laughed, but Faye silenced them with a hand gesture.

'That's a great question. My answer is this: dig where you stand. I love make-up. I understand make-up. I understand women's need for make-up. That's why I chose it. If you're into fitness, do something related to that. If you like… Oh, I don't know … gardening, then maybe garden products or services might be your thing. Or do what I did when I was getting paid for walking other people's dogs: keep your eyes peeled for an unmet need and then find a solution to it.'

'How do you know you're not being cheated?' A big blonde woman whose name Faye thought was Jessika had asked her question without putting up her hand.

'You can never know for sure. We all know how dangerous it is to trust someone – and how little you can rely on others. Most of us only trust ourselves, and sometimes barely even that. You've got to dare to put your trust in others when you're starting up a business, but that doesn't mean you should be naïve. Do your homework on the people you surround yourself with. Never relinquish control completely. Be on your guard, but when people reward your trust in them, be bold and give them freer rein. That's my advice. And try to find the right people to collaborate with, who are good at what you're not the best at.'

More hands shot into the air. After a Q&A session that felt like it would never end, Faye stepped off the gym mat two hours later to a smattering of applause.

Agneta Persson came over to say goodbye. She looked completely exhausted.

Ballbag and another screw escorted the journalist out while Faye spent a few seconds exhaling. Then she left too.

She felt intoxicated with happiness. It had been wonderful to feel like the old Faye – at least for a brief moment. She was smiling broadly as she turned left towards her cell.

'You think you're so fucking special, huh?'

Faye started and found herself struggling to breathe.

Regina was leaning against the wall, staring at her. Faye refused to show her how afraid she was. She began to move as resolutely as she could.

Regina held out her arm as she was about to pass by.

'You think you're so fucking special, don't you?' she said again. 'And you've managed to fool those grinning idiots in there and all. But you're just like us. Same shit. Bottom of the pile. You ain't no fucking millionaire boss or hot shot in here.'

'I know that, Regina,' Faye said in a low voice.

She tried to avoid eye contact to avoid provoking her any further. Regina wanted to show her dominance, and the most sensible thing to do right now was let her.

Regina shoved her hard before walking off. Behind her, Faye heard her yell:

'I've got my eye on you!'

The cell door slammed shut behind her, and Faye let out a

deep sigh of relief. She knew that sooner or later she would have to face off against Regina properly, and when she did she couldn't afford to lose.

Växjö, 1999

Zoran paid off the debt to Ivan relatively quickly. The gambling den in the basement of our restaurant became a great (albeit secret) success. Gambling addicts, crooks and high rollers came from across the county to play poker seven days a week. Zoran was so pleased that he started talking about expanding to other towns. Of course, he forgot that it was me who had thought of it in the first place. Instead, he boasted to his friends far and wide about how he'd devised the strategy to ensure the police didn't rumble us. He was now scouting out suitable premises in Jönköping.

One evening after I'd put the kids to bed, I heard the front door open. I knew it had to be Zoran, but then I heard voices and realised he had company. I got up from the sofa and went into the hall.

The man with him was Ivan.

'Milenka, darling. Come and say hello to Ivan,' Zoran said enthusiastically.

That Ivan had dispatched two of his goons to threaten us just five months earlier seemed to have slipped Zoran's mind.

We kissed each other on the cheek and Ivan admired our home. He wore an elegant chalk-stripe suit and looked like a wealthy businessman rather than someone devoted to a life of crime and violence.

They left me and went upstairs to Zoran's study while I returned to the TV. Ivan's presence made me feel uncomfortable. Zoran hadn't said a word about him coming here. Occasionally there would be peals of laughter upstairs and after an hour or so they came downstairs again, still engaged in cheerful conversation. We said goodbye to Ivan in the hall and once the door had closed Zoran turned to me. I could tell by his face that he was excited.

'Come on,' he said, 'let's sit down in the living room.'

He went over to the drinks trolley, poured two generous whiskies and brought the glasses to the sofa where I was waiting. I reached for the remote control and turned down the volume on the TV.

'Ivan was impressed by our setup down here,' Zoran said.

'Great,' I said hesitantly.

'He wants to partner up on the gambling clubs.'

I'd hoped we'd be shot of Ivan in our lives now that we'd cleared our debt, but I didn't say anything and waited for him to continue.

'He wants to expand. To the big city. To Malmö. To Gothenburg. To Stockholm. He'll source the venues and I'll be in charge. Do you realise what this means?'

He drank the whisky while waiting for my reply.

'Do we have to move?' I said.

'Move?' he said, as if this were a stupid question. 'Yes, of course. He wants us to live in Stockholm. So that we're close by. Milenka, damn it! We'll be able to get out of this shithole. It's where we met – surely you remember that New Year's Eve? You said you wanted to live there someday. Now we have the chance. You'll want for nothing. Nor will the boys.'

I clutched my glass tightly, without tasting the whisky. He was right; I had dreamed of Stockholm. I still did, even though

170

I was happy in Växjö. What worried me was not the move itself, but being too close to Ivan.

He was dangerous. Being accepted into his inner circle could be the end of your life. It was a world of violence in which the strong always prevailed. Worse, Zoran would be pulled even further into shady dealing, which risked us attracting the attention of the police.

This wasn't just about me and Zoran anymore. We had our two boys and … I put a hand on my belly. Another child was on the way. I hadn't said anything to Zoran yet, but once I'd been two weeks late I'd realised I was pregnant. I hoped it was a girl this time.

Zoran moved closer.

'Milenka, darling. I know things haven't been the same between us lately. You know, I've been so stressed. But I've fixed it all now.'

I met his gaze, trying to gauge whether he was kidding himself, whether he actually meant that he was the one who had resolved this.

'Zoran, he's dangerous. Ivan is dangerous. What happens if something goes wrong? You'll be the one responsible.'

'That's not going to happen. I know what I'm doing.'

He caressed my cheek.

'I don't want to do this without you. Sure, you could stay here in Växjö, but I don't want to be without you and the boys. You know how it is for me – family comes first. I'm nothing without you.'

I sighed, took his hand and held it in mine. Luka and Marko would miss him. And he was a good dad when he actually came home. If he lived in Stockholm and we stayed in Växjö, they'd never see him. I couldn't do that to them. Besides, I still loved him. If I stayed here I knew he'd meet someone else in the big city. He'd trade me in for a younger, more beautiful model. Zoran was incapable of being alone and he was charming and handsome. I knew the impact he had on women.

'We'll come with you, but you'd better make sure you find us a big enough house,' I said with a smile.

He leaned forward and kissed me on the mouth.

'I'll get us a palace,' he said with delight. 'It'll be so big you'll need a map to find your way around it.'

I laughed.

'Good. And I want us to move as soon as possible so that we're in safely before the birth.'

He stared at me.

'Birth?'

I placed a hand on my belly.

'We're having another baby, Zoran.'

His jaw dropped, then he laughed and hugged me. He got up to refill his glass, but I put a hand on his shoulder.

'Take mine instead,' I said.

I felt a little bit of the old trust between us. That love that had been the very foundation of my first years in Sweden.

At breakfast four days after Faye's talk in the sports hall, Ines leaned over to her.

'Today's my birthday and tonight there's a party.'

Goosebumps formed on Faye's arms.

'Where?'

'My cell. Let's skip dinner.'

Faye's cheeks flushed. While she wasn't exactly suffering or unhappy in prison, her days were incredibly monotonous and they dragged by. The only things to break the boredom were her brief encounters with Ines. She wasn't quite sure what Ines envisioned by way of a party: she assumed booze was off the cards since it was prohibited and difficult to smuggle in.

After breakfast, Faye headed off to get to work on her sewing. Regina was on her way into the welding workshop. She turned and stared at Faye, who just kept going, pretending she hadn't noticed. She could never show fear. Not here, not anywhere. But in recent days, Regina's staring had still left Faye feeling ill at ease. She really needed to avoid being on her own with Regina.

The day dragged by far too slowly to sate the butterflies in Faye's tummy which had been fluttering away since breakfast. When it was finally time for dinner, there was a knock on the door. It was Ines.

'Go straight to my cell.'

'But they're—'

'It's all sorted,' Ines said, going out into the corridor. 'I've spoken to Ballbag – he's on duty tonight. Just do as I say. Come along in a sec.'

Ines's cell was five doors down. A minute or so later, Faye stepped in and found Miryam was there too. There was someone rattling around in the loo. The door to the ensuite opened and Ines appeared with a bottle of Explorer vodka in one hand and a stack of three plastic glasses in the other.

'Ready to party?'

Faye stared at her, trying to work out how long it had been since she'd had a drink. She concluded it must have been at the Grand Hôtel, moments before the plain clothes police officers had arrested her in the foyer.

That was just over nine months ago. Approximately one pregnancy. She giggled at the mere thought of drinking booze.

'How did you get hold of that?'

Ines distributed glasses.

'Ballbag. Anything and anyone can be bought. Especially him.'

She unscrewed the cap and poured.

Faye contemplated the transparent drink, inhaling the delicate aroma of the liquor. Maybe a little alcohol wasn't such a bad idea. Maybe she needed the madness as a battering ram against the boredom. It might offer her an outlet from grey prison life. The prospect of forgetting she was an inmate in the toughest women's prison in the country and pretending she was at a boozy knees-up, even for a while, was irresistible.

They raised their glasses.

'Happy birthday! Cheers to you,' Faye said, looking at Ines.

They downed their vodka and Ines topped them up. They clinked the glasses together and downed them again.

Without anyone saying a word, they lay down on the bunk. After a few more glasses, the alcohol began to take effect, forming an undulating veil that clouded and softened the clarity of Faye's gaze.

Perhaps because it had been so long since Faye had drunk anything, she felt inebriated after the first glass. She noted the absence of music and other sounds, and savoured her friends' voices and happy laughter.

Ines talked about her upbringing in a strict religious family in the Stockholm suburb of Järva.

'I hardly ever met any Swedes until I turned eighteen and got a job working on the concourse at Stockholm Central Station as a passenger host. I think that was the most fun job I've ever had. People would come up to me and ask where the right platform was or whatever, and I'd smile at them and point them in the right direction. It was all so easy back then.'

Miryam, who had grown up in a 1960s concrete suburb of the provincial town of Västerås, mimicked the man she'd lost her virginity to. He'd been thirty and she'd been fourteen.

'He sounded like a chainsaw that had jammed,' she said, and they bent double with laughter.

Faye thought it was dodgy as fuck for someone that young to have sex with a grown man, but Miryam said it wasn't something that bothered her. Perhaps there were other, worse events that had smoothed over the memory of it all. Faye told them about the terrible moment when she'd walked in on Jack and Ylva in their marital bed.

'That was when my life began,' Faye slurred.

'So just how rich are you then?' Miryam said.

'I'm not really sure, but I think it's three or four billion kronor.'

'What a waste,' said Ines.

'How come?'

Ines and Miryam looked at each other for a few seconds then began to laugh even louder.

'Take a look around you, sweetie,' Miryam said, wiping

away tears of laughter. 'You're drinking fucking Explorer from a plastic glass inside a cell at Stenakull with two lags.'

Faye shook her head and huddled closer to Ines.

'I can't think of any better company,' she said. 'Although it'd be nice if there weren't bars over the windows. And if there was music for us to listen to, I guess.'

'What do you miss most about the outside?' Ines said.

'Freedom,' Faye said.

'Cock,' Miryam said.

Yet more hysterical laughter.

'Okay, I'll second cock,' said Faye. 'But I don't miss men.'

'Imagine being properly turned on. You know, so that your ears pop.'

Miryam rolled her eyes.

They fell silent, each one of them wrapped up in her own fantasies.

She could no longer see the plastic cups, which seemed to have disappeared, so Faye reached out for the bottle and necked it. Then she passed it on to Ines.

'Why does drinking always get me so wet?' Miryam complained. 'Feel for yourself. I'm soaking.'

She reached out and guided Faye's hand into her trousers. Faye became wet between her legs as she ran her fingertips over Miryam's smooth sex, which felt warm and moist.

Ines gazed at them, her eyes full of desire.

'I asked Ballbag for something else apart from the bottle of vodka,' she said.

She stood up and tottered towards the desk. Out of the desk drawer she pulled a pale blue dildo and a red and white device that reminded Faye of a small blow-dryer. She realised it was a Satisfyer.

'Since it's my birthday I want to go first.'

Ines slowly took off her clothes and lay back down on the bunk. She was so fucking beautiful. Faye bent over and kissed her before straddling her and softly holding down her arms with her knees so that Ines couldn't move. She ran her hands along Ines's arms and shoulders, and when she reached her breasts she saw out of the corner of her eye that Miryam was watching them, breathing heavily as she began to touch herself. After a while, Faye picked up the Satisfyer while Miryam grabbed the dildo.

The next day, which was a Saturday in mid-March, Faye received her first personal visit. It felt like a real treat: Christmas and her birthday all in one. She was shown into the same visiting room where she'd met Agneta from *Strömstads Tidning*. Alice was wearing an exclusive leather jacket, tight black jeans and tall boots, while her perfectly styled blonde hair flowed down over her shoulders.

'You look like an angel who's flown in over the walls,' Faye said with a smile.

They embraced. As ever, Alice smelled expensive thanks to her Chanel no. 5. The scent seemed more pronounced to Faye now.

'Did they search you?'

Alice giggled.

'Yes.'

'But not down there?'

'No.'

'Apparently they're not allowed to.'

'Should I have shoved something up there?'

'Next time,' said Faye.

'It's a pity I just had one of those vaginal rejuvenations – I'm afraid there's probably not much space up there.'

Faye laughed and hugged Alice again.

'I'm so happy to see you. Sorry about not wanting visitors

before. I've been focusing all my energy on blending in and getting to know the others, and I didn't want to confuse the two worlds.'

'So have you done it now? Are you blending in?'

In her mind's eye, Faye replayed images of the previous night in Ines's cell. Miryam's big, perfect breasts. Ines's small firm ones. Their naked sweaty bodies. Tightly entwined. The smell of alcohol and sex. Good God, she would never forget it.

She smiled.

'I suppose you might say that.'

Faye reached out for the glass of water.

'How are you all? How are things at Revenge?'

'Better than ever. It's looking amazing so far this year. The attention around your... conviction has only done us good. It seems all publicity really is good publicity. We doubled our revenues for the second year in a row last year. But the question is what we do about the USA launch. There's a tremendous amount of interest. We've got distributors requesting exclusivity on Revenge products.'

'What do you think we should do?'

'I think we should go for it. And let's invite three or four American outlets to come and interview you here in prison as part of the launch.'

'Isn't that risky?'

'Have you been following the debate since the article in *Strömstads Tidning*?'

Faye furrowed her brow.

'No...'

'You've been praised by loads of people. You denied the murder and most people think you're innocent. Swedish women are buying Revenge in their droves. Even if they thought you were guilty, I think they still would, because that would mean you killed the man who killed your child.'

Faye laughed and shook her head. She paused to think for a moment.

'Okay, let's do that then. Pick the biggest media outlets. We'll go ahead as planned with the launch. I'll do the interviews here, show them around, play the grieving mother and so on.'

Alice stood up and went over to look out of the barred window.

'Are you sure you're all right?'

Faye looked at her standing by the window. Beautiful, fragile and completely out of place here.

'Oh yes. You get used to everything. This is my life now. And it's given me time to think about Dad. His next move.'

'You don't think he's given up? Isn't getting you banged up enough?'

Faye shook her head.

'No. He'll never give up. But the more I think about it, the more certain I am that he must be getting help. He wouldn't have been able to stay on the run this long otherwise. Someone's helping him.'

'Who?'

'If only I knew. I wonder if Zoran Rakitic might be helping him. They were in Hall together.'

'The gangster kingpin? Why would he be helping your dad?'

'My father's qualities may well be invaluable in the right context and to the right person.'

'What qualities would those be?'

Alice tossed her blonde hair. She looked exceedingly overdressed and refined in this setting.

'Cruelty. Ruthlessness. No conscience. And he takes immense joy in hurting others.'

Faye shivered. She thought once again about the gang shootings.

Alice turned around.

'Don't you ever think about breaking out?'

Faye hesitated. Ought she to let Alice in on her ideas? No, it was too early.

She shrugged.

'The problem isn't escaping. The tough thing is life on the run – always being hunted. It's really not so bad in here.'

'I would never make it.'

'Yes you would, Alice.'

They sat talking and when they parted an hour later, they embraced for a long time.

The warm water ran down Faye's body and she closed her eyes in pleasure. Her muscles were worn-out and throbbing after the heavy workout session that Miryam had led her through. She lathered herself and thought ahead to the sore muscles she knew were coming. The shower in her cell was small, but right now it surpassed the most luxe bathroom out there.

Faye started. Had she heard something outside the door?

She pricked up her ears. Was it her imagination? No, there was definitely someone going through her things. She put her hand onto the tap but didn't stop the water yet. The sounds were clearer now. Someone was approaching the door to the ensuite.

For a moment, she thought it was Ines who had come to surprise her, but when the door opened Faye almost lost her balance.

It was Louise who was standing there.

'What are you doing here?' said Faye.

Louise didn't reply. She was staring at Faye with a gaze that seemed almost vacant.

Faye's own gaze was drawn to something in Louise's hand – something gleaming. Something sharp. She stopped breathing. Then everything went very fast.

Faye heard herself scream, but the sound of running water

drowned out the sound she was trying to squeeze out. Louise raised the sharp implement and lunged forward to stab her. Thoughtful, happy, jolly Louise was stabbing and stabbing. Faye defended herself with the only thing she had to hand: the shower head.

She cried out for help. She shrieked even more loudly when she sustained a flesh wound on her right arm and she flailed wildly with the shower head, managing to strike Louise's face. Louise lunged again and it was as if all Faye's strength disappeared. A gasp escaped from her and then she felt the pain in her side. She collapsed, with Louise above her.

She heard cries. Not her own. She was unable to make any sound. Arms were pulling Louise away and she was roaring as if she were possessed, but what she was yelling was incomprehensible: 'They'll kill her! No, no! Paula!'

Somewhere amidst the tumult, Faye heard Ines's voice. She looked down and saw a knife. It was still stuck in her. Shocked, Faye stared at the black handle protruding from her body. Someone turned off the water. She moaned. She groped about for the handle, meaning to pull it out.

'No, leave it alone. Otherwise you might bleed to death.'

She tried to place the voice, to understand who was talking to her, but her vision was clouding over. The women who were crowding around her were nothing more than blurry outlines. She was frozen, shaking. She heard herself mumbling Julienne's name; she saw her daughter's bright, beautiful face before her.

Was she going to die? Who would protect Julienne and her mum? They would be completely defenceless.

Someone was holding her hand and talking to her soothingly. But the world was slipping away, faster and faster, until there was nothing left but darkness.

Stockholm, 2002

The first two years in Stockholm were the happiest years of my life. Or at least that's what I tried to tell myself. In the beginning, we lived in a small house in Botkyrka, but after a year Zoran bought a big house for us out in Skuru. Ivan and his family were now just a couple of doors down from us. We had more money than I had ever dreamed of. Zoran kept bundles of cash hidden around the house. If I needed to buy something, I would stand on a chair in front of the bookcase and grope about on the top shelf, and behind the books there would be a thick wad of notes that probably amounted to something like a hundred grand in wrinkled five hundreds. That was my housekeeping allowance.

But that wasn't the only place that money was kept. Sometimes I'd take a box of cereal from the pantry only to find that Zoran had stuffed it full of banknotes. Next to the clear blue swimming pool in the garden there was a wooden deck, and buried underneath it were bags of cash.

As the boys got older, we were able to leave them for a couple of days at a time. Sometimes we had two nannies. Zoran took me on trips to Paris and New York and that made me happy. I saw it as proof that he still loved me. On those trips, Zoran was always the perfect husband.

Zivko bought a new apartment for Mum in Zagreb and invited her to Sweden so that she could see us and her grandchildren. To the outside world, I was the perfect, faithful housewife. But on the inside, my panic was growing. It was as if the stakes were getting higher and so was the drop. It wasn't just the police that I feared; it was the other criminals.

In the space of a year, Zoran had become Ivan's right-hand man and his closest confidant. Ivan was feared. He was already involved in debt collection and gun running. But the gambling dens sprang up all over Sweden and quickly became the cash cow in Ivan's criminal empire.

The first time I realised that not everything was as it should be was on New Year's Eve, 2002. Ivan had thrown a grand party. He'd hired out the Grand Hotel Saltsjöbaden and invited over a hundred guests. Business partners, underlings, his lawyers. Their wives. The dinner went on for ages, with guests spread out around circular tables covered in white tablecloths in the dining room overlooking the sea. It was a cold winter and the snow outside the window was hard-packed.

I was wearing a red Versace gown, while Zoran was dressed in a dark blue Brioni suit that we'd bought in Italy. We were seated at the same table as Ivan and his wife Ivona. She was fifteen years my senior and a haughty, rather cruel woman. She never showed it when our husbands were there, but whenever we were alone she would make digs about how I should watch my weight and not dress so sluttily. They had two children, a son and a daughter.

Unlike Ivona, Mirko's wife Natasa treated me like a sister. After the time Mirko and Dragan had barged in and threatened me, Mirko had shown genuine remorse. Whenever Zoran was away for too long, he and Natasa would stop by to see me and the kids. Now Natasa was waving to me from the next table, behind Ivona's back. She was the only person who knew how I really felt about Ivona.

But it wasn't my relationship with Ivona that was worrying me. It was Ivan's and Zoran's. I first noticed it when Dragan came to our table and asked Zoran if he wanted to have a cigarette with him. They went out into the cold together. I chatted with Ivan, but I noticed that he was constantly glancing out towards Zoran and Dragan. More men had joined them. They were standing on the steps outside, talking and laughing. Irritation began to smoulder more and more obviously in Ivan's eyes. After a while, he stopped talking to me altogether and just sat there with his arms folded, glaring at the group outside.

I knew what that look meant. He felt threatened. Zoran was younger, more charming and easy to like. He liked to talk and joke about with the underlings; he'd give them small gifts when they did well and ask them how their families were and knew all about what was going on in their lives. His manner was in sharp contrast to Ivan's cool relationship with them, which was based on fear and respect.

When Zoran returned to the table, Ivan sullenly asked what he and Dragan had been discussing.

'All sorts,' Zoran said, shrugging.

'You have to be tougher on them. You're their boss, not their friend. Otherwise they'll never respect you.'

Zoran glanced towards me and Ivona. He and Ivan never talked about business or their crew in front of us. It was a breach of etiquette to do so in front of their wives.

He lowered his voice.

'Ivan, we were chatting about football. Hajduk Split are having a good season and Dragan was banging on about bloody Partizan Belgrade who look like they're going to win the Serbian league again this year.'

'Nothing else?'

'Well, Dragan's son Adam. He's met a Swedish chick and now he wants to marry her. Dragan isn't sure how he feels about that.'

Ivan stared at him, far from convinced.

I could tell that Zoran was completely unable to grasp what was behind Ivan's line of questioning. But it began to dawn on me what was going on.

I laid a hand on Zoran's arm, smiling and untroubled, as if I was truly curious about Dragan's dilemma.

'And what did you think, darling?'

Zoran turned to me and smiled.

'There are no better women in the world than Croatians. I said that even though his son is a Serb, he ought to pack him off to Dubrovnik or Split for a week to get that girl out of his head.'

I laughed out loud and kissed him on the cheek, but inside I felt an icy chill sweep through me.

Zoran put an arm around me. I glanced towards Ivan and smiled innocently at him. He didn't respond.

The party continued; there were fireworks on the stroke of midnight, and then it was full steam ahead on the dancefloor. The booze was flowing. We got into a taxi to go home at half past two. The boys were asleep, as were the nannies. We took off our clothes and had sex standing up against the basin in the ensuite to our bedroom.

'Zoran, have you thought about who's going to succeed Ivan?' I asked, once we'd got into bed.

He gave me an astonished look.

'No.' He lit a cigarette and stared up at the ceiling. 'Talk like that's dangerous, Milenka.'

'But...'

He tapped his cigarette against the ashtray on the bedside table.

'Never mention it to me again. Okay?'

Zoran fell asleep quickly. I lay there watching him and thinking that he looked so innocent. So unprotected. Since we'd got home, I'd been meaning to share my thoughts about Ivan, but I kept them to myself. I wasn't sure whether Zoran would understand. He was a lot of things, but he wasn't a woman and he lacked our unique intuition.

Although Zoran lacked any ambitions for power, or at least not ones that included becoming number one, that wasn't something Ivan would ever understand. To him, Zoran was a rival, and I knew all too well how he dealt with threats, regardless of whether they were internal or external.

I would have to make sure that the threat towards Zoran was dealt with.

When Faye woke up, she didn't know at first where she was. There were no bars over the windows and the lighting was dim. She was lying in a bed in a room that she was certain was not inside Stenakull Prison. She whimpered as she remembered Louise standing before her. The brutal attack. The roar. The knife handle buried in her own body.

'They'll kill her! No, no! Paula!'

Faye's hand trembled as she lifted the covers. She gently ran her hand down over her ribs and stomach. There was no knife.

When she turned her head, she spotted a contraption that resembled a stranded spaceship in some sci-fi movie. She tried to sit up but the pain in her side exploded. She sank back down onto the pillow, panting. It slowly began to dawn on her that she was in a hospital.

She spotted a call button and managed to press it. After a while, she heard the shuffle of footsteps in the corridor outside and a nurse aged around sixty opened the door.

'Hello there. How are you feeling?'

'Not great. Where am I?'

Her mouth was dry and she was slurring her words. Her tongue felt weird.

'At Sahlgrenska University Hospital. In Gothenburg.'

Faye took a couple of deep breaths. Just talking took immense effort.

'What time is it?'

'Half past ten in the evening.'

'What's the matter with me?'

The nurse smiled.

'The doctor's on her way – she'll be able to answer all your questions. Is there anything else I can do for you?'

'Water?'

The nurse filled a plastic cup from the tap and handed it to Faye, who raised her head before bringing it carefully to her lips to drink. The cup reminded her of the party in Ines's cell. She found herself smiling faintly. The nurse filled the cup again and set it down on the small table next to the bed before going to the door.

'The doctor won't be a moment.'

Faye stared up at the ceiling. She really wanted to turn onto her side, but she couldn't because of her injuries and because of the handcuffs that were keeping her in a supine position in bed.

She thought about Louise, picturing her desperate face in her mind's eye. The way she'd been screaming her daughter's name as they dragged her off Faye. It was impossible to believe that Louise harboured any sort of grudge against her. They must have got to her. Threatened her family. Whoever 'they' were. Faye knew of only one person who wanted her dead – her father. Was he mixed up in this? Could he get at her in this very hospital? Probably. She wasn't safe anywhere. Not here. Not in prison.

She had to get back to Stenakull and regain her strength, and then she had to escape. Otherwise she'd die in that prison.

There was a knock at the door and it then opened. A woman in a white coat with her brown hair in a ponytail came into the room. She introduced herself as Dr Högberg before pulling a chair up to the side of the bed.

'How bad is it?' Faye said.

The doctor peered down at her through a pair of round spectacles.

'You've got a punctured lung, but we've drained it and it's been responding well to treatment.'

'How long have I been here?'

'Four days. By the way, you've got a gash on your right upper arm that we've also seen to.'

Faye was surprised. She looked at her right arm, which was bandaged.

'How long am I going to be short of breath just from talking?'

'You're going to make a full recovery, but it's hard to say how long that will take. It's down to the individual.'

'When will I be back to normal?'

'In two or three months.'

Faye groaned. That long?

'Is there anything I can't do?'

'You can't drive.'

The doctor smiled.

'That shouldn't be a problem,' Faye said. 'I think they'll sort out a lift for me back to Stenakull.'

The doctor's smile became a laugh.

'When can I go back?' Faye said.

'In a week or so, I should think. Once I think you're healthy enough to manage it. It's my decision and my decision alone.'

Faye returned to the prison a week later. As she climbed out of the car and looked towards the big grey concrete building, she felt a strange mixture of conflicting emotions in her breast. In one way, it felt very wearisome to be returning to captivity and leaving freedom behind. But in another, she was looking forward to being ... home. She'd made friends here. People that she would never have met if she hadn't ended up here.

As she entered the common room, the hubbub stopped abruptly. Hanging over the big table was a handmade sign that read *Welcome home Faye*.

She felt tears pricking the backs of her eyelids. Then Marissa rushed towards her and flung her arms around her neck.

'Ouch! Ouch!' Faye laughed, and Marissa stepped back in horror.

'Sorry! You're hurt.'

'It's okay.'

Faye reached out and hugged her gently.

More and more of the others came to her. A few hugged her softly, while others gave her a pat on the shoulder, a smile or a look of warmth. That went a long way. She looked around anxiously.

'Louise has been transferred,' Ines said, stroking Faye's arm. 'You're safe. No one else here would think of doing something like that. Right?'

Ines fixed her gaze on one woman after another. Everyone nodded. Faye said nothing, but she knew that Ines couldn't guarantee anything. Anyone who could get to Louise could get to anyone else.

'Coffee?'

'Fuck, yes. I never thought I'd say this, but the stuff we've got here is high end compared with what they've got at the hospital.'

Ines came over with a steaming mug of coffee and Faye sipped it carefully. The strong coffee left her reeling.

'I'll help you to your cell. You need to rest,' Ines said firmly.

Faye didn't protest. Supporting herself on Ines, she walked to her cell. Following the shared hospital room where she had always been handcuffed to the bed it felt like the Grand Hôtel.

They sat down on the bunk.

'We would have killed Louise if she hadn't been transferred.'

'I still feel terrible whenever I picture her in front of me,' Faye said. 'She was so desperate.'

'She was screaming her daughter's name when they pulled her off,' Ines said, stroking Faye's arm again. 'Paula.'

Faye let out a deep sigh.

'Somehow, someone must have threatened her daughter's life. They forced Louise to attack me.'

Ines leaned closer to Faye.

'The people we care about make us both stronger and weaker,' she said.

Faye closed her eyes. She pictured Julienne. All she could do was nod.

'Louise, that poor bitch,' Ines said. 'But I'd still kill her if I saw her.'

'I'm pretty sure my dad is behind this somehow,' Faye said. 'But I don't have any proof. Just my own gut feeling.'

'You gonna tell the pigs?'

'No.'

Ines nodded slowly.

'So what are you going to do?'

Faye grimaced as the stitches from her surgery strained. She was getting slowly stronger with each passing day, but she was a shadow of her former self. Her lung ached in response to the slightest effort, and she was pale and anaemic. The simple act of showering was a tribulation.

'I have to get out of here. I've got to deal with this myself. If I stay here then I die. Sooner or later, he'll get me.'

Ines stared at her.

'How are you planning to escape?'

Faye smiled.

'I figured you'd tell me that. Is it even possible? Miryam claims it is.'

'Yes, of course. It's been done before. This is a women's prison – not some maximum security joint. Security isn't very high. As ever, men underestimate women.'

Ines got off the bunk and went to the window.

'When?'

'I need to get stronger first. I have to be able to cope out there,' Faye said, nodding towards the setting sun.

'If you manage to get out then you have to keep your head

down for at least two or three weeks. You have to stay put – you can't go off on adventures. That's how most people get caught – they quickly get restless, do something dumb and then they're found.'

Ines turned and looked at Faye.

'I know a place where you'll be safe. It's not what you're used to – it ain't no Östermalm – but I think you'd like it.'

'Where?'

Ines gave her a wry smile.

'One thing at a time. First we got to talk to Katya.'

Faye furrowed her brow.

'Why?'

'How else were you planning on getting out? Taking hostages and demanding a helicopter?'

Faye laughed.

'It'll cost you, though,' Ines said.

'How much?'

'I don't know. The money's for Katya, not me, see. I would never charge to help you.'

In the week that followed, first Alice and then Kerstin came to visit Faye. She needed to involve them in her plans and neither of them protested when she told them she'd decided to break out. Both of them understood that she was in mortal peril if she didn't, given what had already happened on the inside.

Above all, it was Kerstin who needed to make certain practical preparations. Faye was going to spend the first three weeks in hiding at a location arranged by Ines. She hadn't received any details as yet; she trusted Ines enough not to ask any questions but to assume that everything was ready.

Kerstin's tasks were much more difficult. Faye explained roughly what she had in mind, but it was up to Kerstin to figure it out. She probably wouldn't be able to go and see Bengt in Mumbai for a while, and that pottery class would have to wait.

In parallel with her escape preparations, Faye had been spending an extra hour in the sports hall each day. The governor had given her special dispensation to help her build back her physique, and she was also allowed to work half her usual hours at the sewing machine.

Faye was slowly regaining her strength. She would need it for what awaited her. She had to be in good shape.

After seeing Kerstin in the visiting room, she returned to her wing.

'I've got a number for you,' Ines whispered.

She dragged Faye to the empty phone booth so they could talk in private.

'Three hundred Gs. Deposited to this account.'

Faye peered down at the note she had been handed and nodded.

'Before I go?'

'No, Katya trusts you. Just as long as she gets the money before she gets out you won't have any problems. She's got two years left.'

'Good, that means I can do a better job of disguising the transactions,' Faye said in a low voice.

She looked towards some of the other women. Katya was in conversation with Miryam.

'How's it going to work?'

'Miryam's going to help. Katya's going to ask Ballbag to do a weekend shift so they can hang out – that's when it's quietest around here. She's going to say that Miryam wants in for a threesome. He won't be able to resist. And it has to be in the evening so that he can sneak into her cell and let Miryam out too.'

'And then?'

Ines smiled.

'Then the girls will make sure that the access cards get to your cell, and you'll walk straight out.'

'It's that simple?'

'This is a class 2 prison. It's that simple.'

'In that case I'll make sure Miryam gets the same amount. Can you let me know when and where she'd like the money?'

'Sure thing,' Ines said, smiling at her.

'And then what?'

'There will be a car not far away. It'll be dropped off about an hour before you go to avoid raising suspicions, which it will if it's there too long. It'll have a full tank and be ready to go. The keys will be on the right front-hand tyre. Get in and drive to Skövde. You'll change cars there. Someone will be waiting for you at the Ica Maxi supermarket by the motorway. Drive that car to Husby. Don't stop anywhere until you get to Skövde. If they have time to set up roadblocks then you'll be screwed.'

'Husby?'

Ines nodded.

'There will be a flat there with people waiting for you. It's all been sorted out.'

'Who are these people?'

'My family,' Ines said, grinning.

'Is that really wise? If the cops find me there they'll be in trouble.'

'You're my family too. They know that. And in my family, we stick up for each other.'

Faye gazed into Ines's dark eyes. Then she hugged her – for a long time.

On Saturday May 1st, there was only half the usual shift on duty. There wasn't a better day for Faye to escape. Katya had arranged for Ballbag to come to her cell at half past eleven that evening after first letting Miryam out. In the middle of the act, Miryam would make her excuses saying she needed to fetch a sex toy from her cell – they knew what Ballbag liked. Katya would ensure that his attention was directed elsewhere to allow Miryam to take the access cards that Faye would need from his trousers before hurrying to Faye's cell and letting her out.

Faye put on the prison guard uniform that Ines had bought from one of the female screws and given to her before they'd parted ways. She looked at the clock on the wall. It was eleven twenty-five. She moved silently to the door to try to figure out whether Ballbag was on the way. After a while, she heard his heavy footsteps and the sound of a door slowly opening.

Butterflies fluttered in her stomach. She nipped to the loo before hurrying back to her position by the door. She sank to the floor.

Earlier that evening, she'd said goodbye to Ines in her cell. They'd lain on the bunk holding each other until one of the screws had come and said it was time for lock-up.

'I'm going to miss you,' Faye had whispered.

'And I'll miss you. But we'll see each other when I get out. Though that might be a while...'

Faye had silenced Ines with a kiss and returned to her cell. She had tried to watch TV, but it was hard to focus on the news bulletin that was on. There had been yet another shooting. According to the grim-faced reporter who was standing outside a residential property, this victim had also been an associate of Zoran Rakitic. Once again, the modus operandi meant the police believed it was the same killer. But they didn't want to go into any further detail.

Faye checked the time again. Twenty to twelve now. In about five minutes' time, Miryam would leave Katya's cell – hopefully with the access cards that Faye would need to get out. She stood up. She was ready.

Just four minutes later, she thought she heard the sound of footsteps in the corridor. They stopped outside her door and a moment later the lock clicked. Miryam was standing there, naked and glistening with sweat.

She handed over two access cards, flashed Faye a smile and then nodded before turning and hurrying away again.

Faye headed for the door that the prison officers used. Miryam, who had had sex with a female guard in the staff changing rooms on several occasions, had told her how to get out.

She pulled the cap down low over her brow to make sure her face wasn't clearly visible, then tapped the card against the reader. A green light came on. She took a deep breath. She entered the airlock and tapped the card against the next reader.

Nothing happened.

Beads of sweat began to form on her forehead as she tried again and met with the same result. She began to feel sick. She tried the other card, her hand trembling, and she could have shrieked with joy when the second door silently glided open.

The corridor in front of her was dark but the lights came on as soon as she took a step into it. She consciously made an effort not to start running. It was not likely that anyone would be monitoring the CCTV at this time of night; she knew the screws usually watched TV or listened to music. And if they did spot her, then they would think she was a colleague doing her job. No one would suspect it was an inmate in disguise staging a prison break. At least that was what she told herself.

She made her way down the stairs and reached another locked door. This time she chose the correct access card first time round and continued on her way. She turned right around a corner and passed what she understood to be the changing room before arriving at an entrance hall that represented the final obstacle before she reached the outside.

All of a sudden, she heard footsteps behind her. Faye looked around in panic. If she were discovered here then it would be over. There was no sensible reason or explanation she could provide for why she was here in a guard's uniform. The footsteps were getting closer and panic made the blood rush in her ears.

The changing room. The door was a few metres away and she didn't know whether there was anyone inside it, but she would have to take her chances.

There were voices audible as the footsteps got closer. Two people talking.

Quickly but quietly, she ran to the changing room door and opened it cautiously. Her heart was pounding as she looked in. No one there.

The steps and voices were even closer now. She closed the door behind her and looked around the small room. The only place she could hide was in one of the lockers where the prison officers kept their clothes and belongings.

She threw herself into one of the open lockers. It was a squeeze – she barely fitted – but she managed to pull the door shut on herself. She forced herself to control her breathing so that she wouldn't be heard through the locker door. She had to stay completely still.

The changing room door opened and the voices were suddenly much too close to her. Just as long as they didn't open the locker she was inside... Faye screwed up her eyes. The guards were laughing and gossiping about the inmates. She heard her own name but didn't catch what they said. It sounded as if they were changing. Faye opened her eyes and stared at a point on the inside of the locker door right in front of her nose. It might open at any moment.

The laughter and talking continued and she heard rattling and the rustle of clothing. Two locker doors opened – but not hers. Faye realised that she had been holding her breath and slowly began to exhale. If only they would leave.

After a few minutes that seemed to last an eternity, Faye finally heard the changing room door open and close before the voices and footsteps disappeared. She closed her eyes tightly. She'd been clenching her fists, and she waited another minute or so before carefully unfurling them and stretching her fingers before opening the locker.

The changing room was empty.

Faye padded over to the door and put an ear to it. She could hear nothing beyond. She pressed the handle down and opened it a crack to peer outside. Nothing.

She carefully opened the door and stepped into the corridor. There was no one to be seen or heard. She took a few deep breaths to calm herself and tried to regain her focus.

Now there was just the last door to go – the one used by staff to come and go. She unlocked the door and opened it. At once she was embraced by the fresh night air and she drew it deeply into her lungs. Behind her, there was the sound of voices again and she hurried to silently close the door.

Faye then hurried along the paved path towards the gate in the fence. She tapped the access card against the reader and the lock mechanism clicked.

Her heart pounding, she walked along the verge making for the edge of the forest – just as Ines had told her to. She couldn't help turning around briefly to take a look at the fences, walls and building that had been her home for all these months. Then she hurried on along the road and turned onto a narrow gravel track.

It took her a while to find the silhouette of the green Opel that had been dropped off for her there. She thought of Ines and silently offered her gratitude as she groped about on the ridged top of the front right-hand tyre to find the key.

She opened the door and got in behind the wheel. The car's interior smelled the same as cars had done during her own childhood – sort of old and damp, mixed with cleaning fluid and possibly smoke.

She discovered it was a manual and tried to remember what she had to do before pressing down the clutch and turning the key. The engine spluttered when she put her foot down and she tried to find the biting point. She failed the first time and took a deep breath.

It would hopefully be at least a couple of hours before they discovered she was gone – a head start she would need if she was to avoid being caught at any of the road blocks that the police would be guaranteed to set up. The only question was when. And first of all, she would need to get this car started.

'Come on!'

It went better second time around. After that, it was as if her brain switched to autopilot and she didn't have to think. The car rolled forward under her pilotage.

After a while, she couldn't resist slowing down so that she could turn on the radio. If she was caught before she reached Skövde then at least she would have got to drive a car with the windows rolled down and music in her ears.

PART III

Stockholm, 2003

I set to work almost immediately since I knew I had no time to lose. It was an afternoon in the beginning of January, just a couple of days after that New Year's Eve gathering. The boys were out with the nannies, Zoran was in Malmö and I knew that Ivona was in town because I'd seen her car drive past a little earlier. I put on tight activewear and some lipstick, tidied my hair and put on a coat.

Their huge house, which Ivona was always telling everyone was New England style, was surrounded by a tall white wall. I pressed the buzzer and smiled towards the small camera. The lock clicked and I was admitted.

Ivan was standing in the doorway waiting for me as I padded up the gravel path. He was dressed impeccably in a suit and regarding me sternly.

'I just wondered if Ivona was at home?'

He shook his head.

'Oh, that's a shame.'

'What did you need her for?'

'I'm rearranging the furniture at ours and I needed some help to move a coffee table. Zoran's away. The boys too. You know what us women are like – we get bored. We need to have projects on the go.'

He smiled.

'Ivona's the same. I'll help you.'

'Oh, that's really not necessary. I'm sure you've got more important stuff to do than moving a coffee table.'

'I'm done for the day. I'd be happy to help.'

'Thank you – that's so sweet of you.'

He waved his hand and let me into the hall.

He disappeared momentarily before returning and putting on a coat and a pair of shoes. We walked side by side over to our house.

I took his coat and hung it up next to my own. I led the way into the living room and noticed in the mirror that he was eyeing up my figure.

'What needs doing?' he said, clapping his hands.

'I want the coffee table moving over there. And the rug underneath it too.'

'Well let's get to work then.'

The move was quickly and easily accomplished. Afterwards, I asked whether he'd like a beer and he didn't say no. He sat down in an armchair and waited while I went to fetch him a bottle. I opened it, picked up a glass as well, and handed them to him.

'Aren't you having one?' he said as he poured the beer into the glass.

I shook my head modestly.

'I've got to think of my figure,' I said, brushing a hand across my waist.

He smiled without saying anything.

I sat down on the sofa and crossed my legs.

'I wanted to say how grateful I am,' I said, feigning self-consciousness.

'Oh, it was nothing. It didn't take any time at all,' he said.

'I didn't mean that. I meant for everything. For taking care of us so beautifully. You're like a … father … to us all.'

He didn't say anything, instead raising the glass before taking a long draught.

'It must be a lot of responsibility.'

He nodded grimly.

'Sometimes. But ... we Yugoslavs have to stick together. The war was a long time ago. And if we're going to stick together then someone has to lead us.'

'I'm glad it's you,' I said.

He gave me a long look.

I knew I couldn't move too quickly, but there and then I knew it was going to work.

Faye was standing in front of the mirror. The long dark fabric felt unfamiliar against her body. There was a strong and spicy smell of cooking in the flat. And of lots of people in a small space. This room had been her sheltered world for three long weeks. She hadn't seen anything else and hadn't spoken to anyone outside the flat. Now, for the first time, she was going to venture out onto the streets she had seen from the window in her room.

The flat was on the eighth floor where she could hear the hum of the E18 motorway if she had the window open. She closed the window and went into the hall. She sat down on a stool, raised her skirts and put on her shoes.

'Are you ready?'

Faye looked up at Leila Makhrabi, Ines's mother.

'Yes.'

'We've told the neighbours that you're a very religious relative visiting from Iraq. It'll be fine.'

'I know.'

Faye stood up and looked in the hall mirror, adjusting the niqab's face veil so that only her eyes were visible. Then she embraced Leila, and put a hand on the front door handle.

'Would you like me to come with you?'

Faye shook her head.

'No, this is something I've got to do alone. But thanks for offering.'

She carefully shut the door behind her, lifted the niqab slightly and began to descend the stairs. Her footsteps echoed around the stairwell. Sounds of life came from the other flats she passed. A TV on, a child crying, a couple arguing.

She reached the ground floor and the main door, took a few deep breaths and then opened it. The sunshine dazzled her as she emerged and joyfully inhaled the fresh air, admittedly filtered through the fabric in an unusual way, but still. She was at liberty to move about as she pleased.

A couple of youths were sitting on a bench but barely gave her a glance as she headed for the plaza with shops at Husby Centrum, as per Leila's instructions.

She passed large, run-down blocks of rental flats, enjoying being able to move freely and completely unhindered. It was wonderful. Since her escape three weeks earlier, her exercise had consisted of walks back and forth across the room she'd had at her disposal. And before that she'd been behind bars... She couldn't fathom how she had endured it.

Faye had followed the intense police-led search for her in the early days on the small TV in the living room. It had now abated and resources had been redirected. But what was apparent was that she was more famous than ever. The escape had given her cult status – that much had been clear when she had viewed both the news and the social media platforms from the family computer. She knew there were hashtags and memes alluding to her escape.

A roaring moped made her start as it passed by her on one of the footbridges crossing the motorway. Faye made herself calm down. Before long she arrived at Husby Centrum, which was full of people. At first she was anxious, having become unaccustomed to crowds, but she soon relaxed. In the plaza, there were market traders selling fruit and vegetables, while men stood in clusters smoking and children were running around and playing. No one seemed to pay her any attention.

She went over to one of the men selling fruit, glad that

Leila had given her some cash. She pointed at the apples and held up two fingers. He put two shiny pieces of fruit into a paper bag and handed it to her. She handed over a twenty and took the bag, not bothered about getting any change.

She walked on and spotted an empty bench which she sat down on. She didn't know whether it broke any unwritten rules, and she was ashamed by her own ignorance, but she carefully lifted the bottom of her face veil and took a big bite from the juicy red apple. The pulp crunched inside her mouth and juice ran down her chin. She couldn't remember when she had last eaten something so delicious.

Once Faye had finished her first apple, she immediately took out the next one and bit into it. She was about to meet the person who would give her what she needed. First she just wanted to enjoy this moment.

People began to emerge from the entrance to the underground station. Two girls in their early teens passed by the bench.

Faye's jaw dropped when she spotted her own face on one of the girls' t-shirts.

Beneath the picture it said 'Run, Faye, Run'.

She smiled.

Then she began to cry.

Faye sought out a small mobile phone shop in the shade on the ground floor of a grey block of flats. The windows were barred. She opened the door, which chimed, and stepped inside. There was an assortment of mobile phones on display inside several glass cabinets. Some looked used, while others looked new. On the wall there was a black and white poster of Steve Jobs. Behind the counter there was an open door and music coming from the room beyond. A bald man in his forties emerged, wiping his mouth with a green napkin as he eyed her.

'Ines sent me,' Faye said.

The man crumpled the napkin into a ball and threw it into a wastepaper basket behind the counter.

'I've prepared things for you. Would you like me to show you how they work?'

'Please.'

He nodded, glanced towards the door behind Faye and then went over and locked it.

'Come into the office,' he said, beckoning her to follow.

It was hot and stuffy in the small room. Lying on a basic-looking table were the remains of the man's lunch in a plastic box. There was a pleasant smell of cumin and fried onions. He put the lid back on and placed the lunchbox on a shelf. Then he bent down and pulled out a Lidl carrier bag which he put down on the tabletop. He pulled up another chair so that they could sit side by side.

'Please sit down,' he said.

Faye sat down while the man pulled a Hello Kitty-emblazoned laptop case out of the bag. He removed the laptop from inside it. He put his hand back into the bag and brought out two mobile phones in boxes, as well as chargers, headphones and a payment card.

'I don't suppose I need to explain the computer to you?'

'I don't think so.'

'The password is Amina.'

'Why?'

'Because she's my wife,' he said and Faye smiled, even though the stuffy air made breathing difficult beneath the niqab.

He took one of the phones out of its packaging.

'I took the liberty of charging them and installing the… apps that I gather you need.'

'Which apps would those be?'

'First of all, Telegram. It's encrypted. But nonetheless, please avoid communicating in plain language. You never know. Your username is VeronicaMalmsjo47.'

'And who's that?'

'My Maths teacher,' he said, without batting an eyelid. 'There's only one contact saved on it, which is for the phone that an Uber courier delivered to the address that I was asked to send it to. It's been activated so that you can communicate with each other.'

He cleared his throat before continuing.

'It's probably most secure if you make calls. As I say, the other person's number is already saved to the contacts.'

He flipped the phone over. On it, there was a Post-it with a mobile number and various combinations of numbers and letters written on it.

'This is your number, password and other bits. Learn it all

by heart and then throw the note away. Same goes for the payment card.'

'Okay. Is that it?'

It was very hot underneath the black fabric. She wanted to get out into the fresh air again.

'It's set up so that you can download more apps if you need to.'

He made to return the phone to the box, but Faye put out her hand.

'I'll take that.'

He handed the phone to her and returned the other items to the Lidl bag before handing that over too.

'What do I owe you?'

'It's already been paid for.'

Faye raised her eyebrows beneath the veil.

'Ines?'

'I never ask questions, but I've got my money.'

Faye said goodbye to the man and exited the shop. The sun had disappeared behind the clouds, she noted with relief. It was cooler now. She refrained from pulling out the phone to call Kerstin, even though that was all she wanted to do. She realised it might seem strange if someone heard her speaking Swedish without the slightest accent while wearing a niqab. She'd already waited three weeks, so she could wait another couple of hours.

But for some unfathomable reason, her feet didn't carry her back towards the Makhrabis – instead they conveyed her towards the underground station.

Stockholm, 2003

I made sure that I bumped into Ivan as often as I could.

As soon as Zoran was away and I knew Ivona was out, I would pop over to theirs on minor errands. Ivan didn't mind. The relationship was a friendly one. He was fatherly in his indulgence towards and protection of me, and I gladly took on the role of the innocent, feminine daughter. We became increasingly familiar. When we met in other contexts where it wasn't just the two of us, we were polite and cordial. But I noticed that Ivan's looks towards me were getting longer and more covetous. Especially if Zoran touched me.

It was April by the time I took the decisive step. Zoran was away again and the nannies were keeping the boys busy. I saw Ivona's car drive by so I went to the phone. Ivan and I hadn't seen each other for a while as they'd been back to Croatia for a week. And before that, Zoran hadn't been gone much.

'Hi, Ivan,' I said in a bright, childish voice. 'What are you up to?'

He laughed.

'I thought it might be you.'

'We never hang out anymore,' I said, feigning a hurt tone. 'Perhaps you're sick of me?'

'Never. But I've had a lot on.'

'Well, you do have a lot on your mind. I won't disturb you. But I do miss our chats.'

Silence for a while.

'What are you doing tomorrow night?'

'Nothing much,' I said.

My heart began to pound in my chest. There was a new tone in his voice. I was actually supposed to be going to the cinema with Luka and Marko, while our youngest son Dejan was tended to by one of the nannies. But that could be changed.

'Why don't we have dinner?' he said.

'At yours?' I said, hoping he would suggest something else.

'It's nicer to eat out. How about the Grand Hotel Saltsjöbaden, where we had the New Year's Eve party?'

I contemplated the intent behind his question. I was convinced that he hadn't told anyone about our relationship. So far, it hadn't crossed any lines, even if it was obviously flirty. His wife would never believe that he was just hanging out with a much-younger woman. Nor would Zoran appreciate our friendship, to say the least. Ivan's men would turn against him if they found out he was spending time one-on-one with the wife of his right-hand man. Ivan would never take the risk of being seen alone with me. The risk of bumping into someone in the restaurant at the Grand Hotel Saltsjöbaden was far too great.

No, he had no intention of being seen there. There wasn't going to be a dinner. He would most definitely book a hotel room and seduce me. And he wouldn't tell anyone that he was going there to see me or that we had been in each other's company for a couple of months already, even if nothing had happened. He couldn't take that risk.

'Sure, but it'll have to be after the kids are in bed,' I chirped.

'Nine o'clock?'

It would be dark out by then, which was perfect.

Faye got off the underground at Östermalmstorg. It had been very trying to come all the way into town amidst all those other people. In the city's smartest postcode, practically everyone stared at her. A woman in a niqab was as alien as a giraffe roaming around the posh covered market nearby. Many of the looks she received were angry or even downright hateful. A woman with a big, blow-dried hair do and a small feisty dog in tow hissed at her as she passed by:

'Why don't you go back to where you came from?'

Faye ignored her and kept walking. Her feet were automatically directing her towards the old flat on Narvavägen where she and Jack had lived. Once there, she stopped for a while and looked at the windows on the top floor, her gaze fixed on the bedroom window where she had found him in bed with Ylva.

Then her thoughts turned to her father – just as they had done every other minute since her escape from Stenakull. But out here in the open in her old neighbourhood, it was as if those thoughts were sharper.

She was sure that he was behind the murder attempt on her behind bars – that he still wanted her dead. The only question was how.

She had spent hours doing research on Leila Makhrabi's computer. She had particularly devoted herself to reading up on Zoran Rakitic and the connection to the so-called gangland killings. The victim who had been shot shortly before Faye's prison break was a man by the name of Zivko Mikolic, who had been close to Zoran for a long time. Unnamed police sources in the press were convinced that Rakitic was putting his own house in order – and that he was using an outsider to do it.

She couldn't disregard the fact that the murders had taken place while her father had been on the run. Faye didn't want to think about him – not now that she was finally able to move freely. She needed a break from those thoughts if she was going to cope. But he was a constant presence.

She sat down on a bench on Narvavägsallén, pulled out her mobile and downloaded a popular true crime podcast that she had been bingeing on in the flat in Husby. It was called *Gangsterland* and was hosted by a woman called Caroline Sterner.

After struggling with the niqab, she managed to insert the earbuds she'd been supplied with in her ears. To her surprise she heard Sterner say that in two weeks' time she would be posting a special episode on the murders connected to Zoran Rakitic, in which she would reveal something that the police had missed.

'I've spoken to a witness who has actually seen the man suspected of at least one of these murders,' said Caroline Sterner. 'But that's in two weeks' time. Today we'll be talking about other things, including the recent wave of scams targeting the elderly...'

Faye jumped as she received a message on Telegram. She looked around and then opened the app. It was from Kerstin.

Everything's ready.

Faye checked once again that no one was nearby. She so longed to hear Kerstin's voice. Finally, she gave in. She opened her contacts and pressed the call button.

'Hello,' she said when Kerstin picked up.

'Oh my dear, hello! How are you? Where are you?'

Faye looked around. A nanny with an Eastern European appearance was leading a small girl with a rucksack across the street.

'Right now I'm on Narvavägen outside my and Jack's old flat.'

'Are you out of your mind? Someone might recognise you and call the police.'

Faye let out a low laugh.

'Don't worry. I'm in disguise.'

'In what way?'

'I'm wearing a niqab.'

'Oh gosh! Isn't it ... rather hot?'

'Very much so. And I might be attacked at any moment by some angry, Sweden Democrat-voting Östermalm bitch. How are you?'

'Good. I miss you. But I'll see you soon. Like I texted, everything's ready.'

Faye thought about the assignment that she had given Kerstin. Of course she had delivered, and in less time than Faye could ever have imagined. She'd thought it wouldn't be ready until after Midsummer.

'Thanks. You must have worked night and day.'

Kerstin disregarded the praise.

'I'm here now. It's actually pretty cosy, even if I do say so myself.'

'Where is it?' Faye said.

'The place we discussed.'

Faye sighed. Part of her was terrified of abandoning the safety of the Makhrabis, while another part of her was desperate to get to work in the fight against her father – before he tracked down her mother and daughter, as he would, sooner or later. Once she'd started, there would be no going back. She would win or die.

'I'll be there tomorrow. I'll let you know when I'm close.'

She ended the call and stood up. She glanced back at her old bedroom once more, then headed for the underground station to return to Husby for what would probably be the last time in a long time. Perhaps ever.

She thought about what Caroline Sterner had said about the witness. She wanted to know more about the killer in order to confirm the suspicion that had begun to germinate inside her. She had to contact Sterner before the episode dropped, and she knew she had something that would attract the podcaster's attention.

Faye had borrowed a battered green suitcase from Leila in which to put her belongings. They looked paltry, making her think of small fish inside the belly of a whale. Together with Kerstin, she had decided she would go to the Meatpacking District late that evening so that as few people as possible saw her out and about. Now she was sitting on the bed that she had neatly made and staring out of the window at the early summer sun that still hadn't set. She heard a quiet knock on the door.

'Come in,' she said.

Leila stepped into the room and sat down next to Faye on the edge of the bed.

'I've been to see Ines,' she said.

'How's she doing?'

'Good. She says hello and hopes it all works out.'

Faye smiled.

'I miss her. We were close on the inside. I don't know whether it's possible to explain what that isolation does to you. Bad things, of course. But good ones too. It makes your relationships stronger. You endure, side by side.'

Leila cleared her throat.

'I miss her too. But there's a lot that I miss.'

'Your homeland?' Faye said tenderly.

Leila shrugged.

'More like my home. We lived in the countryside surrounded by nature and greenery. And so many animals. Here, all I see is concrete.'

Faye nodded and took Leila's hands in hers. Her eyes were shiny with tears.

'I really want to thank you for everything you've done for me – you opened up your home to me and protected me. I'll never forget that.'

Leila smiled.

'It's been an honour to have you. You're a special woman – very different to me and the people I'm used to. But I'm glad you're my daughter's friend and that she had you close by for a while at Stenakull.'

Faye pictured Ines's dark eyes in front of her; remembered what her lips tasted like.

'Once she's out we'll see each other again.'

They stood up and embraced. Faye held back her tears. It was horribly difficult to leave this protective cocoon.

She felt like a soldier getting ready to leave on a campaign as she donned her niqab, picked up the suitcase and put on her shoes in the hall. Leila waved at her sadly as she stepped into the stairwell.

The taxi Faye had booked was waiting for her outside the main door.

The driver put the bag in the boot and Faye climbed into the back seat. She handed him a note with the address. Then he started the engine and they slowly began to make for the E18 motorway.

Faye wasn't sure she felt ready for what awaited her – but she had to be ready, otherwise she and her family would soon be wiped out.

Stockholm, April 2003

As soon as the kids were asleep that evening, I got ready. The plan was in place; now all I had to do was implement it. No one would suspect me – of that I was sure. But my biggest issue was ensuring that there was no call history connecting me and Ivan. Neither the landline nor my mobile could be among the last numbers he had called. This was something I had already dealt with, or so I hoped.

Once I'd put on my make-up and a provocative black dress, I put on a tracksuit over it and donned my coat. I'd have to leave my mobile at home. I checked that I had everything I needed in my big handbag. I'd be gone for about an hour and a half, and the kids would be alone throughout that time. But they rarely ever woke, so I would just have to hope everything would be fine.

It was ten degrees Celsius. I pulled up the hood on my tracksuit and cycled down towards Nacka Forum. There were two payphones in the square outside the shopping centre. I propped my bike up on a bike rack and looked around before making for one of them. There were people around so I made sure that my hood was covering me as much as possible. Then I pulled out my phonecard and inserted it into the slot. It was half past eight. From my handbag I retrieved the note of Ivan's secret mobile number that he used for business and which he'd given to me.

'Yes?'

'It's me.'

Ivan fell silent.

I could hear a woman's voice in the background and realised that Ivona was at home. That made me wonder if he was going to cancel. I didn't have my mobile with me, so he could well have called it already to let me know. I could tell that he wanted me to say something.

'Pick me up from Nacka Forum instead. I'm by the cab rank. I'll explain later.'

'Okay,' he grunted before hanging up.

I stood there with the receiver in my hand for a few seconds before I returned it to the hook. Then I went over to the nearest bin and threw away the phonecard.

I positioned myself a short distance away from the rank to ensure the drivers wouldn't be able to identify me after the fact. It began to dawn on me what I was going to do. I'd spent all my time until now trying not to think about the moment itself.

I discreetly slipped my hand down into my bag and fumbled for the Mora knife I'd bought using cash two weeks earlier. I ran through the story I was going to tell Ivan again. He had to believe it. I was a woman. He was underestimating me. That was my biggest advantage. He didn't know that I had realised he thought Zoran posed a threat to him – and this meant a problem for my whole family. Luka, Marko and Dejan were in danger, but Zoran would never be able to deal with Ivan. His being away was the perfect alibi.

'No one will suspect you,' I muttered to myself. 'You're a woman. You're insignificant.'

I gazed towards the road, but Ivan's Mercedes was conspicuous by its absence.

Two cabbies were leaning against one of their cars, smoking.

I stifled the impulse to go over to them and ask for a ciggie to calm my nerves.

It was five past nine when the black Mercedes finally pulled into the car park. I emerged from my hiding spot and quickly made for the car, opened the back door and got in.

Ivan turned around and looked at my outfit.

'Drive,' I said, laughing.

He smiled in amusement.

'What happened?' he said once he was back on the main road.

'I had to fool the nanny. I said I was going out running, so I couldn't take the car. That's why I cycled here.'

'Why did you lie?' he said, giving me a probing look in the rearview mirror.

He began to indicate to pull onto Saltsjöbadsleden. I realised he was testing me.

'Because I'm not the kind of girl who goes out for dinner with handsome men while my kids are asleep and my husband is away,' I said.

'Then why are you doing it?'

I stretched the seatbelt as far as it would go and leaned forward so that my face was almost beside his.

'Because I don't think you're taking me for dinner,' I whispered.

I felt him freeze.

'Or am I mistaken?' I said.

He didn't reply. I leaned back and looked out the window. Traffic was sparse.

'So what do you think is going to happen?' he said, scrutinising me in the mirror again.

'I don't know. All I know is that I like spending time with you, Ivan. You're … a real man. I like being by your side. Being able to feel weak. All women do – you know that. Zoran… He doesn't have your strength.'

I could tell he was satisfied with that answer.

We drove past the grand houses of Saltsjöbaden and across the level crossing in silence.

The white façade of the Grand Hotel loomed in front of us in the darkness and beyond there was a glimpse of the dark waters of the bay.

'Please park away from the building. Over there where there aren't as many cars.'

'Where?' he said.

'Over by that tree. With the bonnet towards the bushes. I need to get changed.'

He stopped in the most desolate corner of the car park, where I had indicated. The tinted windows hid us from the world outside.

'Is Madam happy now?' he asked, switching off the engine.

'Nearly. I just need to get out of these clothes. Surely you didn't think this was what I was going to wear for our *dinner*?'

He turned and looked at me. I let the coat fall onto the back seat and pulled the zip down on my jacket. His gaze stopped at my cleavage.

'We are having dinner, but I've booked us a room. We'll eat in there,' he said in a low voice.

'I suspected as much,' I said with a smile. 'Turn around, please. It's not very glamorous getting out of a tracksuit in the back seat of a car. Not even a car this smart. You'll get to the see the whole dress later.'

He reluctantly did as I asked. He was sitting upright, but I realised that the angle was wrong. I bit my lip and worked out how to make him move slightly. I preened and tugged at the tracksuit bottoms. I wasted no time, reaching into my bag and grabbing the knife by the handle. He looked at me in the rearview mirror and I met his gaze with a smile while trying to thrust out my cleavage. I took care not to let my face show what was about to happen.

'Ivan,' I said. 'Give me your right hand.'

He obeyed immediately. I gripped it softly with my left

hand and guided it slowly to my leg and upwards along my thigh. His breathing became more strained and he leaned to the side in order to go higher.

When his fingertips reached my groin, I squeezed his wrist hard and stabbed him with the knife, right in the neck.

He cried out and I stabbed again. I felt the blade penetrating tissue. I pulled it out and struck again. The cries stopped and he fell silent.

I pulled out the knife but remained at the ready in case he wasn't dead. I turned around and peered out of the tinted windows. In the distance, a man and a woman were walking away from the hotel. They didn't appear to have noticed anything of what had happened in the car.

I had to stifle the impulse just to open the back door, hurl myself out and run. I waited until the couple were out of sight. I pulled up the tracksuit bottoms, zipped the jacket back up and then put on the coat and gloves that I'd had with me in my bag.

I looked around again, checked that the car park was empty and opened the back door. I got out and opened the driver-side front door.

Ivan's body was lying diagonally across the centre console. I took a deep breath, grabbed hold of his legs and heaved. I pushed with all my might to try to get him into the passenger seat, but it wasn't enough. He was too heavy.

I tried to stay calm. I checked that no one else had arrived in the car park, then I went around to the passenger side and opened the door.

I bent forward, grabbed him by the arms and yanked him towards me. He shifted slightly and finally I managed to push his head down into the footwell. His body was still soft, so he was lying on his stomach on top of the bloody seat.

A pair of headlights was approaching. I hurried to walk around the car and get in behind the wheel, pushing his legs out of the way. I started the engine and reversed out of the parking space.

As I was about to drive away, another car pulled into the car park and I held my hand up in front of my face as if the headlights were dazzling me.

I checked the time: nine thirty-five. First, I pulled over by a drain on the road where I dropped the knife through the grate. Even in the unlikely event that it were ever recovered, it would be impossible to trace it back to me. Then I continued calmly towards the location where I planned to leave the car. It was a small clearing in the woods west of Fisksätra, overlooking the island of Mårtens Holme in the strait. It was just ten minutes' walk from the nearby railway line.

I pulled onto the narrow forest track, found the clearing and drove the car into the vegetation. I got out, opened the back door and retrieved my bag. Inside it I had a change of clothes – another tracksuit without blood stains. But before I put them on, I took out a pack of baby wipes from my bag and swapped my leather gloves for latex. I wiped down the car's interior, trying to cover every surface that I had come into contact with. In the end, all that remained was Ivan's wrist where I had held him while guiding his hand back to me just before I stabbed him.

It worried me that I couldn't find a mobile phone. I had searched his pockets and the car, but assumed he must have left it at home. I changed out of my tracksuit and pulled off the dress too, shivering as I stuffed the clothes into the bag I had brought with me for the purpose. Then I put the bundle into my handbag.

'Never threaten my family,' I said, gently closing the door. Then I started walking towards the station.

Faye waited until the taxi had disappeared from sight before she picked up the suitcase and carried it towards the building. It was a ramshackle place. She wondered whether she'd come to the right address. She pressed a small white bell that was skew-whiff, but she didn't hear anything. She shifted from foot to foot for a while before she heard the sound of footsteps. A moment later, the door opened and Kerstin was there, looking at her.

Faye took a step back. It was almost as if Kerstin had aged since the last time she'd seen her, but that couldn't be true.

'It's me,' she said.

'Come in,' said Kerstin.

Her warm smile was still just as beautiful.

Faye carried her bag across the threshold into a large entrance hall. Once the door had closed behind her, she pulled off the veil so that Kerstin could see her face.

They hugged for a long time, Faye pressing Kerstin's delicate, indomitable body against hers.

'I'm so glad to see you,' she said in a low voice.

'Me too.'

They detached themselves and looked into each other's eyes. In the end, Kerstin shook herself.

'Come on, we can't just stand here. You've got to see everything.'

Faye looked around. They were standing by a disused reception area.

'Do we own the whole building?'

'Yes. It's the old administration building for one of the abattoirs. I got it on the cheap.'

'Of course you did. You're the best negotiator I know.'

'Oh, shucks. Come on.'

Kerstin beckoned eagerly. Faye picked up the suitcase and brought it with her.

'I really want to show you what I've done,' Kerstin said.

She opened a thick iron door. Behind it, there was a set of concrete steps leading down into a subterranean area.

'They had store rooms, archives, a gym and a sauna down here,' Kerstin explained while Faye hauled the bag down the stairs. There was a smell of fresh paint.

They reached the basement and Faye looked around, wide-eyed. The walls had been painted in a light shade of blue-grey, and the floor was covered in pale beige carpet.

Kerstin smiled at her.

'With some help from a reputable builder, I've transformed it into… Well, a big apartment. I left the sauna and gym in place.'

Faye was stunned. She gazed at the plush carpet. It really was an apartment, and a cosy one at that.

Kerstin showed Faye into a living room that was furnished with an inviting sofa, armchairs, table, lamps and a big flat-screen TV. The air was fresh and easy to breathe so she realised Kerstin must have had a new ventilation system fitted.

Astonished, she dropped her bag there before they moved on. Kerstin showed her a study with an empty desk and a chair. She was already holding the door open to show her the next room, where she switched on the lights.

'This is where you'll sleep.'

A big bed with loads of cushions and fluffy throws on it dominated the room. There were nightstands either side of it, each with a pretty blue lamp on it.

'This is the only room with wallpaper,' Kerstin said.

Faye ran her hand lightly over the beautifully patterned walls.

'This is the best part,' Kerstin said with a look of satisfaction.

She went over to a built-in piece of furniture at the foot of the bed and pressed a button. It opened up and a TV rose out of it.

'Handy, right?'

'I love it.' And you, Faye thought.

'It's one of those smart TVs. It's got Netflix and all the rest. Come on, let me show you the bathroom.'

Kerstin turned off the light before leading Faye into a large bathroom. Behind a glass door she caught a glimpse of a sauna, but it was the vanity that really attracted Faye's attention. Next to it there were two packs of hair dye and a big hair trimmer that was plugged in to charge. Faye picked up one of the packs and stared at the bright red colour. The other was green.

'I've watched a couple of YouTube videos,' Kerstin said. 'I think we'll be able to get you looking really cool with one of those Mohicans. I've also got hold of lots of make-up – Revenge, of course – and I've done my best to find out how those gobs like to make themselves up. The new clothes are all in the wardrobe in your bedroom. You'll be absolutely gorgeous.'

Faye laughed.

'Goths, Kerstin, not gobs. And I'm sure it'll be great. Will you be staying here too?'

Kerstin nodded.

'Yes. I took the liberty of making up another bedroom.'

'Great. It'll be just like the old days.'

Kerstin reached out and caressed Faye's cheek.

'Just like the old days. Except...'

'Julienne ... but she's best off where she is.'

'I know, but I do miss that little girl.'

'Me too.'

Faye's throat constricted and she coughed to clear it. She pulled out her phone to check the time. 23:17.

'Tomorrow we'll give you your makeover,' Kerstin said, stifling a yawn. 'But I think it's best we get some sleep. I should, at least. The people who claim you need less sleep as you get older are lying.'

Faye put a hand on her shoulder.

'Thanks for sorting all this out. I don't know what I would have done without you.'

Kerstin shrugged.

'It's been a lot of fun. Well, not the circumstances themselves, but you know I like to be useful and helpful. And I'm not sure I was all that into pottery anyway.'

Faye and Kerstin ate a hearty breakfast comprising porridge, cheese sandwiches, boiled eggs and coffee. After they'd cleared the table and loaded the dishwasher, they went to the bathroom. Faye brought a kitchen chair with her.

'Are you ready?'

'No,' Faye said, positioning the chair in front of the mirror before sitting down. 'I feel like Britney Spears.'

Kerstin grabbed the scissors.

'At least you don't have to do it yourself.'

Faye closed her eyes as she felt Kerstin's fingers grasping her locks of hair. She heard the scissors get to work and hummed the melody of 'Toxic' to herself. When she opened her eyes after a couple of minutes, her hair was chin-length and hung in lank clumps. Kerstin put down the scissors and reached for the trimmer. She switched it on and the room was filled with a low rumbling sound.

Faye kept her gaze fixed on the mirror while Kerstin shaved her head, leaving a broad strip of hair down the middle. That was going to be used for the mohawk.

'You actually look younger now,' Kerstin said appreciatively when she put down the trimmer and washed her hands.

Faye saw that she was right. The new hairstyle accentuated her face.

'Now we just have to decide which colour you're going

for,' Kerstin said, her brow furrowed. Then she smiled. 'Both of them, right?'

'Red and green?'

'Yes. It'll be harder to do but look way better. You'll look like that Salander woman.'

'Lisbeth Salander? Haha, okay.'

It was an hour before they were satisfied.

There was a ten-centimetre red and green mohawk protruding from the middle of Faye's head.

They laughed so hard that their sides almost split as they admired the results of their handiwork.

'No one is going to recognise you. Especially not once I've done the next step,' Kerstin said.

'What's that?'

Kerstin opened one of the drawers in the vanity and got out a piercing gun.

'I've already read the instructions and the full process is well documented on YouTube, so there's no need to worry.'

'Is this really necessary?' Faye said, staring anxiously at the contraption in Kerstin's hand.

'Yes. Don't be a coward now.'

A wry smile crossed Faye's face.

'I've always secretly harboured the dream of having a nipple piercing.'

'In that case, this is the day your dreams come true. Let's start there.'

Faye unbuttoned her shirt and unclasped her bra to reveal her breasts.

'The left or the right one?' Kerstin said.

'Why not both while you're at it?'

Kerstin dabbed both nipples with disinfectant before bending forward, taking aim and pulling the trigger.

Faye screamed.

'Jesus fucking Christ.'

Kerstin smiled.

'And the right one?'

'Yes, but make it quick,' Faye said grimly. 'Before I change my mind.'

Kerstin gripped the nipple with a look of concentration before pulling the trigger again.

'Bloody hell!'

Kerstin wiped off the streaks of blood running down Faye's front.

'There we are. That's quite enough fun for one day. I was also thinking one on your nose and one in each eyebrow. That's what gobs – sorry, goths – look like. I've seen them on YouTube.'

Faye rolled her eyes.

'Stop banging on about YouTube. If you carry on like this, we'll have to limit your screen time. Do what you must and stop looking so pleased.'

'There's no getting away from it – this is sort of fun.'

'Yes, you've made that quite obvious. Maybe I should stab your tits too?'

Kerstin brought her palms protectively up to her breasts.

'Certainly not. I'm not that young anymore. Besides, fine motor skills deteriorate with age. Bengt would get stuck.'

'We'll see. Maybe I'll sneak in while you're asleep.'

Kerstin snorted.

Faye closed her eyes as Kerstin took aim at one of her eyebrows.

Before long, they were done and she had jewellery inserted into all her fresh piercings.

Faye leaned towards the mirror. She was happy with the result, even if her nipples were aching and the new piercings in her nose and eyebrows were throbbing. She'd let those grow back later.

'There's just one more thing,' said Kerstin.

'What?' Faye said in surprise.

Kerstin opened the bathroom cabinet and took out a package.

'Tattoos.'
'You're going to tattoo me?'
She nodded.
'But don't worry. It's the kind of tattoos they use in films. They're ready-made designs that stay in place for a couple of days, so I'll have to touch them up later. But those will be the icing on the cake – you'll see.'

After Alice had descended the stairs to the subterranean apartment that Faye had begun to refer to as the bunker, she came to a halt and stared – then she burst into roars of laughter that almost felled her to the floor.

'I can't believe it's you. Kerstin wasn't exaggerating. You really do look like Lisbeth Salander.'

Kerstin and Faye exchanged satisfied glances.

Faye was dressed in a black leather jacket, a black t-shirt emblazoned with a pentagram and black jeans with braces. On her feet were a pair of Dr Martens and there was a tattoo winding its way up her throat towards her jaw.

'To be honest, I think Lisbeth Salander was probably more discreet than this,' Faye said with a shrug. 'But the important question is this: would anyone recognise me?'

Alice shook her head firmly.

'No, I would have walked straight by if I'd seen you in town. And I would have held onto my Balenciaga bag a little more tightly.'

She went over to Faye and inspected the tattoos and piercings with fascination.

'It's incredible,' she murmured, running her fingertips along Faye's shaved head before gingerly touching the mohawk.

Faye and Kerstin showed Alice around the bunker and she was just as full of admiration for Kerstin's work as Faye had been the night before. After they had finished the tour, Kerstin withdrew to her room while Faye and Alice sat down at the kitchen table.

Faye got out a bottle of red wine that Kerstin had – with a degree of foresight – left in one of the cupboards. She opened it and poured them a glass each.

'I'm so bloody happy to see you,' Alice said. 'Even if I'm still having a hard time believing it's you. Couldn't you have gone with a more contemporary look? Punk went out of fashion in like ... the Eighties? What is it the kids call themselves these days? Goths? Emus?'

Faye laughed.

'I think you mean emos. But I wanted to be a punk when I was a teenager, so this was my chance. And the main thing is that this is way different from my usual appearance.'

'You've definitely succeeded in that.'

Faye smiled and took Alice's hands in hers.

'How are you doing, Alice?'

'Good.'

'And Revenge?'

'Better than ever. Your prison break bought us a load of free publicity across Scandinavia and boosted sales by fifty million kronor.'

Faye gazed at her in amazement.

'And tomorrow we're launching a new lipstick colour: Runaway.'

Faye laughed and raised her glass towards Alice, who clinked hers in return.

'Good idea.'

Alice shrugged.

'Well, it's my job, isn't it?'

They drank in silence and the atmosphere became more serious.

'What are your plans now?' Alice said, setting down her wine glass.

'To find my father.'
'How?'
'By cutting off his livelihood.'
'How do you mean?'

Faye ran a hand over her mohawk. She wondered how long it would take to get used to the feeling. When she brought her hand back down again, she realised she had forgotten to paint her nails. She reached for a bottle of bright red Revenge nail polish on the table and smiled when she saw the shade was called Escape. Was that coincidence, or had the marketing department been extremely quick off the mark? She started to paint her nails while concentrating on her answer.

'I suspect he's collaborating with a major player.'

She outlined the murders of people in orbit around the gangster Zoran Rakitic. There was no lead suspect, but according to police statements to the media they thought the killings had been carried out by the same person. Possibly a contract killer from abroad.

'Well, how are you going to succeed if Zoran Rakitic is backing him?' Alice said.

Faye raised a hand to touch her sore eyebrows, but the gesture made her topple the small bottle and nail polish began to run across the table.

'Shit.'

'Forget about it; you can take it off with acetone later,' Alice said dismissively.

Faye quickly righted the bottle, ignoring the spreading patch on the tabletop, and carried on applying polish to her fingernails as she replied.

'First I have to make sure that I'm right. That's where I'm going to start.'

Alice shook her head.

'But the question still remains – how?'

'Have you heard of the true crime podcast *Gangsterland*?'

'No.'

'It's run by a woman called Caroline Sterner. I'm going to contact her.'

Alice leaned forward and stared at Faye.

'Why are you going to do that? What are you on about?'

'I meant what I said. I'll offer her an interview in exchange for advance information about an episode she's putting out in two weeks' time, where she'll be revealing new details about the gangland killings. I have a feeling it might be important.'

'Faye … is this really…?'

Faye held up her hands to parry her off. Her nails were gleaming red and she waved them briskly in mid-air to get the polish to dry more quickly.

'A good idea? I don't know, but it's the only one I've got. I've got to stop him or he'll kill me. And it won't just be me. He'll kill Julienne and Mum too. I know it.'

Alice nodded.

'Okay, I get it. When are you going to get in touch with her?'

'Tomorrow.'

'And what are you going to say?'

'I'll ask her whether she'd like an exclusive interview with Sweden's most wanted.'

'Just like that?'

'What else am I supposed to do? Send the PR department round?'

Alice sipped her wine.

'No, you're right. There's no way she'll turn you down. An interview with you is a scoop. A massive scoop.'

In order to contact Caroline Sterner, Faye pulled out the second burner phone she had been given in Husby. She would dispose of it immediately after the call, and she would take care not to be in or anywhere near the bunker when she made it. She walked to the underground station by the Avicii Arena, feeling safe in her new disguise. No one would connect Faye the businesswoman with a leather-clad, tattooed woman with a mohawk. She grinned as she recalled Alice's reaction the day before.

She took the underground to the city centre and got off at Hötorget. She sat down on the sunny steps in front of the Stockholm Concert House and watched the crowds and market traders from behind a pair of sunglasses. She pulled out the mobile and created a throwaway email address that she used to send a message to Caroline Sterner, asking her to call and giving her first and last name and her number.

Faye waited for an hour while the greengrocers proclaimed their wares to the square.

Eventually, she began to feel pangs of hunger and decided to make for McDonald's. She stood up and was crossing Kungsgatan when the phone began to ring. She answered it while standing on the corner by the Kungshallen food court.

'This is Caroline Sterner. Who am I speaking to?'

'Are you alone?'

Faye realised how idiotic this question was – Caroline could say anything; it wasn't as if Faye was able to check her answer.

'Yes.'

'I'm the person I claimed to be in the email I sent to you.'

There was a moment's silence.

'What do you want from me?'

'I want to be interviewed on your podcast.'

'Is this a joke?'

'No, not at all.'

Caroline fell silent again. Faye gazed longingly towards the sign with the golden arches further down the street.

'I can't do the interview by phone. You could be anyone.'

'Exactly. I was going to suggest we meet in person.'

Another silence ensued. Faye could practically hear the cogs turning at top speed in Sterner's brain.

'What do you want from me? I mean – why do you want to talk to me when every single newspaper and TV channel out there would happily give you a big platform?'

'Because I like your podcast. But you are right: I do want something in return.'

'What?'

'The information that you mentioned on the latest episode of *Gangsterland*, that you're going to release in two weeks' time. I want to be given that information when I see you for my interview. And I want my interview to take place as soon as possible.'

A group of teenage girls were looking at Faye and she turned around and began to move slowly along the street towards the McDonald's.

'I'm free tomorrow,' Caroline Sterner said.

'Good. I suggest we meet at your place. Where do you live?'

'Fruängen. At 12 Bergtallsvägen.'

'Alone?'

'Yes.'

'I'll come round at two o'clock tomorrow afternoon. Does that work for you?'

'Yes.'

'And you accept my terms? A flash drive with your next episode on it.'

Faye held her breath.

'Yes, although I still don't understand why you're so interested in it.'

A blue bus stopped at the adjacent bus stop and let off a handful of passengers. A beggar sitting on the pavement gave her a pleading look and extended his hands.

'My explaining that isn't part of our deal.'

'Fine. See you tomorrow at two o'clock.'

'One last thing. Under no circumstances are you to reveal what I look like. To anyone. Is that understood?'

After a few seconds, Sterner meekly confirmed that it was.

Faye sighed. She would just have to trust her.

Stockholm, October 2003

I was in the waiting room at the Nacka maternity clinic waiting for an ultrasound. I'd suspected I might be pregnant for a while, and I'd had this suspicion confirmed a couple of weeks earlier when I took a test, but I hadn't said anything to Zoran. This time I was convinced it was a girl.

In the months after Ivan's murder, I'd had nightmares about stabbing him to death in that car. I was constantly afraid the police would arrest me, but they didn't even question me. And even if they had questioned me, they would have struggled to tie me to the crime. I'd burnt the clothes I'd worn that very same evening in the fireplace. Zoran, Zivko and the others in the gang had been questioned and as far as I could tell the investigators had one main avenue of inquiry: they believed Ivan had been betrayed by one of his own, given the execution of it. He would hardly have been in the car with an enemy. But they seemed convinced that the perpetrator was a man. Over the summer, I'd noticed that the investigation seemed to be losing steam. The tabloids, which had referred to it as the 'gangland killing', had lost interest after just a fortnight.

'Milenka Rakitic?'

The midwife wore round glasses and had curly brown hair. I got up and followed her into an examination room. She asked me a couple of routine questions before asking me to lie down on the couch and smearing cold gel on my slightly distended belly.

She guided a transducer across my stomach and focused on the black screen.

'You're in the fourteenth week,' she said, making a note.

'What sex is the baby?' I said.

She smiled.

'Would you like to know now? Or should I write it down so that you and the father can open it and find out together?'

'I want to know now.'

'It's a girl.'

I laughed. It had been a long time since I had been so happy.

As I left, I felt a sense of relief. Finally a girl. I really had been missing the company of a girl in this masculine world where I was surrounded by men of all ages.

I went home and as I pulled onto the drive I saw Zoran's car was there. He was back from his trip to Malmö and I decided to tell him the good news.

Ever since the murder, our relationship had been increasingly strained. Zoran had assumed Ivan's position and was now head honcho, but responsibility weighed heavily on him. He had become increasingly unkind towards me. He would often snap at the boys and be dissatisfied with them. Although he had drunk a lot before, that was nothing compared with the way he was tipping the booze back now. Sometimes, I'd see him having his first drink before lunch. I'd tried to talk to him about it, but it had only led to rows that ended with him getting into the car and driving off. Then he'd refuse to speak to me for several days afterwards.

I hoped the news that we were having a baby girl would make him happy. Perhaps it would be a fresh start for us.

I unlocked the door and called out his name. There was no answer. I heard noises coming from upstairs and realised that he must be in his study.

I examined my expectant face in the hall mirror, adjusted my hair and then went up.

'You're home early,' I said, smiling at him.

He stared at me but didn't say anything. I could tell by his eyes that he'd been drinking, and the room stank of alcohol. His eyes were filled with hatred and his face was contorted into a grimace.

'How long did it go on for?'

I didn't understand what he meant.

'How long did what go on?'

Zoran stood up.

'How long did it go on for?'

'What...?'

'How long were you spreading your legs for him? How many times?'

I shook my head.

'Who?'

He was bellowing now.

'Ivan! You banged him. I know you banged him. Did you do it here too? Under my roof? While the boys were asleep? Well, did you?'

'No, we never did anything,' I whispered. 'I never betrayed you. Why would you think I did?'

'Because I know everything... A taxi driver found Ivan's phone in the car park outside the Grand Hotel the day after the murder. He could see the last number that had called so he dialled it from his own phone. It was Ivona's number, and she did what was expected of her – she went to see the driver and then she passed the phone on to me. We knew there might be things on it that needed to be hidden. The phone died but we kept it. We couldn't get past the PIN request, so it was sent down to Croatia and a specialist there finally managed to crack it. So I've seen the texts you sent each other.'

I remembered how I'd frantically searched for the phone

but been unable to find it and how I'd decided Ivan must have left it at home.

He stood up. He came closer to me. He looked out of his mind.

'You cheated on me, you whore. You fooled me and humiliated me. After everything I've done for you.'

When I opened my mouth to protest, he hit me.

This time it wasn't a slap – it was harder, with his clenched fist. I fell backwards.

Dizzy and dazed, I lay there on the floor. I didn't have time to react before he kicked me hard in the stomach. I was completely winded and gasped for air as I curled up to protect myself; to protect my little girl. Once I had air back in my lungs, I shouted that he had to stop, that I was pregnant, but he didn't listen and just carried on.

When the kicking had stopped, he grabbed me by the hair and dragged me out of the study.

'You should be grateful I don't kill you.'

Then he slammed the door shut.

My insides were burning and when I put a hand to my crotch I found it was bleeding. I knew I'd lost my daughter.

Faye had butterflies in her stomach as she passed the Långbro Inn on her way to Bergtallsvägen. She'd always loved verdigrised copper roofs – the way the gleaming green contrasted with the white façade. The inn itself was buzzing with life. Families, older couples, newly-in-love younger couples – all of them looked so carefree as they sipped coffee, chatted and lived their lives, free and happy. At least that was how it looked on the outside, through the windows. No one seemed to pay her any attention, apart from a few people who did a double take at her appearance.

Faye walked past a pond and on through the park, where multiple dog owners were keeping their pets on short leashes. It was an open park with an avenue and clusters of trees. The greenery had just begun to show itself and all the tree branches were sprouting small green leaves. She knew the park had previously been part of the grounds around the Långbro mental hospital, but that institution had been closed long ago.

She made for Bergtallsvägen, continuing to observe the people she encountered. A part of her was unsure about Caroline Sterner. What if she'd contacted the police? Perhaps she was so hard-nosed that she'd cut a deal with them: as soon as the interview was over they would storm her flat and arrest Faye, before taking her back to Stenakull, the whole thing immortalised by tabloid photographers.

No, the world didn't work that way. She had to trust people, she told herself silently. At least, right now she did. She had no choice.

She took a deep breath and tapped in the entry code for the main door that Caroline had sent to her burner email account, then she entered the stairwell. Caroline lived on the ground floor. She must have heard her, because the front door opened before Faye had made it all the way over.

Caroline stared at Faye, who nodded in return. Caroline shook her head sceptically as she admitted Faye, and then shut the door and locked it behind her. She was struggling to tear her gaze away from the mohawk, the piercings and the black clothing.

It was evident that Caroline had tidied up in anticipation of her visitor – there was a powerful smell of cleaning products.

'Welcome to my humble abode,' she said, looking around apologetically. 'I'm afraid it's rather small.'

A cat brushed past Faye's legs and she bent down to scratch it between the ears.

'I think it's lovely. And it's all relative. After my time inside, everything seems big.'

Caroline leaned forward and examined Faye's piercings.

'It really is you. Wow.'

Faye nodded as she took off her boots.

'In the flesh. I've got a new stylist. I'll give you her number.'

The corners of Caroline's mouth twitched.

'I can tell. Are those piercings real?'

'Yes. But you've got to keep your word. You can't tell anyone what I look like or where we're meeting. If you do, the detectives will review all the nearby CCTV footage and then they – and everyone else – will know about my new appearance. That can't be allowed to happen.'

'I promise.'

Caroline showed Faye into a cosy kitchen. She had prepared

for the interview: there were two microphones on the table opposite each other, and the curtains were closed.

'I've made a pot of coffee, if you'd like some.'

'Yes, please.'

Caroline began to rummage in the cupboards while Faye sat down by one of the microphones. Caroline filled two mugs with the *Gangsterland* logo on them and set one down in front of Faye.

'Nice mugs.'

'Thank you,' Caroline said with a grin. 'By the way, I'll do a rapid edit on the interview and post it as a special episode as soon as possible. You're hot news right now, so people will go completely bananas.'

Faye nodded and sipped the coffee. She had more or less assumed the episode would be uploaded almost right away.

Caroline adjusted the microphones for a moment before asking Faye if she was ready. Faye nodded.

Caroline leaned towards her microphone.

'I'm speaking to you from an undisclosed location where I'm joined by Faye Adelheim, who broke out of Stenakull Prison almost a month ago and who has been on the run since,' she said in her best broadcast voice. 'Faye, welcome to *Gangsterland*.'

'Thanks.'

'Why did you break out from prison?'

Faye had decided to adopt a sober, businesslike tone.

'Because I should never have been there in the first place. I didn't kill my ex-husband. But the final straw was when another inmate tried to stab me to death. I really don't want to die right now. Life is short enough as it is.'

Caroline gazed at her wide-eyed.

'How would you describe life at Stenakull?'

'In one way, it was almost the best time of my life. In other ways, it was the worst. I met people who have become friends for life, but being locked up takes its toll on you. So I look back on it with mixed emotions, although I'd prefer not to return, as it were.'

Caroline paused for a moment before speaking again.

'I've got to say you really do seem to be very, very calm even though every police officer in Sweden is looking for you.'

'That's why I've got to be calm. Otherwise my freedom won't last for long.'

'How did you escape?'

Faye thought through her answer. She didn't want to unmask the people who had helped her.

'I happened upon one of the guards' access cards and made a quiet exit.'

'And then?'

Faye laughed.

'Since then I've been lying low.'

'What's the plan now?'

'Keep lying low.'

'For the rest of your life?'

'Until I manage to prove that I didn't kill my ex-husband. I've been wrongly convicted, and to top it off the prison service didn't even manage to protect me from a murder attempt while I was in their custody. I therefore felt I was fully entitled to get out of there – to survive. I would say it was my downright duty to abscond. Don't you agree?'

Caroline gave Faye a wry smile.

'I couldn't comment. I'm neutral and not in possession of all the facts.'

'Okay. But that's what I think and I believe that most of your listeners will agree.'

The interview then turned to more detailed questions about the escape itself that Faye didn't want to answer out of consideration towards her accomplices, as well as questions about life on the inside.

Eventually, after forty-five minutes of conversation, Caroline began to wind up.

'You undeniably have a lot of support, particularly from women. Have you seen the t-shirts paying tribute to you? And all the posts, memes and hashtags that have gone viral?'

'It's been hard to avoid them. I'm both touched and proud. We women have to stick together. So thank you to everyone offering me your support. I promise to do the same if any of you are ever treated the same way I have been.'

Faye meant every single word. She often thought about the girl in Husby with the *Run, Faye, Run* t-shirt.

'Thanks for sitting down with me for this interview,' said Caroline.

'Thanks for having me,' said Faye.

Caroline switched off the recording equipment and they sat in silence for a while before Faye stood up to refill her mug with coffee.

'Now it's your turn,' she said after she had sat back down.

Caroline pulled a flash drive from her breast pocket and pushed it across the table.

'There's the whole episode that's going to be uploaded.'

Faye eyed the USB stick – she would have liked to listen to the episode here and now, to confirm her suspicions. She picked the drive up and tucked it into the pocket of her jeans, wondering whether Caroline had noticed how affected she was by it.

They both got up and Caroline escorted her back into the hall. Faye was startled by her own reflection in the mirror; she still hadn't got used to her new appearance.

Once she'd put on her boots, she proffered her right hand to Caroline.

'If you have any questions about the episode then get in touch,' Caroline said as she shook Faye's hand. 'How are you feeling? Do you want to sign a contract?'

Faye looked at her. Making an assessment.

'No need for a contract. I think I can trust you.'

Caroline nodded and smiled. 'You can.'

As Faye emerged from the building, she inhaled the clear air. She felt it penetrating deep into her lungs. She didn't look over her shoulder as she crossed the pretty park – she wasn't afraid. All her instincts told her that she was safe, at least for now. She set her sights on Fruängens Centrum. It was time to go home.

Faye inserted the USB stick into the computer and sat down on the living room sofa with a pair of big headphones she'd bought on the way home. She pressed Play on the episode. It turned out to be an interview with a policeman whose voice was distorted to prevent him from being identified.

'We're certain that Zoran Rakitic is using a new hitman – an outsider – to clean up in the ranks.'

He went on to talk about how the suspected killer had known what times the victims would be at home and alone. The approach had been similar in all cases. The victims had been shot with a sawn-off shotgun at point-blank range. It was an unusual weapon for those circles.

It was twenty minutes into the episode that the big revelation dropped.

'There's one witness who's actually seen the killer,' the police officer said.

'How did the witness describe the killer?' Caroline asked matter-of-factly.

'He was described as a male in his sixties, seemingly white Swedish. As you can tell, this doesn't sound like one of Zoran Rakitic's usual hired guns. We don't know who this man is, but we're going to find him – sooner or later.'

Faye's hand was trembling as she stopped the podcast and closed the laptop. She took off the headphones and put them down on the sofa, clasping her hands over her stomach and staring up at the ceiling.

It was as she had feared.

Now there was only one thing to do: find out everything she could about Zoran Rakitic's criminal empire. The next question was *why* he'd turned to Faye's father. She would somehow have to figure out what their agreement was. But her questions would have to keep. First, she needed to find out as much as possible – find the weaknesses that were to be found in every organisation.

She fiddled with the two rings attached to her eyebrows, but quickly reminded herself to stop. She couldn't let them get infected.

She would proceed methodically, as if this were a competitor she was thinking about acquiring. At first, she considered going to the National Library and looking up all the newspaper articles and information there was out there, but she knew there was someone who knew more than she would ever find at the library: Marissa – Zoran's mistress. The woman who had given birth to his child and was banged up at Stenakull. Faye recalled her words: *'I dare say he's keeping tabs on his entire operation. His men are loyal.'*

She decided to arrange for Kerstin to pay Ines a visit. She would in turn approach Marissa to try to find out what weaknesses there were in Zoran's organisation.

On the same day that the episode featuring her interview dropped, Faye headed to the National Library in the centre of Stockholm, where she spent most of her time in the reading room, just as she had done in recent days. First she read up on everything that had already been written about her appearance on *Gangsterland*. The response had been immediate and huge. The struggle between law enforcement and journalism had been brought to a head with countless statements made by both sides arguing their respective cases hard. The police were angry that Caroline wasn't helping them to track down Faye. Some even thought that they should search Caroline's home to look for images and other evidence. Journalists, on the other hand, were pleading for her right to protect her source. If she began to reveal things about the people she interviewed, no one would appear on her podcast ever again. Besides, there was always the risk of threats and violence towards those who passed on information to the police, some argued.

Faye closed the news articles and went about her real business, ploughing through every single article there was about Zoran Rakitic.

He'd arrived in Sweden from Croatia in 1993. He had built up a small restaurant empire in Småland before moving to the capital around the turn of the millennium. A few years later, he'd been regarded as the most important and dangerous player in Stockholm's underworld. His foot soldiers smuggled cigarettes, drugs and weapons in from the Balkans while he outwardly devoted himself to charity work and glad-handing events organisers and politicians. Five years ago it had all fallen apart when the police had managed to bug a call in which Zoran gave the order for a rival to be gunned down. The trial had received widespread attention. But despite the fact that Zoran was serving a sentence at the maximum security Hall Prison, business was booming. Not only that, but his status as the boss of the powerful and shadowy organisation he had built up remained unthreatened. The police officers quoted in the articles thought he was maintaining an iron grip over the gang via family members on the outside.

Faye examined several recent photos of Milenka, his wife. She was as beautiful as Faye remembered her being from the pictures she had seen before. She was in her fifties, with a tough, penetrating gaze and expensive-looking attire that reflected her good taste.

Faye glanced up quickly when she heard footsteps.

'We're closing,' she was informed by a librarian with a pair of glasses on her nose and a second pair pushed up onto her forehead.

On her way to the underground station, Faye could still see Milenka's face in her mind's eye. It was hard to explain why, but she could tell instinctively that Milenka wasn't a trophy wife – she was deeply embroiled in her husband's business affairs. Perhaps she was the one who was running the show in his absence. If so, was she aware of her husband's escapades? Did she know about the much-younger Marissa who had given birth to his child, and who'd gone down for Zoran's right-hand man?

Kerstin had gone to Stenakull that day to speak to Ines, so Faye would have more information by the evening. Maybe it would be possible to create a rift between husband and wife. Extramarital relations tended to do that.

It was half past five in the afternoon when Kerstin tapped on the door to Faye's bedroom. They went into the kitchen, where Faye had made spaghetti Bolognese. As she was laying the table, she asked Kerstin how she had got on.

'Your friend Ines is a funny lady.'

The corners of Faye's mouth twitched as she considered how Ines would have taken it if she'd been called *a funny lady*.

'Isn't she just? But what did she say?'

'Marissa confirmed that it's the wife, Milenka, who's running the show while Zoran is on the inside.'

Faye nodded impatiently while plating up the spaghetti. She remembered that Marissa had hinted something along those lines to her when they'd been discussing Zoran.

According to what Faye had read, Milenka and Zoran had three sons together. She added the Bolognese sauce and put the plate in front of Kerstin, who began to devour it.

'My God, you know how to cook, woman. This is absolutely delicious. What else do you do?'

'I'm afraid that's my whole repertoire,' Faye said. 'It's Julienne's favourite.'

Her hand instinctively went to her breast when she mentioned Julienne's name. Faye took a few deep breaths and sat down opposite Kerstin with her own plate.

She prodded her food but she didn't seem to have any appetite. She needed to find a way forward and she was increasingly sure that it would be via Milenka. She understood women and what drove them. She would have to try to win her over. But how?

There was only one way to find out: seek her out.

In one of the articles, Milenka had said she was a regular visitor to the spa at the Grand Hôtel. Although this snippet was now a few years old, Faye doubted she would have changed her habits. Grand Hôtel regulars usually remained regulars. Perhaps that would be the right place to approach her? But how to go about it? She'd only get one chance and she couldn't fail.

'What are you going to do next?' Kerstin said, wiping her mouth with a napkin.

'I don't know. That's what I'm trying to work out.'

Faye twirled spaghetti onto her fork.

'Is there anything I can do?'

'Yes, there might be. How do you feel about a trip to the spa?'

Kerstin perked up.

'That sounds nice. When?'

'Every day until Milenka turns up. It's on me.'

The boosted episode of *Gangsterland* was due to drop the next day, including its description of the notorious killer. It had been brought forward because the topic was so hot. Faye was curious to see whether Caroline Sterner had managed to find anything else in the imbroglio that had eluded the police – something that hadn't been included in the version of the podcast she'd been given on the flash drive. Once she had listened to the official episode when it was posted tomorrow, she would make her final decision on how to approach Milenka.

Once they had eaten and filled the dishwasher, they watched an episode of *Succession* that Kerstin hadn't seen before, and then turned in for an early night. Faye fell asleep with a sense of tense anticipation in her breast, and nipples that still ached from being pierced.

Stockholm, October 2003

'Natasa? Can I come in?'

I knocked loudly on the door. Mirko's wife let me and the boys in without question. She took one look at my bloody trousers and stepped aside.

'Milenka?'

Mirko came out from his study and perked up like he always did when he saw me. He had been one of Zoran's closest lieutenants over the years, and he and his wife Natasa had always been a safe place in a chaotic world. But when he too saw the blood the smile faded.

'Milenka? What's happened?'

Natasa held up her hands towards him.

'Don't start cross-examining her.' She looked at me. 'First we need to get you into some clean clothes. And you need coffee. Mirko, put the coffee maker on while I find some clothes. I'm a lot chubbier than you, so they'll probably be a bit on the big side, but it's better than…'

Natasa's gaze was fixed on the blood stain at my crotch. Then she looked at my sons.

'Boys, why don't you go upstairs to Dragomir's room? He's playing there.'

They quickly scurried away while I glanced gratefully at

her. The boys didn't understand what was happening, and I didn't know how to explain it to them.

I'd gone into the bathroom when I'd heard the nannies arriving back home with them. Zoran had given them the rest of the day off and once they'd gone he'd shouted to me that I'd have to take care of them. I heard the front door slam shut.

As soon as Zoran's car was gone, I'd quickly hustled them into my car and driven away. He'd be angry if he came back and saw we were gone, but I had no choice. I had to get away. Away from the blood stain on the carpet in Zoran's study, away from the bloody lump that had slid out of me and into the toilet. Away from Zoran.

Natasa's face was a mask of worry when she returned.

'Here's a pair of joggers I haven't worn in years. If you pull the drawstring they should fit.'

I took them and the pair of knickers lying on top and went into the bathroom to change. After I'd done that and washed, I stood there clutching my bloody garments. The trousers were from Max Mara. Expensive. Elegant. I never wanted to see them again.

'Can we chuck these out?'

Natasa took the clothes and put them in the bin under the kitchen sink.

'Take a seat and have some coffee,' Mirko said kindly, pouring me a piping hot cup.

I took a couple of sips. My stomach ached but the hot liquid helped to thaw some of the icy cold I felt inside myself.

'Let's talk,' Natasa said, sitting down next to me. She glanced at Mirko to indicate he should also sit down at the table.

It was as if they were embracing me with their warmth. The feeling made me want to cry, but I couldn't allow myself to. If I started, I wouldn't be able to stop. I'd dissolve. I'd be destroyed. Like a sheet of wet paper.

'Zoran?' Mirko said in a low voice, peering at me from beneath his fringe.

He was an unusual man in this world. A man of honour. And heart.

'Yes. He punched me and kicked me and I lost the baby.'

'You were expecting another little one?' Natasa said, and I saw her clench her jaw.

She'd never liked Zoran. I knew it without her ever having said a single bad word about him.

'A girl.'

The words made the icy cold return inside me, and I quickly took several more sips of the coffee. From upstairs I could hear the boys laughing loudly and that helped me to breathe a little more easily. I'd do everything I could to protect them – from Zoran, from the world. Even though I hadn't been able to protect their sister.

'What can we do, Milenka? Do you want me to talk to him?'

Mirko's voice wrapped itself around me like a blanket. I knew he meant well, but I also knew what the reality was.

'No, Mirko. I've got to go back. Zoran went out, but he could come back at any moment. I just needed to come up for air. To see some kind faces.'

'We're always here for you. You know that,' Natasa said, squeezing my hand.

'I know that. But you know just as well as I do what it's like. The rules. There's nothing you can do. There's nothing I can do. I just want to sit here in your kitchen for a while with you and drink coffee. Then I've got to go back home with the boys again.'

Neither of them protested. We were all in the same system. They knew what I was saying was true. I was going to stay for a while – then life would have to move on.

When Faye woke up, she reached out for her phone to play the new episode of *Gangsterland*. She frowned when she opened the Spotify app – it still hadn't dropped. Odd. Had Caroline changed her mind and decided to publish it later?

She sat up and blinked the sleep from her eyes, yawning as she got out of bed. She went to the bathroom and was about to get into the shower when Kerstin knocked on the door.

'Have you seen?' she shouted, her voice shocked.

'Seen what?'

Faye wrapped herself in a towel and opened the door. Kerstin held her laptop towards Faye, who squinted at the display.

True crime podcasting queen murdered read the headline.

Above it was a picture of Caroline Sterner.

Faye snatched the computer from Kerstin and put it down on the vanity so that she could read the article.

'What the hell...' she muttered, suddenly feeling icy cold.

Podcast star Caroline Sterner was shot dead late last night in her flat in southern Stockholm. Police are currently very reticent about the course of events leading up to Sterner's death and have not made any comments. However, Expressen's sources can confirm that it appears to have been an execution-style killing. Sterner was reportedly found with her hands tied behind her back and had been shot at close range with what is believed to have been a shotgun. Sterner was best known for her popular podcast Gangsterland in which she talked about and examined crime from a variety of perspectives. Her last episode featured an exclusive and highly acclaimed interview with the convicted murderer Faye Adelheim. Sterner had stated in a previous episode that the podcast due to drop today would reveal new details about the three murders that have shaken the Stockholm underworld to its core over the last year. Police have, for the time being, prevented the publication of the episode. Police have refused to comment on whether they believe that Sterner's death is connected to this episode or her interview with Adelheim.

'We're pursuing a number of lines of inquiry, but have chosen not to disclose these for operational reasons,' said police spokesperson Solveig Vahnfelt.

It felt as if Faye's legs were going to give way. Her father was behind this murder – he had to be. And that meant the police would intensify their search for her.

Caroline's hands had been tied behind her back, so Faye's father had presumably been trying to extract information from her. What she looked like, where she was staying, what she'd said apart from what had been broadcast. Faye had to assume that he'd been successful. He might even have planted something at the scene to make it look like Faye had been behind Caroline's murder.

Apart from her appearance, there was nothing else that Caroline could have revealed. Faye thanked her lucky stars that she'd been so careful when contacting her.

She started when Kerstin laid a hand on her shoulder.

'What are we going to do?' she asked.

Faye swallowed.

'I need a couple of wigs that look completely different. And we're going to have to shave off the mohawk and take out the rings. And then it's time for you to get along to the Grand Hôtel. Book a room for a week and spend as much time in the spa as you can.'

'We carry on as planned?'

'What other choice do we have?'

Kerstin squeezed Faye's shoulder.

'What do I do if I run into Milenka?'

'Call me and I'll get down there.'

Kerstin seemed surprised.

'Is that it?'

Faye nodded grimly.

'That's it.'

Kerstin nodded, picked up her laptop and left the bathroom.

Once she was alone, Faye took a couple of deep breaths and then dropped the towel before getting into the shower. She probably seemed more confident than she felt. That was the only way to get through this. Yet the truth was that she was worried, afraid even. It was as if a noose were tightening around her neck. Her father was demonstrating that anyone in her proximity was in mortal danger.

Faye was waiting in the van that Kerstin had rented. They had parked it at the rear of the Grand Hôtel. While Kerstin was in the spa keeping an eye out for Milenka, Faye read the latest media updates on the killing of Caroline Sterner, which was still dominating the news some two days after the murder.

Faye had been in the van for three hours when a message arrived via the encrypted app Telegram.

She's here.

Faye stared at the two words for several seconds.

On her own? she finally replied.

Yes

She'd initially feared that Milenka would bring bodyguards but had then dismissed that concern. If she had, then they would surely wait outside rather than being inside the spa itself. Even if they saw Faye entering they wouldn't perceive her as a threat since they wouldn't recognise her.

Faye chose between the two wigs and settled on being a short-haired platinum blonde. The mohawk had been seen off with a little help from Kerstin and the trimmer and her head was now completely shaved. Like Sinéad O'Connor, she thought as she donned the wig. She wore a black turtleneck to conceal the neck tattoos, which hadn't completely disappeared. The piercing jewellery had been removed from her nose and eyebrows, but she'd left the ones in her nipples.

Having put them in and gone through all the pain, it would be a pity if no one else saw them.

She touched up her red lipstick, put on a pair of large sunglasses, slipped a small stiletto knife into her jacket pocket and then opened the door.

Faye entered the hotel via the back entrance, moving purposefully towards the spa without giving the impression she was agitated. Her heart was pounding so hard in her chest that her field of vision almost blacked out. She was exposing herself to a huge risk, but this was the only way forward. The disguise wasn't as effective as the punk get-up, but the hotel wouldn't have let her in if she didn't look like she belonged there.

She needed to talk to Milenka one-on-one, and she needed to get her onside.

Faye reached the changing room. There were two women there. Damn it. They needed to get out. Faye sat down on a bench and waited impatiently. The two women were discussing what had apparently been an incredibly fascinating padel match as they changed. When they finally left the changing room, Faye pulled out her phone. *Go* she wrote to Kerstin.

In her mind's eye, Faye pictured what would happen next. Kerstin would stagger in front of Milenka and ask her for help back to the changing room.

Faye stood up, pulled off the wig and sunglasses and went into the toilet without locking the door. After a while, she heard footsteps approaching. Kerstin cried out loudly in the changing room.

'Could I have some water?' she groaned.

Faye heard them coming closer. She pressed herself to the wall by the door. It opened. Milenka stepped in. Faye pressed the tip of the knife to her throat and locked the door behind her.

Milenka showed no signs of fear, instead meeting Faye's gaze in the mirror.

'I'm not quite looking myself, but I think you know who I am,' Faye said.

Milenka nodded slowly.

'I do,' she said. 'What do you want?'

'To find out why you're trying to kill me.'

'I don't know what you're talking about.'

Faye glanced towards the door. People might enter the changing room at any moment, but right now it was still quiet out there.

'This is what we're going to do. I've got a room at the hotel. You and I are going to stroll to it for a quiet chat. We're going to walk there arm in arm, like really good friends do. You're going to smile and seem happy. Otherwise I'll bury this knife in your liver.'

There wasn't even a flicker of emotion on Milenka's face.

'Sure.'

Faye reluctantly admired her. She wondered how calm she would have been in Milenka's place.

There was a light tap on the door.

Faye unlocked it and Kerstin handed them two white bathrobes.

Milenka put one on without any fuss and Faye put on the other.

'Let's go,' she said, slipping her arm through Milenka's.

They reached the suite that Kerstin was staying in on the fifth floor. Of course, she'd booked under a different name – it was reasonable to assume that the police would be monitoring all Faye's nearest and dearest. There was a risk that she'd been flagged in the hotel's reservations system. But both of them had multiple cards issued in other names. They sometimes came in handy.

Kerstin opened the door and Faye gestured towards the sofa facing the windows overlooking the Royal Palace, indicating that Milenka should sit down.

'Thank you,' she said to Kerstin. 'Now please leave us and wait in the foyer.'

After the door had shut behind Kerstin there was absolute silence. Nervousness coursed through Faye's body as she scrutinised Milenka's face to see whether there was a flicker of fear or anxiety. There was nothing to be seen. On the contrary: the woman seemed to be getting calmer with every passing second. Milenka appeared to be completely unaffected by the situation, which wrong-footed Faye. Was she mistaken? Was this a trap orchestrated by her father? Had he figured out her next step? But no – if he had then she'd already be dead. She was sure of that.

Faye held the knife in her hand and kept it pointed at Milenka.

'I want to know why you and your husband are trying to kill me.'

'I still don't know what you're talking about.'

Milenka regarded her calmly. It was as if she hadn't even seen the knife.

Faye licked her lips; they were completely dry.

'You may have noticed that people around you are dying. Important people in your husband's empire. I know who is carrying out those murders. I don't know why they're happening, but from the outside it's hard to escape the impression that you've lost control.'

'I'm in full control of my empire and my people.'

Faye looked straight into the woman's eyes while making up her mind to play her trump card, even though she had been planning to hold it back.

'Even over your husband's illegitimate daughter?'

For the first time, Faye glimpsed a crack in Milenka's cool, composed face. It only lasted a microsecond, but Faye saw uncertainty.

'The girl is five years old and living with her mother's relatives. She was born just before Zoran went to prison. I was in Stenakull along with the mother. She told me everything.'

Milenka shrugged.

'Men are men. What do you want me to do about it?'

'We've both been working in the world of men for long enough to know that if you let them walk all over you then you end up being a doormat. I don't think you want to be a doormat, Milenka Mikolic.'

As Faye uttered Milenka's maiden name to prove she had done her homework, she realised something that had escaped her before: Mikolic was also the name of the man who had been murdered most recently. Zivko Mikolic. Was he a relative?

'You're probably right, but I don't know what you're looking for. All I hear is empty talk.'

Faye decided to take a chance.

'Zivko Mikolic. Gunned down in his own home. My father committed the murder. Did you really authorise him to kill your ... relative?'

Milenka pursed her lips.

Faye could tell that she was surprised – affected by the change of direction and Faye's knowledge.

'What do you want?' Milenka asked at last.

Faye thought she could make out a different tone – a more conciliatory one. Less haughty.

'I'd like your help to find my father before he kills me and my family.'

'And if I did happen to know where he was, then what would be in it for me?'

Faye moved the knife from one hand to another, buying herself more time.

'You'd put a stop to the man who killed your relative. You'd show your husband can't make decisions over your head. I assume that's what happened.'

Milenka scrutinised Faye for a few seconds before slowly

standing up. She snorted when Faye tentatively raised the knife.

'I don't think you want to use that thing. I'm leaving now. For your sake, I'll forget this ever happened. I think that'd be best for all involved.'

She turned her back on Faye, headed for the door, opened it and left the suite.

Faye sat there, completely unable to do anything. Her chin slumped onto her chest and her shoulders began to shake. *Pull yourself together, damn it!* she said quietly but angrily to herself. *Pull yourself together!*

She shook herself and then finally managed to pull out her phone and call Kerstin to tell her they needed to leave – right away.

The situation was darker than ever. The previous day's attempt to win over Milenka Rakitic had been an outright failure. For the first time, she began to doubt whether she would defeat her father.

She was on the sofa watching TV. A police press conference broadcast live from police headquarters had started at ten o'clock that morning in relation to the murder of podcaster Caroline Sterner. A troubled-looking male detective in his sixties explained that there was a credible suspect in the case, and that individual was none other than escaped prisoner Faye Adelheim. The supposed motive for the murder was to prevent Sterner from revealing Faye's current appearance following the interview she'd given at the podcaster's flat. He urged the public to contact the police immediately if they had any information on Faye's whereabouts.

'This woman is dangerous. We have to stop her,' he said.

Faye switched off the TV. It was as she had feared.

She put down the remote and sat there on the sofa, staring vacantly at the black screen.

She'd really thought she would persuade Milenka to help her. She'd spent countless hours reading up on her and trying to get close to her and Zoran. But it had all been in vain. Could she contract an underworld hitman to take out her father? She wasn't short on cash. But it felt wrong. She wanted to be the one who put a stop to her father. She felt a desire to kill that she had never felt before – not even with Jack. Or Sebastian. Everything that her father had done to her mother, the abuse, the torture. The years he'd spent breaking her bit by bit. The way he'd let Sebastian – Faye's own brother – rape her.

She was crazy with anger. No – she wasn't just going to survive. She was going to have her revenge too.

'Pull yourself together, right now,' she said aloud to herself.

She got up and went into the kitchen to make some coffee. She needed to find a new way forward. There was too much at stake to simply give up. Both her mother and Julienne would die.

She was resignedly scooping ground coffee into the machine when there was a pounding on the thick iron door. She knew it couldn't be Kerstin, and Alice wouldn't just show up. She quickly put down the scoop, grabbed a knife and crept into the hall. She checked the monitor with the CCTV feed. She instantly recognised the person on the other side of the door and goosebumps began to form all over her body.

Stockholm, October 2003

I don't remember much about the days following Zoran's assault, which had made me miscarry our daughter. I wandered about in a daze, like the living dead. The boys noticed that something was wrong and tried to comfort me.

Zoran hadn't rushed back since leaving in his car. He hadn't actually been home at all since then.

After five days, I began to think he had left me. I'd taken the older two kids to school and dropped Dejan off at nursery when I returned to find his car on the driveway.

I went into the house and found him on the living room sofa. I felt nothing but hatred towards him. Yet at the same time, he was the father of my children. I couldn't hurt him – even though I wanted to kill him.

'So you're back?' I said.

He looked at me in surprise.

'What do you mean?'

'You kicked me in the stomach and made me lose our daughter.'

He snorted.

'If it was even mine. I've come here to tell you what happens now.'

I sat down at the far end of the sofa.

'Out with it then,' I said.

'We'll continue living together – for the boys' sake. But I'll never touch you again. You've been sullied, you whore. Do you understand?'

I stared at him, trying to discern whether his words hurt me. I concluded they didn't.

'If you do anything to displease me, I'll have the boys sent to Croatia where they'll be properly brought up. Got it? Then you'll never see them again.'

I began to laugh.

He stared at me in disbelief.

'What the fuck are you laughing at?'

I ran a hand through my hair and fixed my gaze on him.

'He squealed like a pig when I killed him.'

'Who?'

'Ivan.'

'What are you talking about?'

I indulged myself in another smile.

'I killed him, Zoran. I stabbed him in the neck outside the Grand Hotel. I killed him because he was going to kill you, but you didn't get it. I pretended I wanted to sleep with him to lure him there. That was all. I killed him for your sake; for the sake of our boys. Because you were too weak to do it.'

'I—'

'Shut up. Because now I'm going to tell you what's actually going to happen.'

He remained silent but glared at me.

'If I meet with an accident then an email will be sent to the police describing your business affairs in detail. How the clubs work, which accounts you use, the names of various players. I've picked up plenty down the years.'

'You fucking—'

I held up my palm towards him.

'I'm not done,' I said, grimacing as I felt a stab of pain

in my stomach. 'You're no longer the sole leader of the organisation, except outwardly. I'm to be involved in all major strategic decisions. What you tell your boys is up to you, but if I suspect you're trying to get round me or keep me out then I'll crush you.'

His face was pale as he spoke in a low voice: 'How would you do that?'

'Never forget that the gambling dens were my idea, even if you've taken the credit for them all these years. I gave you everything without demanding anything but love in return, but that's over and done with.'

He didn't reply.

I leaned back on the sofa, crossing one leg over the other and folding my arms.

'You're right about the fact that we're going to keep living under the same roof for the boys' sake. But from now on, I'll be the one making the decisions – not you. You can devote yourself to drinking and pretending to be the one in charge. That's all you're good for. And one more thing: if you ever touch my brother I'll kill you.'

Faye eyed Milenka Rakitic on the black and white screen while she evaluated the situation. Milenka was dressed in a dark skirt and white blouse. Her hair was neatly arranged. If she'd come to kill her then she would hardly have come alone, and she wouldn't have sought Faye out in this manner. Instead, she would have given the address to Faye's father and left him to do the job. Or perhaps it was a trap after all? Faye couldn't see whether there was anyone behind her. There was only one camera and it didn't cover the full area outside the door. A minor oversight in the planning.

Faye put her hand on the lock but hesitated for a second before turning it. Then she opened the door and looked at Milenka, who met her gaze without blinking.

'Come in,' said Faye.

Milenka took a step forward and looked around.

'A bunker?' she remarked.

'Something like that. But this bunker has coffee.'

Milenka smiled briefly.

'Every time we meet you're holding a knife,' she said, nodding towards the chef's knife that Faye was clutching.

'You bring out the worst in me,' Faye said, putting it down on the console beneath the monitor after locking the door again.

'That's better.'

She showed Milenka into the kitchen, picked up the scoop and finished filling the machine before pressing the button.

They waited in tense silence for the coffee to be ready. While Faye poured two cups for them, Milenka didn't take her eyes off her.

'Why don't we go into the living room?' Faye said, and Milenka raised her eyebrows at the choice of words. A smile began to form as they went through the door.

'A bunker with coffee and a living room,' Milenka said in surprise as they sat down opposite each other in armchairs.

'How did you find me?' Faye said.

'I assumed you hadn't been hiding out at the Grand Hôtel all this time, so I waited until you left your suite yesterday and followed you here.'

Faye nodded. How banal. And how incredibly clumsy of her.

'And now you want to have coffee with me?'

Milenka cleared her throat.

'I couldn't stop thinking about her,' she said.

'About whom?'

'Zoran's girl, with the mum in Stenakull.'

Faye started. If Milenka demanded to know where Sara was in exchange for helping Faye then what would she do?

'I have three sons. I've always wanted a daughter. But now I'm too old.'

Faye didn't say anything while Milenka sipped her coffee.

'I know Zoran had other women. He always has. Of course, I kept tabs on Marissa but I didn't know she'd had a daughter. Is it Zoran's fault she's doing time?'

Faye nodded. She had to bite her tongue so as not to interrupt. She realised she was winning Milenka over.

'But that's not all,' Milenka said. 'Zivko was my little brother. It goes without saying that his murder was not something I condoned. Zoran knew that. He did it without my knowledge. He sent your father to take him out. Then he pretended nothing had happened.'

'So it is my father who's the murderer?'

Milenka nodded.

'Do you even need to ask? You seemed so sure yesterday...'

'I'm a good actress,' Faye said.

'Evidently.'

'Why is my father helping Zoran?'

'They met in prison. Your father offered to help us put our house in order in exchange for us helping him to stay off the radar and giving him what he needs to get rid of you.'

'Just me? He doesn't just want to kill me. He also wants to kill my ... family.'

A silence descended between them.

'And now?' Faye said after a while.

'Everything's changed now.'

'Does Zoran know that?'

Milenka smiled grimly.

'No. Not yet.'

Faye and Milenka had moved onto the sofa and swapped coffee for wine as they worked out how to achieve the goals they had chiselled out together.

Milenka wanted to know the location of Sara, Marissa and Zoran's daughter. Not to hurt her, she emphasised. On the contrary, she wanted to take care of her. The girl was the half-sister of Milenka's own sons and would become part of the family.

She saw Faye's hesitation.

'My life with Zoran is over. I can't forgive him. I'll never let him back into my life again. But the girl needs me. I'm pretty sure I can give her a more stable childhood than the relatives she's staying with right now, and I promise to take care of Marissa too when she gets out. I'll make sure they're all safe. And that they stay together. You have my word.'

Faye could tell from the steely look in Milenka's eyes that she meant it. She weighed up the pros and cons.

As soon as Marissa was out of prison, she would be back under Zoran's control again. Both her and her daughter. Milenka was her only way out.

Faye nodded slowly.

'I believe you. I'll find out where she is. But what do we do about my father? Do you have any control over him?'

Milenka raised the wine glass to her lips and drank a big mouthful.

'Yes, for now at least. But that's not enough. We need to get him out of the way. He's on Zoran's side and it's not just you he poses a threat to. He's a dangerous, sick man.'

'I know that better than anyone,' Faye said quietly.

'I realise that.'

Milenka swirled the wine in her glass.

'Are you able to contact him?' Faye said as Milenka took her eyes off the wine.

'I've got a phone number,' she said.

'What if you summoned him to a meeting? Somewhere secluded?'

'That might work,' said Milenka.

Faye nodded.

'But I'd need a weapon.'

Milenka raised the wine glass as if making a toast.

'That can be arranged.'

Faye sighed with relief.

Suddenly, she could see an end to this nightmare. Soon they would be safe. She'd be able to return to Italy, fetch Julienne and her mother and then move to somewhere else in the world. Somewhere the Swedish police couldn't get at her. Perhaps that was how it would have to be.

She didn't ask how Milenka was going to escape Zoran's grip. That was Milenka's concern, not hers.

Milenka drained her glass and stood up.

'Good wine. Thanks.'

Faye didn't reply.

'I'll contact your father, then we'll get this over and done with.'

Faye stood up and shook her hand. They gazed at each other mutely for a while and then Milenka spoke again.

'You're an interesting person. I hope we'll have the

pleasure of each other's company in calmer, more pleasant circumstances some other time.'

'Me too.'

Milenka made to leave, but then suddenly stopped.

'If you're deceiving me, Faye, then I'll kill you.'

Faye nodded, meeting Milenka's gaze.

'And I you, Milenka.'

The day after Milenka's visit, Faye headed out onto the streets of southern Stockholm. There was a football match on at the Avicii Arena and she encountered thousands of bare-chested young men drinking beer and singing for their team. She wasn't worried about the police monitoring the crowds, given that they had their hands full preventing the various groups of young men from clashing.

For the first time since her prison break, she felt calm. She had done what she could, and now it was up to Milenka to lure her father to the scene of his death. Only then would the ball be back in her side of the court.

Faye had no doubt she was going to succeed, nor was she afraid that she would lack what it took. It was either him or her family. And it wasn't as if she were the one who had triggered this vendetta – he had started it when he'd tormented her and her mother for all those years in Fjällbacka. Everything Faye had done and experienced in life had been preparing her for this moment when she would confront her father.

She sat down outside a café bar and ordered a beer. She remembered her Stockholm School of Economics years when she had met Jack and they'd hung out at the dives in the part of the city they referred to as Chinatown. Back then she would never have believed that one day she'd end up here – one phone call away from killing her own father. Back then he'd been a closed chapter. Locked up; forgotten.

She'd thought that she and Jack would conquer the world together. It hadn't turned out that way. Jack had deceived her, humiliated her and thrown her out without a penny to her name – even though it had been her know-how that had built his company, Compare. But she had recovered. She'd met Kerstin, she'd walked dogs to get back on her feet and salvage her finances, and she'd built Revenge. She'd even escaped from prison after being convicted of murder.

Nothing could stop her.

Her phone's angry ringtone derailed her train of thought. She was immediately worried. Only three people had the number: Kerstin, Alice and Milenka.

'Hello?'

'Hello – it's Milenka.'

Faye could tell right away that something was up.

'Did you get hold of him?'

'We'd better meet – I don't want to do this on the phone.'

Faye gazed towards the young men marching towards the stadium in a cloud of red smoke from flares.

'Where?'

'Your place. In twenty minutes.'

Faye took a last sip of her beer before getting to her feet and hurrying home.

Milenka was sitting behind the wheel of a black Mercedes parked up by one of the loading bays adjacent to the bunker. Faye looked around hastily before getting into the passenger seat.

'What's happened?' she said.

Milenka took off her sunglasses and folded them up.

'I've been calling your father since last night on the number we gave him, but he's not answering. The phone's switched off.'

'Do you think he knows that you and I...'

Milenka shook her head slowly.

'I find that hard to believe. If he did then I've no idea how.'

A lorry reversed from one of the loading bays, turned around and drove off. Faye tried to think clearly, but she felt hampered by something bordering on panic.

'Are we in danger?' she said, swallowing.

'I don't think so. No one but you knows what I'm planning to do, and I've been extremely careful when making contact with you.'

This calmed Faye somewhat. She looked up at the inside of the car's roof and sighed heavily.

'What does this mean for our deal?' Milenka said.

'It still stands.'

'Good – I wanted to be sure of that.'

Two men in work clothes passed close by the car without paying them any attention. When they had gone, the women resumed their conversation.

'I never trusted your father. There was something about his eyes and his manner that aroused my suspicions. Perhaps he even scared me a little. And there's only one man I've ever been afraid of before: Zoran.'

Faye said nothing – she knew exactly what Milenka meant. Even as a child, her father's gaze had been capable of making her blood freeze. Nothing had been more frightening than his wrath. And the fact that he seemed to have enjoyed hurting her.

'I installed spyware on the phone I gave him,' Milenka said. 'It's been showing me his position all along but then yesterday afternoon it stopped.'

Faye raised her eyebrows.

'And where was it when that happened?'

Milenka drummed her fingers on the steering wheel.

'In Italy, oddly enough.'

Faye stared at Milenka, then pulled out her phone, opened the car door and stumbled out.

Her hands trembling, Faye dialled the number for the house in Italy. All concerns for her own safety were gone in an instant. They would be able to trace the call, and it might lead her father to her mother and Julienne in their hiding place in Ravi, but that couldn't be helped.

Her heart was pounding. It took an eternity for the call to connect and it rang for a long time. No one picked up. She ended the call and tried again. Just as she was going to end the call again, a man answered and said something in Italian.

'Hello! Who are you?' Faye said after recovering from the shock.

'I am police officer,' the man said in accented English.

'What has happened?' Faye heard her own voice breaking.

'There has been an incident. Who are you?'

'You are answering my mother's phone. It's my house in Ravi. They live there.'

'Well, something happened here.'

The policeman's slow way of speaking was driving her mad.

'My daughter? My mother?'

'We have four dead bodies. Only men.'

The relief made her reach out to the car for support – it felt as if her legs were going to give way.

'And my daughter and mother? Where are they? Are they okay?'

'There is no woman and child here. Just dead men.'

Faye slowly lowered the phone from her ear. Julienne and her mother were missing. That could only mean one thing. She had underestimated him.

It had been a week since Faye had received the awful news. During that time, she had stayed locked in her room. She had barely left the bunker and barely eaten, even though Kerstin had tried to get her to. It was now the day before Midsummer's Eve and Faye got out of bed to go to the toilet. When she looked at her face in the mirror, she barely recognised herself. The shaved hair had grown into stubble. There was almost no trace of the piercings any longer, and the tattoos were completely gone. Her face was pale, and there were big, dark rings under her eyes. But nothing mattered.

There was a tap on the bathroom door.

'I don't feel like talking, Kerstin,' she called out mechanically.

It was all pointless. The Italian detective she had spoken to had told her that they had found four dead men in the house. The security detail, Faye gathered. But the house itself had been empty. No dead girl, no dead woman. The CCTV had been switched off shortly before the first of the bodyguards had been killed. Where were Julienne and her mother? Were they dead too?

The worst thing was that Faye couldn't do anything. She couldn't call the Swedish police to report two people missing, given that as far as the law and the public were concerned, they were already dead. Instead she was afflicted by terrible apathy. She was paralysed by grief and fear.

'You're going to want to see this.'

There was something about Kerstin's tone that made Faye turn around and open the door anyway.

Kerstin mutely proffered her laptop. Faye looked at the screen.

'He's your mother's brother, isn't he?'

Faye squinted as she read the headline.

Her kind Uncle Egil who had helped Mum to flee from her husband all those years ago had been found dead. Faye blinked a couple of times, and then took the laptop from Kerstin and began to read. According to the journalist, he'd been murdered. Shot in the head. The corpse had been found in the woods a couple of miles from his house.

She knew it couldn't be anyone other than her father who was behind it. That meant he was in Fjällbacka. She immediately realised what that meant. Hope made her heart thud in her chest. Hope and despair. Julienne and her mother might be there too.

She slammed the computer shut and handed it back to Kerstin.

'I've got to go,' she said.

Kerstin looked at her askance.

'Where to?'

'Fjällbacka. My father's there. I can't risk losing track of him again.'

She made her way out of the bathroom and went into the bedroom. She picked up a plastic bag from the floor and began to stuff it with a random assortment of clothes. Why she was doing it she had no idea; she wouldn't need them. Maybe it was just to avoid travelling empty-handed. Perhaps packing before a journey filled her with some deceptive sense of normality.

Kerstin followed her, looking sceptical.

'Do you... Do you really think Julienne could be there? How would that have happened?'

Faye put on a pair of jeans and stuffed a jumper into the bag.

'The Carabinieri didn't find their bodies. And it doesn't matter. My father knows where they are and what happened. I need an answer. I can't die not knowing.'

'And what if he hurts you?'

'That's what he wants. That murder is a message for me. He wants me to go there.'

'So why are you going to go?'

'Like I said, it's the only way for me to find out what's happened to Julienne and Mum.'

'But... Where in Fjällbacka is he? Are you just planning to go there and wait for him?'

Faye stopped and turned to Kerstin.

'I think he's at my childhood home. Where it all began. I bought the place. I own it. It's standing empty. And it's pretty secluded. It's the perfect hiding place.'

'I don't know whether...'

Faye began to move again.

She had to get there.

'I don't know much either, but I have to do this. Without Julienne, nothing matters. What happens to me, if he kills me, how he does it... Those are just the details, the punctuation. I'm already dead.'

Kerstin scrutinised her silently before nodding.

'I understand.' She stroked her chin. 'We've still got the van I hired. I took it on a long rental. I thought it might come in useful. It's in visitor parking by the paint company along the way. The keys are on the hall console.'

Faye paused briefly, wondering whether there was anything else she needed with her, but nothing sprang to mind. Instead, Faye put the carrier bag down, went over to Kerstin and wrapped her arms around her.

'I love you, Kerstin,' she said. 'It's all thanks to you that I've made it this far. It's thanks to you I was able to pull through after all the business with Jack. I don't know whether I've said this properly before, but that's how it is. You saved me.'

Faye felt Kerstin's tears on her neck as she pressed the fragile, aged body tightly to herself.

'I wish I could save you now,' Kerstin said into her shoulder.

Faye smiled.

'Me too. But no one can. Not even you.'

Hall Maximum Security Prison, June 2023

'Does Zoran know?'

Mirko looked at me sadly when I asked. I struggled to keep my sympathy under control. Outwardly, he'd been one of Zoran's lieutenants for all these years. But he'd actually been one of my confidants. We were close. He understood Zoran. He understood me. And his entire family was under my protection.

'No. Zoran doesn't know,' he said.

'Three months? You're sure?'

I wanted to take his hand but I stopped myself. I couldn't allow myself to become weak. I knew what I had to do. Zivko was dead and I had to keep the promise that I'd made to Zoran all those years before.

Mirko shrugged.

'As sure as they can be. Maybe less. They're giving me what treatment they can in prison, but...'

'Mirko, have I been good to you? Have I been good to your family?'

He nodded.

'You've always been good to me, Milenka. And to my family.'

'I'm going to take care of your family, but I need something in exchange.'

'I would do the same.'

Mirko knew the rules of the game. He knew that it had nothing to do with the trust between us. We both lived in a world where emotions and personal relationships always came second – the top priority was survival.

'And you swear you didn't have anything to do with Zivko's death? Do you swear on your children?'

'Milenka, I loved Zivko too. He was too good for our world. I would never have touched a hair on his head. Zoran knows that. And you know it too. That's why I didn't know what was going to happen.'

'Who did it?'

I heard my voice become steely sharp. I still couldn't think about Zivko without a hard, cold shell forming around my heart. Hatred. It was pure, glowing hatred.

'You know who it was. Dragan blindly obeys everything Zoran says. It was him and that Swede. Dragan shot Zivko with his gun. The other bloke used his shotgun.'

'Do you know what Dragan did with his gun afterwards?'

'Of course. I'm the cleaner. The one who deals with all the shit afterwards. I was supposed to chuck it in the water. But it's in my safe. Natasa has the combination. Ask her for it and she'll tell you.'

'And his fingerprints are still on it?'

'You think I was born yesterday or something? Of course his prints are still on it. I've bought myself some insurance over the years, but it's no good to me now. A higher power has dispensed its judgment.'

'But it's good to me.'

Mirko shrugged.

'All that is mine is yours, Milenka. As long as you take care of Natasa and the kids.'

He hesitated.

'But … the new guy. Be careful. He's not like us. We live by rules. He's…'

He did circles with his finger beside his temple.

'He's crazy.'

'I know. I'll deal with him. With a little help. But to do that, I have to know: the necklace that was planted. The one that got Faye Adelheim sent down. Who was that?'

'That was me.'

'Can it be proven?'

'How am I supposed to know? Do you think I'm a cop or something?'

There was a twinkle of laughter in his eyes. It was a glimpse of the Mirko I'd known for so many years.

'Did you have your phone with you?'

'Of course I had my bloody phone with me.'

'Then it can be proven.'

Mirko didn't ask me why I was asking all this, instead waiting silently for my next question. The one he knew would come.

My heart was pounding as I looked him in the eyes. I felt no grief. Only determination.

'Zivko's death must be avenged. If you help me with that then I'll ensure your family always has what they need and then some. And ... you'll need to testify.'

Mirko's gaze didn't waver. He nodded.

I stood up.

'Goodbye, Milenka. May God be kind to you and yours.'

'Goodbye, Mirko.'

As I left Hall Prison, I knew it was the last time I would ever visit. A new era was dawning.

The two women sat in silence. Milenka had parked by the Rosendals Trädgård gardens. There were mums with pushchairs and elderly couples and dogwalkers wandering past them. The peacefulness was in marked contrast to Faye's inner tumult. She had told Milenka everything. About her mother, about Julienne, about Jack. About what she thought was going to happen now.

Milenka laid her hand on top of hers.

'Keep calm. Otherwise, he wins. Don't assume the worst. The game isn't over yet. They're his best hand. He wouldn't play them early.'

'I know. I think he's taken them with him to Fjällbacka. But I'm not sure. He's not right in the head. I can't fathom the way he thinks.'

'Yes, you can. You know how he works. You've lived with it. You've learned him. Just like I learned Zoran. And if you'll let me help, I've got a plan. One that might help us both. One that might get them out of our lives – for good. I've got a trump card. One of Zoran's closest henchmen has terminal cancer. He's only got three months left to live. Zoran doesn't know about it even though they're in the same prison. And I know how to use this to my – to our – advantage.'

Faye nodded.

'I'm listening.'

Milenka spoke calmly and methodically, explaining her idea. Faye let it sink in, ruminating upon each step until she finally said:

'It could work.'

'It will work.'

Milenka bent down and pulled something out of her handbag.

The object was inside a transparent zip bag and Faye carefully accepted it before putting it in her own bag.

Two small brown birds had settled down in the tree directly in front of them. One was bigger than the other. Faye couldn't help but think it was a sign. That the birds were her mother and Julienne. Waiting for her.

'Be careful.'

Milenka's hand was on top of hers again. The warmth from her hand made Faye notice how cold her own was. She'd been freezing ever since the phone call from Italy.

'I won't let him win.'

'If you do your bit then I'll do mine,' Milenka said, staring through the windscreen. 'I can't go on living like this. It has to end.'

'You may have to pay a high price,' Faye said.

'There's no price higher than having to carry on like this. I have no option.'

'Very well. Let's do this.'

When Faye got out of the car to return to the van, she didn't turn to wave goodbye.

Faye headed west in the van, driving through a night that never grew dark. Around her, Sweden was readying itself to celebrate Midsummer; cars were stuffed to the brim with luggage and awaiting families who would get into them to drive and visit their nearest and dearest. In a couple of hours' time, the roads would be rammed.

Faye passed Örebro. Around her, the forest began to grow thicker. She thought about the time she had left Fjällbacka for Stockholm; when she had still been called Matilda. On that occasion she'd taken the train. There was much to suggest this was her final journey. That she would die in Fjällbacka, where it had all started. She'd always imagined that in the autumn of her years she'd return to the village to die. But not this early. Not now.

She harboured the hope that Julienne was alive and that she would be able to find out where her beloved daughter was. Her father had defeated her; he'd resorted to the nuclear option of going after Julienne. In the devastation left in its wake, there was only emptiness and sorrow.

Faye wondered whether there was anyone she ought to speak to – to say goodbye to. Only Alice, she realised. It was five o'clock in the morning. She dialled Alice's number from memory on the burner phone.

'Hello?' Alice's voice was groggy and absent.

'It's me.'
'Faye?'
'Yes.'
She smiled.
'Where are you?' Alice said.
'Driving to Fjällbacka. I was thinking of you.'
'Why are you going there?' Alice said in surprise.
'He's there.'
There was a moment of confused silence in which Faye heard the rustling of sheets.
'Who?'
'My father. I need to find out what's happened to Julienne and Mum. And there's a chance they're there with him. As decoys.'
'Faye, he's going to kill you.'
Alice's voice sounded tense. Faye realised she must be beside herself with worry, but she couldn't bow to that. She just wanted to tell her friend what she meant to her before it was too late.
'Possibly yes. But then at least I won't die not knowing. The alternative is that he finds me in a week, in a month, or in a year, and just kills me. And I can't live in uncertainty any longer. I've done that for a week and it's unbearable. This is no way to live. And if there's even the slightest chance that Mum and Julienne are there then I've got to go.'
Faye had thought that Alice would object, but to her relief there were no attempts to make her stop.
'I understand,' was all Alice said.
Her voice sounded clearer and more alert now.
'So this is a goodbye,' Faye said. 'A goodbye and a thank you.'
'A thank you?' Alice cleared her throat. 'My dear, I'm the one who should be thanking you. You got me to leave Henrik – to leave that gilded cage that we were both captives in. You got me to understand my worth. And these last few years

with you and Revenge have been the best ones of my life. You got me to accomplish things I'd never believed would be possible. The self-confidence that some people get from their parents in childhood is what you gave me.'

Faye said nothing; she knew her voice wouldn't be up to it.

'And if I didn't have kids then I would be sitting next to you in the car right now.'

'I know,' Faye said thickly. 'You don't even have to say so.'

'You're going to make it through this. You'll be back.'

Faye smiled to herself.

'You've always believed in me.'

'We've always believed in each other,' said Alice.

'Yes, we have. Give Ylva my best. I love you.'

'I love you too.'

Faye ended the call and threw the phone onto the passenger seat. The only sound in the cab now was the engine and she blinked away the tears.

She accelerated to overtake a lorry before the dual carriageway ended, while thinking back to everything that had happened since she'd left Jack. They really had been some great years. She'd had a better life than she could ever have imagined. There had been setbacks and failures too, but on the whole she'd lived a life that she could only have dreamed of as a teenager. And she had no one to thank except herself and the women who had helped her rise to the top.

Now she was on her way back to the place she'd hated so much, to confront the man she hated most of all. But to her surprise, she realised she no longer felt any fear. Terror – the weapon her father had always held over her head to repress, to humiliate, to abuse – had been wrung from his hand the very moment he'd gone after Julienne.

Fjällbacka was asleep when Faye drove into the village.

She drove along the old lanes past familiar buildings and for a moment she lost her grasp of time. It might just as well have been 1988 or 1999. Everything looked the same. The rocky, picturesque community had been her whole world.

Faye rolled down the window to inhale the familiar scent of the sea. This was where she'd been conceived and shaped and this was where it would all end – one way or another. She knew that her father was in the house and that only one of them would come out alive.

The houses were gradually set further apart and before long she pulled over to the verge and stopped. She sat behind the wheel for a while before getting out and walking towards the small wooden house. She opened the gate silently, but her footsteps crunched in the gravel. She came to a halt in the garden. Then she climbed up the steps in a few large strides. She put her hand on the door handle and pressed it down.

Her father was sitting at the kitchen table and her mother was standing over the hob. Despite the fear she hadn't felt since she was a child gripping her when she saw her father, Faye exhaled. Mum! Julienne might also be in the house. Alive.

As Faye stepped into the room, her father pointed a gun

at her. Her mother put a hand to her cheek to wipe away a tear when she spotted Faye.

'Where's my daughter?' Faye said. Her voice was steady.

'Upstairs,' her father said flatly. 'Sit down, Matilda.'

Faye concealed her relief, even though all she wanted to do was to call out to her daughter. Her girl was alive. Julienne was alive.

'I'm called Faye now.'

'It doesn't matter what you're called – you're still a whore. Sit down.'

He gestured towards the chair on the other side of the table, which meant that Faye's back was turned to her mother.

'Your dear mother is just making me some breakfast – just like the good old days. Do you remember?'

Faye drew out the chair and sat down. She turned her head.

'Mum, are you okay?'

Her mother mumbled something that sounded like an affirmative. Her face was tense with fear and worry, but Faye was relieved to see there were no physical injuries.

Her father chuckled.

'It's so good to see the family back together again – one last time.'

Faye swallowed.

'How did you do it?'

'Get us back together?'

Faye nodded reluctantly.

'If that's how you see it, yes.'

Her father chuckled again.

'I picked up my wife and granddaughter in Italy and brought them here with a little help. I made sure there was food in and the house was ready so that it would be just like it used to be. How are those pancakes coming along? I'm starving!'

Faye's mother turned around with a plate of pancakes in her hands. She set it down on the table between them.

'Jam!' said her father.

She went to the fridge, opened the door and took out the jar. She twisted off the lid, inserted a spoon and stirred it.

He grabbed her wrist.

'Are we supposed to eat this with our hands like savages then? Fucking tramp. Cutlery and plates, now!'

He let go of her and she hurried to retrieve crockery and cutlery. Faye noted with sadness that her mother was once again in check and completely in his power.

Her father reached for the fork and held it in his right hand while he kept his relaxed left hand on the gun.

'Eat,' he said, without looking up.

Faye made no move to obey.

Her father let go of his fork, raised his arm and slapped her. The pain and the shock were immediate. She raised a hand to her stinging cheek and closed her eyes. There was something about the smells, the place and the pain that made her almost lose track of what year it was.

Her father was hunched over his plate. The fingers of his right hand were splayed after the hard blow. Faye reached out for a pancake and lifted it onto her plate before eating it in silence. Her mother watched them from her position by the worktop.

'Why are we here?' Faye said.

'To die together.'

'In what way?'

'You'll see. You've always been a nosy little slut, but now it's time to shut your mouth. Can't you see that I'm enjoying your mother's pancakes? It's been much too long.'

Faye glanced discreetly at the gun.

If she were to try to take it from him he would just shoot her. No, she would have to think of something else. She didn't want to die – not now that she knew Julienne was alive. One way or another, she was going to kill her father.

The zip bag with its contents that she had hidden in the waistband of her trousers made itself felt when she turned.

There was too much that might go wrong if she yanked it out now. It was only to be used when she was fully in control.

She resolved to wait him out. If he'd gone to the trouble of bringing them there, then he wasn't just going to shoot them. He had something planned. It would surely be painful and humiliating, but it would also be Faye's chance to kill him.

Once her father had finished eating, he licked his lips before wiping his mouth with the back of his hand. He stood up and raised the gun, sweeping it through the air before aiming it at Faye.

'Now we're going to go upstairs to your old room. All three of us. You'll wait up there until I come to get you.'

He cleared his throat.

'You two first. If either of you tries anything, I'll shoot the other.'

Faye and her mother complied and left the kitchen. Faye grabbed the stair banister and began to climb, her mother following and her father bringing up the rear. The steps creaked under their feet. Soon she would know what he was planning and then she could prepare her own countermove.

Once they got upstairs, Faye went straight to her old bedroom door. She opened it and nearly cried out when she spotted Julienne in the dark. The girl's chest was rhythmically rising and falling. Her eyelids were shut.

Her father had removed Faye's old bed and instead laid three thin mattresses on the wooden floor. The bedroom otherwise looked just as she remembered it.

Julienne seemed to be sleeping heavily. Her face was peaceful and Faye suspected she had been drugged.

Her father pulled out some cable ties from his back pocket.

'Put these on, Matilda,' he said, holding out a couple of them to her mother. 'Make sure you tighten them properly around her hands and feet, otherwise I'll thrash you harder than ever before.'

Faye held out her hands and smiled at her mother soothingly as she did as she was told. Then she sat down and allowed her mother to apply the next cable tie to her ankles. Her father bent down and checked they were properly tightened.

Once he was satisfied, he stood up again. He tucked the gun into his waistband while he attached the cable ties to her mother's wrists and ankles. He returned the remaining ties to his back pocket.

He stood in the doorway contemplating them with a smirk on his face.

'My beautiful girls,' he said. 'The next time we meet it will be to die.'

He closed the door behind him. The room went completely dark. Faye blinked a couple of times to adjust her eyes, but when she opened them again she still couldn't see anything.

They waited until his footsteps had disappeared downstairs before they dared to speak to each other.

'What do you think is going to happen?' her mother whispered.

Faye couldn't see her face.

'I don't know. I don't want to think about it. The only thing we should think about is how to get out of here.'

'How are we going to do that?'

Faye didn't reply. Instead, she laboriously inched towards Julienne. She could feel the girl's warmth on her skin as she reached out and gently caressed her face.

'She's got so big.'

Her voice was barely audible. She leaned forward, inhaling her daughter's scent before kissing her on the forehead. She was going to get her out of here. Julienne would live. What happened to her didn't matter, but her daughter had to live.

Julienne's mattress was in roughly the position where Faye's bed had previously been. She remembered the cavity behind the loose piece of skirting board. The shard of glass that she'd hidden there when Sebastian's advances had become too much. The one she'd never been able to use against him. If she was lucky, it would still be there. It would surely be just as sharp today. Hopefully it would be enough to cut through the cable ties. Then she'd have to improvise.

She remembered how she'd managed to kill Jack even though she'd been terrified and certain that he was going to take her life. The memory gave her the strength to do this too.

'Mum, you've got to help me,' she whispered.

'With what?'

'To pull the mattress that Julienne's on, so that I can get to the wall.'

'Why?'

'Because there's something hidden there.'

She heard her mother move closer. They groped for each other's hands. Faye guided her mother's hands down to the mattress and together they carefully pulled it outwards. Whatever it was that she'd been given meant that Julienne was sleeping soundly.

'I think that's enough,' Faye whispered although she wasn't sure.

She scrambled across the floor towards the wall the bed had been adjacent to. She fumbled along the skirting board with her bound hands and found the spot where it was interrupted. She was panting with the effort. She managed to loosen the skirting and insert her fingers into the cavity.

The pain at the tip of her finger when she cut herself made her smile. She wanted to shriek with joy. Perhaps they had a chance after all. She raised her finger to her mouth and sucked it, tasting blood. She reached out again and grasped the jagged shard of glass. As far as she could remember, it was green – but she was no longer sure.

'Mum,' she whispered. 'You have to come over here.'
'Where are you?'

She scraped her foot gently against the floor to help her mother to find her. Presumably her mother understood, because after a while Faye felt a hand on her leg.

'Be careful – I've got a shard of glass.'
'Why did you hide that?'
'For Sebastian…'

There was a moment's silence. No words were necessary. The air between them quivered with the pain they had both been forced to experience during all their years in this house.

'You have to use it to cut the ties off my wrists,' Faye said at last. 'I can't do it to myself.'
'Do you think it will work?'
'We don't have a hope otherwise, so it has to.'

Faye groped for her mother's hands, put her hands around the clasped hands and guided them carefully to her thigh where she had put down the piece of glass.

'Have you got it?'
'Yes.'

Faye straightened her arms so that her mother would be able to get at the cable tie between her wrists. Then her mother carefully began to move the shard of glass back and forth.

Faye's shoulder joints ached and there was sweat soaking through her top. She couldn't see how her mother was doing, but judging by her heavy breathing the work was taking its toll on her too. It was hard to gauge how much time was passing – it seemed like hours since her father had shut them into the bedroom.

She told her mother to take a break from her attempts to cut off the cable ties and then she gingerly ran the tip of her tongue along the slit in the plastic. It had got deeper, but she estimated that so far they weren't even halfway through.

'How are you doing?' she whispered. 'Can you manage?'
'Do we have any choice?'
'No.'
'Then I have to manage. Are you ready?'

Faye proffered her wrists, her mother groped with her fingers until she found the indentation and then she resumed the monotonous cutting. Faye kept her gaze fixed on the closed door, terrified that she might hear her father's footsteps and then see the door open at any moment.

A drop hit her hand and Faye didn't know whether the sweat was from her mother or herself. Her lower back and shoulders ached, but she gritted her teeth. If they didn't manage to cut through it then they would be executed by her father.

She wondered what he was up to downstairs, or wherever

he was. Wondered what preparations he was making to kill. The madness in his head. Could someone really be so evil that he would take the lives of three people, one of them a little girl, without any remorse? A child. His own granddaughter. Yes, her father could. That was why she had hated him her whole life. She knew what he had done first to her mother and then to her. If she didn't put a stop to it then a third generation would encounter his cruelty. Faye couldn't let that happen. She couldn't let Julienne die by her grandfather's hand.

She turned her head in the direction of her daughter and thought she could make out the contours of her small body.

'You're going to live without knowing what evil is,' she whispered.

Her mother stopped her efforts; her panting was heavy.

'What did you say?'

'Nothing. Carry on.'

Her mother resumed her sawing.

After a while, the movements began to slow before stopping entirely.

'Close now,' she whispered.

Faye raised her wrists to her mouth and ran the tip of her tongue over the slit. Her mother was right. It was much deeper now. The question was whether they would make it before her father returned.

With one final movement, Faye's mother freed her from the ties. Then she fell onto her side, exhausted. Faye didn't rest. She grabbed the piece of glass again and set to work on the ties around her feet. This went much quicker – the better angle meant she could apply much more force to the task than her mother had on her wrists. Soon she was free.

Faye stood up. Before she moved, she bent over and took off her shoes to make sure that her father didn't hear that she was on her feet and moving about. She crept across the dark floor and positioned herself by the door to listen. From downstairs she heard nothing. What should she do? How long could she wait? It all depended what her father was preparing for. Perhaps he'd temporarily left the house? But in that case she would surely have heard the front door open and his footsteps on the gravel outside...

'Faye?'

Her mother's wheezing voice interrupted her train of thought.

She turned around and made her way back across the room before crouching.

'I want to be there.'

'What do you mean?'

'When you kill him.'

Faye could see the outline of her mother's face in the dark. She paused to think for a moment. Then she reached out and caressed her mother's cheek. It was moist. She didn't know whether it was from sweat or tears.

He had made his wife's life hell. She was the greatest victim of his violence and sick mind. It would take a while to free her mother, but Faye couldn't deny her that. Not after all the years of physical and psychological violence. Not after all the horrors she'd had to suffer.

'Hold out your arms towards me,' she said.

She picked up the piece of glass and set to work on her mother's cable ties. She clenched her jaw, breathing rhythmically to oxygenate her muscles while fantasising that it was her father's body that she was cutting into.

After a while, her mother's hands and feet were free. She slowly got up, stumbling before Faye managed to catch her. She was weakened, but kept reassuring Faye that she would manage.

'I've got to be there,' she mumbled.

Faye sank down by Julienne's side, gently caressed her face and then kissed her cheek.

'I'll be back soon to get you,' she whispered, even though she knew her daughter couldn't hear her. She pressed her lips hastily against the girl's forehead before standing up again. She crept over to the door where her mother was already waiting. She slowly pushed down on the handle and carefully opened the door.

The steps creaked in protest as Faye slowly worked her way down them. Behind her, her mother was moving just as carefully. Faye was holding the jagged shard of glass in her hand and her mother was armed with a metal vacuum cleaner nozzle she had found outside the door. She could hear her father moving about downstairs. She wasn't exactly sure what he was doing. However, she could smell the pungent scent of petrol. So this was how he pictured it ending. They were to be consumed by the flames. But why had he waited? Had he been struck down by qualms of conscience?

When Faye reached the bottom step, she stood there. She tried to work out where her father was. In front of her, the floorboards were glistening with petrol. She grasped the piece of glass in her hand and quickly peered around the corner. She glimpsed her father's profile in the living room. He was sitting in the armchair with his hand around a bottle of liquor. He seemed to be drunk. Good God. The man wasn't even brave enough to carry out his plan without drinking a skinful. That spoke in their favour.

She wondered where the gun was. She hadn't seen it, but she assumed he had it within reach.

She turned around and signalled to her mother where her father was. She got a quick nod in response. She scrutinised her mother's face. She was committed; determined. Faye flashed a smile at her to infuse courage before turning back again. Her heart was pounding hard. How were they going to get close to him without being detected and then inevitably shot?

The floor was too creaky, no matter how carefully they crept across it.

There was only one way: the way you moved across fragile ice. Every Swedish child who had grown up in cold winters knew how to distribute their weight to ensure the ice beneath them didn't break. You did it lying down.

Faye lay down on her belly on the floor that stank of petrol. Then she began to inch forward. Out of the corner of her eye, she caught a glimpse of her mother shadowing her. The threshold that separated the hallway from the living room pressed hard against her ribs. She heard the sound of her father clearing his throat and she stopped. She pressed her face against the floor and lay still to make sure he didn't spot the threat. The zip bag at the back of her trousers was slick with her own sweat. She couldn't get it out now, even if it might help her. There was too much that could go wrong and then she would be done for.

Her father took a few audible swallows from the bottle before mumbling something.

After a while, Faye dared to move again. She was now only a few feet away from the armchair. If she stood up and hurled herself forward then she would probably have time to stab him in the neck with the piece of glass. Or was it too far? Her father's reactions would probably be inhibited by the alcohol, but how much? Would it be enough? She swallowed. It would have to be.

She took a deep breath and tensed her body. She pushed with her feet and leaped up with the shard of glass in her hand like a knife. She took aim at his neck as she lunged forwards. But something made her father sense the danger and despite his intoxication he managed to get out of the way. Faye lunged towards him again, trying to see where the gun was. The armchair toppled over. They fell to the floor, Faye landing on top. She pressed the piece of glass against his face with all her might, but the bastard was too strong.

He was dogged, his eyes shining with hate. He was heaving with his upper body and he had a firm grip on her wrist, preventing her from driving the shard of glass into him. He managed to get her onto her back, ending up on top instead.

She heard someone cry out and realised that the roar was coming from her own throat. Every muscle in her body was tensed; her sole focus was ensuring the shard of glass didn't slice into her. Her arm was shaking with exertion. But her father's strength was overwhelming. He'd managed to twist her hand so that the sharp tip was now pointing towards her eye. It was inching closer.

She closed her eyes when she felt it touch the skin just below her eye. She knew it was all over. She was going to die.

Then she heard a shot.

There was fluid running over her cheek. The strength in her father's arms disappeared and his head fell onto her chest.

She opened her eyes.

Standing above her was her mother with a two-handed grip on the gun. Faye's jaw dropped. Her mother let go of the weapon, which fell to the floor with a dull thud. Then she fell to her knees at Faye's side. Together, they managed to push aside her father's body.

They stood there, side by side in silence, looking at his lifeless, contorted body. Faye bent forward to remove some unused cable ties from his back pocket. Then she took out the zip bag from Milenka that was tucked into the waistband at the back of her trousers. Her hand perfectly steady, she carefully opened it so that just the barrel was protruding. She couldn't leave any prints.

Then she fired two shots into her father. One to the forehead and another to the chest.

She turned to her mother.

'Listen to me. You have to tie me up again using the cable ties. Here. Then take the phone that's in my van in the road outside. There's no PIN. Call the only number saved to the contacts, tell them who you are and say that I'm asking for help. Do exactly as she says. I'll see you in Italy when this is all over.'

'No, sweetheart, it's over now.'

'This isn't over until you're both safe. You can't stay here. And I have to get my freedom back. Do exactly as I say.'

Faye held out her hands. Reluctantly, her mother began to secure her wrists and ankles.

Epilogue

The sun was setting, its final rays sparkling in the pool. Faye sipped some ice water while marking the end of the day. It had been almost a year since her father's death in Fjällbacka. Faye, her mother and Julienne had adapted to life in Ravi again and were enjoying a few lazy days of sunshine and swimming. Julienne was playing happily in the water. As ever, Faye pushed away the image in her mind's eye of her daughter lying drugged on the mattress.

'Mum,' Julienne called out.

Faye turned her head and saw her daughter come running.

'Yes, sweetie?'

'Can we go into town and eat at that nice place by the promenade?'

'What's wrong with my cooking?'

'All sorts of things.'

Faye laughed.

'Fine then. Ask Grandma and Kerstin if they want to come with us.'

Her phone lit up with a new text message. It was another picture from Leila Makhrabi. Ever since Faye had bought her the small farm outside Sigtuna, she'd been bombarding Faye with photos of her new home. A home with animals and greenery. And no concrete.

Faye smiled and stood up, taking her glass as she crossed the lawn. As she rounded the pool, she couldn't help stopping to admire the beautiful house that she'd thought she would never see again. She briefly afforded a moment of gratitude to Milenka Rakitic.

Eight months earlier, her husband Zoran had been found dead at Hall Prison. He'd been killed by one of his lieutenants, who had died of cancer before he could be brought to justice. The murder had been splashed across the media, and photos taken at the gang kingpin's funeral had been in the tabloids. Faye smiled when she saw the photos and noticed how well Milenka was playing the role of the grieving widow. She'd been standing there hand-in-hand with Sara, Zoran's illegitimate daughter. She'd kept her promise to Faye. The girl was safe and loved – that much was apparent.

Marissa was still in Stenakull, but when she was released she would become part of the family that Milenka was now ruling with an iron fist, even outwardly. Milenka had also promised to make sure that word got to Louise that there was no longer any threat to her daughter.

And Faye was free. Mirko Herceg, the man who had stabbed Zoran to death in the showers at Hall, had provided the police with a detailed statement before he died. About how he and Faye's father had planned it all together. About how he'd been the one who had stolen Faye's necklace and planted it at the scene of Jack's murder, which had been proven after his phone was tracked. About how Zoran was responsible for the murder attempt on Faye in prison, and how she'd been living with death threats from her father after she escaped.

He'd testified that Faye had finally been kidnapped by her father and found in Fjällbacka beside his dead body, bound and helpless. She'd been saved by the fact that Zoran had ordered his men to follow and kill him. Two guns had been used. One had been Faye's father's own gun, and the other had been a gun that had been traced back to Dragan Maric, a man in Zoran's gang, thanks to fingerprint evidence. Dragan had, however, been found stabbed to death before he could be brought to justice.

The evidence had been compelling and Faye had eventually been exonerated and released. The nightmare was over. And the family of the man who had testified before his death had been extremely well taken care of in financial terms.

No one was convicted of Jack's murder and the mystery remained unsolved, but a rumour had begun to spread in the media that there was a connection between him and Zoran Rakitic. No one knew how the rumour had started, but once it took hold it quickly grew to become an accepted truth.

Revenge's American launch was just around the corner and Faye was soon going to make her return as the figurehead of the company. She had missed it. But the thing she had missed most of all was what she had around her now, thanks to Milenka, who had helped to get her mother and daughter safely back to Italy again, following a plan hatched by Kerstin. All without anyone finding out that they were alive.

'Mum! Kerstin and Grandma are waiting for us in the car,' Julienne called out from inside the house.

'I'm coming.'

She couldn't help but turn around to take another look at the setting sun. The future was bright.

Three months later

The big conference room in New York was packed, with every seat filled and people lining the walls. Faye's return to Revenge had been followed with great interest by the public and media, and they had timed it to coincide with the company's major launch event in the USA.

The spotlight was blinding, but Faye loved it. The world was hers again. She was free, she was happy and she had her army of women at her back. She cleared her throat to silence the hubbub while discreetly checking that the small microphone attached to a band around the back of her head was in the right position. The Fuck Cancer wristband that she always wore as a reminder of Chris brushed against the band and she felt the presence of her best friend. She gazed at the audience and smiled.

'We've created a revolution,' she said, and she meant every word of it. 'We've shown that women can do anything when they work together. Through sisterhood we can create an empire. Revenge is heading for its most successful year to date and now that we're launching in the USA, we'll take the market by storm. And I'm so grateful to be standing here in front of you today. Like many of you, life hasn't always been easy for me. I started with my two bare hands as a woman in a man's world. That's the world we all live in. I was oppressed. I was broken. But I refused to accept my fate. I refused to accept that I didn't have the power to create my own world.'

She paused for a moment.

'But I couldn't have done it alone.'

For a moment, the audience in front of her disappeared and she saw instead the faces of the women who had shared her journey. She saw them all flickering past. Kerstin. Alice. Ylva. Ines. Marissa. Miryam. Katya. Milenka. Mum. And Chris. Always Chris. So many women who had carried her, who had supported her, and who had helped her when she was out for the count. She would always be there for them. And for all the other women she encountered who needed her. She'd kept her promise about the foundation to support start-ups that she'd thought of in prison. Faye had put Kerstin in charge and she was loving every minute of it.

Faye was free now. She was strong. And she was loved.

She glanced briefly into the wings before continuing. Johan gave her an encouraging wink. She'd tried to persuade him to buy a smart-looking grey Hugo Boss jacket for this event, but he'd insisted that his old brown corduroy job with the leather patches on the elbows would do just fine now that he was no longer CEO. And she loved him for it.

She loved everything about him. It was something that had grown slowly, surprising them both. But it was beautiful. And in her heart of hearts, she knew they had Chris's blessing.

She didn't need a man. She was fine on her own. But that was why she was free to dare to love Johan. And tomorrow he was going with her to Ravi and would meet Julienne for the first time.

When she had finished her address, which had been met with deafening applause, she walked towards Johan. He took her hand and kissed the back of it. His lips were warm on her skin, and she loved that the sensation was becoming a familiar one.

'You were incredible.'

'This was my swansong. I've done everything I set out to. Everything I needed to do. This is where a new life begins. But I'm still a little ... afraid. You know everything about me now. Can you still love me?'

Faye didn't dare look at him as she asked the question. She'd wanted to ask it ever since she'd told him everything the night before. All the darkness. Everything she'd experienced. Everything she'd done. She had spared him no details.

Johan took her face in his hands and looked into her eyes for a long time before answering. Then he said slowly and clearly:

'There's nothing about you that I don't love. And that's never going to change.'

She could tell he meant it.

She was finally free. There were no secrets between them. Never again would she have to settle for dreams of bronze.

Acknowledgements

It takes teamwork to write a book and that team needs to be made up of incredible people. Once again, I've had the privilege of working with my Swedish publishers Ebba Östberg and John Häggblom at Bokförlaget Forum – as always, it's been a pleasure. Their ability to deliver compliments and criticism in equal measure helps me to improve my skills constantly and makes me a better writer. I also want to extend my profuse thanks to my editor Kerstin Ödeen, who has deftly and intelligently picked up my mistakes and plot holes while guiding me whenever I've gone linguistically astray. In addition to Kerstin, my friend and colleague Pascal Engman has helped me in my quest to use more direct, journalistic language in Faye's stories. Pascal has exhibited angelic levels of patience with my linguistic excesses and has gently but firmly got me back on the right track.

There are many others I wish to thank at my Swedish publisher Bokförlaget Forum: none of you are named but none of you have been forgotten. Many people were involved in getting this book into your hands, dear reader, and I am deeply grateful to them all.

In addition to my publisher, I had expert help in getting this book out into the world and launching it. Thank you to

Lili Assefa and the rest of the team at Assefa Kommunikation, as well as Joakim Hansson, Anna Frankl and everyone else at Nordin Agency.

On the home front, I benefit from the tremendous support offered to me by my wonderful family in the form of my beloved husband Simon and my children Wille, Meja, Charlie and Polly. And thank you to my in-laws, Anette and Christer, who are always ready to lend a helping hand.

I also have the world's best staff: Natasa Maric, Frej Vahlström and Johan Hultman. And where would I be without Martin Junghem, who handles my finances and whose patience I am always trying through the purchase of new homes?

Finally, I would like to thank my father Jens for giving me my love of books.

Camilla Läckberg
Stockholm, March 2024

If you enjoyed *Dreams of Bronze*, don't miss the first two books in the Faye's Revenge trilogy

People would kill to have Faye Adelheim's life. She lives in an ultra-swanky apartment in the most exclusive area of Stockholm, she has a gorgeous husband who gives her everything she's ever wanted, and she has an adorable daughter who lights up her world. Faye's life is perfect.

So how is it, then, that she now finds herself in a police station?

The truth is that Faye's life is far from what it seems. The truth is that Faye isn't even her real name. And now she's been caught out. There's no way she's going to go down without a fight. The only question is – who will escape with their life?

'A sexy, sensational novel with intoxicating vengeance and an unexpected tenderness'
Karin Slaughter

She is safe . . .
Faye Adelheim deserves the life she has. After fleeing from a violent marriage, she has built her business into a global brand and is living in a beautiful villa in Italy with her daughter.

Or so she thought . . .
But Faye's life is turned upside down when her murderous ex-husband escapes from prison. Faye has no choice but to return home to confront him.

This will be the fight of her life . . .
Faye will do anything to keep her family safe. But when the dark secrets of her childhood come back to haunt her, she will have to battle like never before to stop her deepest fears from coming true . . .